TERE MICHAELS

Forever & Ever

A COLLECTION OF STORIES

Published by

DREAMSPINNER PRESS

5032 Capital Circle SW, Suite 2, PMB# 279, Tallahassee, FL 32305-7886 USA
www.dreamspinnerpress.com

Forever & Ever – A Collection of Stories
© 2018 Tere Michaels.

Cover Art
© 2018 Aaron Anderson.
aaronbydesign55@gmail.com
Cover content is for illustrative purposes only and any person depicted on the cover is a model.

Trade Paperback ISBN: 978-1-64080-952-9
Digital ISBN: 978-1-64080-951-2
Library of Congress Control Number: 2018962510
Trade Paperback published December 2018
v. 1.0

Printed in the United States of America
∞
This paper meets the requirements of
ANSI/NISO Z39.48-1992 (Permanence of Paper).

Readers love the Faith, Love, & Devotion series by TERE MICHAELS

Faith & Fidelity

"A lovely, poignant story with heart. I recommend this to any m/m reader, especially if you're just venturing into the genre."

—Sinfully Sexy Book Reviews

Love & Loyalty

"Be prepared to laugh a bunch, shed a few tears, and jump for joy when these two find their happy ever after."

—Love Bytes

Duty & Devotion

"Those familiar with this author are aware of her talents and her strengths for writing multi-dimensional characters, intelligent dialogue and believable story lines… she has quickly become a favourite author among many readers within the sub-genre."

—The Indie Reviewer

Cherish & Blessed

"Reading these stories was like visiting with a best friend. I just couldn't get enough because my appetite for them is insatiable."

—The Novel Approach

Truth & Tenderness

"Michaels brings her Faith, Love, & Devotion series to a stunning conclusion that is sure to please fans…."

—Library Journal

By TERE MICHAELS

Groomzilla
Groomzilla & Groomzilla Does Vegas Anthology
The Heir Apparent
One Holiday Ever After
One Night Ever After

FAITH, LOVE, & DEVOTION
Faith & Fidelity
Love & Loyalty
Duty & Devotion
Cherish & Blessed
Truth & Tenderness
Forever & Ever

THE VIGILANTE
Who Knows the Storm
Who Knows the Dark

Published by DREAMSPINNER PRESS
www.dreamspinnerpress.com

TABLE OF CONTENTS

ACKNOWLEDGMENTS

THIS BOOK is a thank-you, and a final coda, to the Faith, Love, & Devotion series.

We finished the journey in *Truth & Tenderness* with a wedding (and a secret wedding!) and anticipating a baby, but a few things were missing that I know my lovely and passionate readers really wanted. And while I didn't have another complete book to tell, I did have little bits and snippets of their lives post "happily ever after" that I wanted to share, a newsletter story that needed a follow-up, and questions I wanted to answer. What would it be like when the kids grew up and started families of their own? How did this devoted group of friends handle getting older, changing lives, and elderly parents? When things got rough, how did they rise up to help one another?

Oh right, and you wanted a wedding. *The* wedding. That's in here too.

Please enjoy this last walk past The End into the future, where Matt, Evan, Jim, Griffin, Helena, Shane, Daisy, Bennett, and all the kids (and their kids!) are living their lives with love and witty retorts.

Thank you to my readers, including the many who have become friends because of this series. What an incredible silver lining to all this! You are the *best*.

Thank you to everyone at Dreamspinner Press, especially Elizabeth North, Lynn West, and Amelia Vaughn. All hail Ginnifer Eastwick, the wonderful editor for this series, who has the patience of a saint as she deals with my "process"—I would be lost without you! And Aaron Anderson, for all the gorgeous covers.

Thank you to all the wonderful bloggers, librarians, and booksellers who supported this series. I appreciate your recommendations through these years.

Thank you to those who were there from the very genesis of this idea, especially Beth and Linda, who made sure I finished *F&F* all those years ago.

I have the best tribe in the world and cannot go further without saying thank you to: Elle Brownlee, Elizah J. Davis, Agatha Bird, Rayna Vause, Kate McMurray, LaQuette, Harper Miller, Adriana Herrera, and

Geoff Symon. There are so many more people to list! I just appreciate you all—thank you.

Damon Suede gets his own paragraph, for reasons. Thank you, my friend, for reasons professional and personal, for long lunches and good advice, for both kicking and saving my butt repeatedly. You both rock and also roll. When a stranger in a kilt runs toward you at a signing, sometimes it's a good thing.

And finally, to my husband and son, who gave me the freedom to pursue this writing life. I believe in love and happy endings because I have you.

Here's to the next ten years of telling stories!

Tere Michaels
September 18, 2018

INTRODUCTION

WHAT MAKES a book unforgettable? Extraordinary characters, intense emotion, inspired worldbuilding, and a larger sense of how the greatest love stories extend beyond two people to enrich and extend a community. Oscillating between snuggletimes and hot boning punctuated with stretches of "names doing stuff" never suffices. The best heroes save the world from itself while they're solving themselves. No, special books deliver something unexpected.

I met Tere Michaels because of my deep respect and affection for *Faith & Fidelity*. I had no idea who she was and her cryptic website convinced me she was an elderly virtuoso living off Pop-Tarts in an attic somewhere, surrounded by feral cats. That didn't matter and it was wrong besides. Her book resonated so perfectly with my own hankerings that whatever her circumstances I knew we lived on the same page. I knew we would be instant friends, to be honest. Chance had nothing to do with it because the obvious, overwhelming overlaps in our experience and inclinations made it a fait accompli. I adore and admire her unreservedly. As different as we are, we are cut from the same crazy cloth.

The first time I read *Faith & Fidelity* I thought, "This Tere Michaels person knows what an ending actually is and how people can live past it." Talent and skill smoked off every page. The second time I read it, pulling it apart like a watch to see why it worked so perfectly, I could see on every page that she knew that "happy" and "ever" can only come "after" things that pull folks inside out. Every time I read the book I find something new buried there. I should, because Tere buried so much for us to find.

Faith & Fidelity begins in grief and disappointment, and with one deft stroke roots itself in the kinds of unhappy endings that can break spirits and crush lives. It charts a dangerous path to hope. And because Tere knows what she's about in every sense, this dazzling story carries its readers into the light one gratifying step at a time with measured, mindful grace.

One of the greatest things about all of Tere's books is the way they weigh happy endings as an idea... never for a moment glossing over the hideous U-turns life expects of us and the terrible costs of real joy. The thing about Happily Ever Afters is that they must be all three: they must offer real happiness, they must be everlasting, and they must come after things which are neither. Time passes, people grow, and the things that please us change because we change. What comes after happiness and how can we survive it?

HEAs are an odd monolith in the landscape of Romancelandia. The only things every romance must include are a relationship and a hopeful ending. That might sound simple, but in a world where fools can rule and you can be murdered for marrying the person you love, happy endings have a real cost and depicting them requires serious skill. Every happy ending comes at a terrible cost—otherwise who would care?

What Tere's fiction does, like all great romances, is remind us of the impossible hope buried in the darkest moments of our lives, the beginnings which flow around and through us when we pay attention. Like water underground, joy surges up through the cracks in our concrete. If we have faith, if we show fidelity....

If you have read Tere's work, you know exactly what I mean; if you have never read it, I envy you the overwhelming pleasure before you.

Damon Suede
Manhattan, September 2018

1
MATT AND EVAN GET MARRIED. SECRETLY.

MATT HAD taken the subway to the city, so he and Evan walked to his car shoulder to shoulder. The kids were waiting; dinner had to be eaten. They had plans for the weekend to check on their friends and plans for the summer, when all the family could arrange a week or two to be together.

Evan felt the pieces falling slowly into place: another year, another lesson, another way to make things easier. Maybe they'd never find the perfect solution to everything. Maybe it would never be easy.

"I love you," Evan said when they reached the car.

Matt paused at the passenger side, his expression pleased. He leaned his arms against the roof of the car. "I love you too."

"You know this is it, right?" Evan matched his position from the driver side, the rush-hour traffic buzzing behind them. "Us."

"Yeeees," Matt said slowly. "I've known that for a while."

The thought had come to Evan quietly and insistently as the day progressed. Some days he believed Matt had brought him back after Sherri died, but really, Matt made him so much better a person.

Better father. Better cop.

A better man.

"I need you to know that. I want to... to... show you how much this is forever...."

Matt's expression went from concerned to amused to a sweet reddening on his cheeks that Evan found to be his favorite reaction, ever.

"The first time you did this—please tell me it was more romantic," Matt murmured.

"Sherri was sitting on the bathroom floor with a pregnancy test in her hand," Evan said ruefully.

Matt started to laugh.

MATT NEVER expected to play a direct role in a marriage proposal—giving or receiving. The foxhole front seat to his parents' marriage left him commitmentphobic for most of his adult life, then boom, Evan, which seemed to take matrimony off the legal table, if it ever even crossed his mind. Besides, these years with Evan, making a home and a family, seemed far more concrete than a piece of paper.

Hell, they'd even discussed this, at length. Discussed and dismissed. They considered themselves "married" in the sense that this was it. Till death and all that stuff. When they bought a house together. When Matt became the twins' guardian. Evan had risked his mother-in-law's wrath and legal ramifications because he knew Matt would do anything to keep his kids—their kids—safe and sound.

They were it. As it was for their friends who were married or getting married. They didn't need the hoopla or anything official to make it more so.

But.

Matt couldn't lie to himself. He didn't expect it, but apparently he didn't mind it either. Surprise!

When the follow-up to Evan's proposal of forever included making dinner, a discussion of early admission college applications with the twins, and a downstairs clogged toilet, he felt no disappointment. The space between "huh, okay" to "where's the good plunger" barely made a dent in his mood.

Unexpectedly, the underlying feeling of "wow" tingling below his skin through all of it was what threw him. Every once in a while their eyes met across the room, Evan got a little grin on his face, and Matt felt bubbles of happiness in his gut.

So weird. They'd talked about it. It didn't matter! Except maybe it did.

"I believe it's traditional to celebrate an engagement with shower sex," Matt said as soon as the bedroom door closed behind them. They'd handled both teenagers and the toilet, and now it was time to have some adult fun. He leaned against the wall, trying to look sexy, but Evan kept moving through the room and into the bathroom. Without him.

"That wasn't the reaction I was dreaming of," he called as Evan shut the door.

"Checking the toilet!" Evan yelled from the other side.

"Romantic," Matt muttered to himself as he started to strip down to his underwear. He even threw his clothes into the hamper, because he was considerate like that and it felt like the right move when one a) accepted a marriage proposal and b) wanted to get laid.

The shower didn't go on—a good sign; maybe that meant wet sex was still on the table—but Evan took his sweet time coming out. Matt turned on the air conditioner, then crawled under the covers, after a brief consideration of making a sexy pose at the edge of the bed.

For men of a certain age, there just wasn't a way to disguise one's stomach sprawled out, so he quickly ruled that out.

Minutes ticked by. Matt's hopeful erection began to lag, and the remote fit in his hand so perfectly….

"I'm turning on the game!" he announced to the empty room and the rattle/hum of the AC.

When the clock registered fifteen minutes, Matt began to suspect food poisoning or a freak-out.

He rolled out of bed, grabbing his T-shirt from the hamper as he walked by. Neither of his potential theories had a mostly naked dress code, to be sure. A quick knock on the door, a pause, and Matt waited patiently.

The response came in the form of a heavy sigh that practically vibrated the wood between them.

"Stop freaking out, please," Matt said cheerfully. A lesser man—a man who had not recently seen his life pass across his eyes on a highway on Long Island—might panic, but Matt knew Evan, and if he was honest with himself, he had seen this coming. "If you want to take it back, I think you're fine. Unless you got me a ring, in which case you owe me double the shower sex for my broken heart."

The door opened so quickly, Matt almost fell on the floor.

Evan's face registered "pissed." "You're an asshole."

"True, but you're hiding and that's usually because you've gone all…" He made a wild flailing motion with both hands over his head and an expression to match. Sticking out his tongue like a winded bulldog was an artistic flourish. "…Evan."

"I wasn't freaking out, and I have never, in my life, made that face." He exhaled. "I'm just thinking."

"Lucky for us the fire alarms didn't go off."

With a little shove to the middle of Matt's chest, Evan stalked out of the bathroom.

"I just had this moment of thinking about engagements and weddings and telling people," Evan said, doing his traditional pacing circuit around the bed and toward the door. "And—before you think this is about shame or anything else, shut up."

Matt leaned on the doorjamb. "I said nothing."

"You thought it."

"Briefly. A blip," Matt said lightly, crossing his arms. "Listen, I understand if the proposal was a reaction to the whole Tripp debacle and feeling scared. I get it. I won't hold you to anything because at the end of the day, I'm not going anywhere. Broken engagement or not."

Evan squinted as if trying to read his mind to see if he was telling the truth.

"What? Have I, at any point, made you think it was something I needed? I hate weddings—tight shoes, tiny slivers of cake, no seconds on whatever weird chicken-in-sauce dinner they serve. They give you like three potatoes—who only eats three tiny potatoes? And oh Jesus, the music...." Just the thought of enduring it made Matt shiver in horror. "You know I'm buying an industrial-size flask just to survive Jim and Griffin's wedding, and I *love* them!"

"I don't want a wedding," Evan said, stopping midpace. "I mean, I want to be married, but I don't want the... spectacle. That's for other people."

"Okay." Matt shrugged. "You want to do something here, with just the family?" They could fix up the backyard. Maybe get a tent.

Evan started pacing again.

Matt's good nature began to slip a bit. "You think the kids won't go for that? Or... for any of it?" Katie's reaction, he knew, would be 100 percent supportive. Elizabeth and Danny, he had a good relationship with them. No reason to suspect anything other than a couple of woo-hoos, and Elizabeth might get weepy. Which led them to Miranda.

"Miranda and me are on good terms now," he offered, shifting uncomfortably. The game murmured low in the silences. Matt thought about turning it off or lowering the AC or doing anything, but he felt rooted in his spot. "When we were having our—difficulties—recently, she was totally on my side," he said jokingly. "I could talk to her, if you're worried. Maybe a bribe is in order."

"No, no." Evan stopped again, looking across the room to lock gazes with Matt. "This isn't about Miranda. I know she's come to terms with us being together. But even if I thought she'd react badly, this"—he made a motion between them—"this is it. I meant what I said when I asked you to marry me."

The tension knotting Matt's stomach unclenched slightly.

"Well, okay." His body unfroze; he pushed off the wall, approaching Evan slowly. "Okay. No regrets, the kids'll be all right. I don't want a wedding either. So why are you at full freak-out?"

"This is barely a normal freak-out. I've been worse," Evan muttered. He let Matt put his arms around him, resting their foreheads together.

Matt snickered, rubbing Evan's back in comforting circles, trying not to seem sarcastic when he said, "Yes, dear."

"Jerk." Evan tilted his head back. "Can we just… let's do this for us. Alone."

"Elope?" Matt rubbed his hands up and down Evan's back. "I'll get Bennett to send us to the Keys."

"Then Bennett would know."

Evan's words—and the ultimate meaning—finally sunk into Matt's brain. He cycled through a multitude of emotions: confusion, concern, and then delight. "So when you say just us…."

"I mean…." Evan pushed against Matt's body in a way that signaled the end of the conversation rapidly approached. "You, me, a judge. This isn't for anyone else."

Matt's hands slid from comforting to suggestive as he grabbed Evan's ass. With purpose this time. "My terms are shower sex and going away for the weekend to be noisy and rowdy," Matt said, throwing in a suggestive grind for punctuation. "In bed, in case that wasn't clear."

A smile finally broke across Evan's expression. "My terms are you can't write your own vows because I'm fairly sure you'd mention my ass."

"An ode to fucking Evan Cerelli, by Matt Haight," he said sweetly, then cut off Evan's laughter with his tongue.

EVAN LIVED in his head, a constant stream of concerns and worries and self-reflection, imagined reactions and potential pitfalls. Some days he worried about his kids to the point of distraction. He got caught up in cases, stewed over the ones that didn't resolve quickly. He thought about his friends, torn sometimes between stepping in with advice and minding his own damn business.

All that time meant he knew himself with an uncomfortable level of detail. People thought him oblivious, but Evan could diagram every emotion and reaction he had down to the root cause.

Nothing happened without checking on that diagram.

Asking Matt to marry him was probably the most spontaneous thing he'd ever done. He tried to scrutinize it, come up with a reason for the secrecy, and all he could come up with was…

Mine.

Just one word. It was maddening, unreasonable—this purely selfish feeling coursing through his veins. He felt almost giddy with delight, carrying his secret around like a prize. Evan found himself checking his face in the mirror. Was he smiling too much? Did he look ridiculous?

He distracted himself with the change in the weather, upcoming holiday conversations beginning to crop up over the dining room table.

During dinner at Jim and Griffin's house a few weeks later—over steaks and far too many bottles of red wine—Evan listened to them discussing their wedding, wiping his mouth every time he feared the urge to smile like a crazy person. Matt seemed outwardly fine with it all, throwing out jokes about penguin suits and offering to have the getaway car revving in case Jim changed his mind.

"You're just jealous," Griffin said, leaning against Jim's shoulder. They'd been affectionate all night, touching and smiling, sharing quiet moments that started to ping Evan's radar.

The engagement wasn't new. The easy display of love wasn't either. But the spark and crackle between them spoke of a secret of their own.

"We have most of the details worked out, but the actual execution— Daisy said she'd take care of it since we have other things to worry about," Griffin said as they were scraping the last pieces of chocolate cake from their plates. God, their housekeeper created magic with sugar and flour and forty pounds of butter.

"I'm giving Daisy a credit card and free rein," Jim muttered as Griffin petted his head and made soothing noises. "On purpose."

"Why? Why would you do that?" Matt asked, leaning back in his chair. "Griffin has forty-four sisters and a hundred and eleven nieces. They can probably whip up something in a week. You may have some money, trust-fund baby, but Daisy's used to gold toilets. You're going to end up getting married on the moon."

"There is so much to unpack there, Matthew. I'd start with the idea only the female members of my family could plan an event." Griffin shook his head, but Evan picked up on the slight flush on his cheeks.

"What are you two going to be working on?" he asked finally, and was rewarded by the bashfully delighted grins Jim and Griffin exchanged.

A wordless conversation commenced; Griffin nodded and Jim rolled his eyes with a grin.

"Okay—this is for your ears only. Just the parties involved have the poop, and Daisy, because she is my platonic life mate…," Griffin began, sitting up straight in his seat while still holding on to Jim's shoulder.

"Nosy," Jim interjected. "She's nosy and currently emotionally compromised. She basically lives here."

Griffin gave him a slight shove. "Shut up, she's going to be fine." He cleared his throat. "We can't finish planning a wedding because we'll be busy with more important things. My sister Farrah has agreed to be our surrogate. We're uh—having a baby. Officially."

Matt's arms went over his head to call the touchdown of his life; he knocked over a half-empty wineglass getting up, then pulled Jim out of the chair to give him a lung-busting hug. Evan felt his entire face cracking with a smile as he got up a little less exuberantly to congratulate Griffin.

"I had a feeling something was up," Evan said, giving Griffin a tight hug. "You looked like you had a secret."

"The best secret! I mean, we said we were going to have a baby, but now it's officially official, with a doctor and a schedule because we have a date to start fertility treatments. I want to tell *everyone*. I'm in the grocery store like, 'Hey, these apples are great! My sister is having my baby! Or rather my future husband's!' But that sounds so… bad reality TV!" Griffin bounced a little as he pulled out of Evan's arms. "So yeah, that's our news!"

"You're going to be wonderful fathers." A profound gratitude settled into Evan's bones: he and Matt deciding to get married, their friends having a child. He felt the satisfaction at a cellular level. "And I think it goes without saying, we are always available for babysitting."

"When the baby is out of diapers, of course," Matt added smoothly as he finally released Jim from his grip and moved over to do the same to Griffin. "And can eat wings without assistance."

"You're an idiot," Griffin said fondly before being swallowed up into Matt's excited hug.

Evan dodged the lovefest and ducked around to where Jim was standing, looking slightly rumpled from Matt's congratulations.

"Exciting news," Evan said, unsure of going for a handshake or a hug or—

Jim spared him the internal strife, offering his hand. "Thank you. We're not really spreading it around until things are a done deal and Farrah has passed the three-month mark."

"Of course, of course." The handshake tapered off, and Evan made an impulsive decision to pull Jim a bit closer for a one-armed hug. "It'll be nice to add another little one to the family."

When Jim pulled back, he offered Evan a slight nod and a curious expression.

"That wine was great," Evan murmured, feeling self-conscious, like Jim had taken his attempt at casual affection as an invitation to probe Evan's mind. "But whew! Not used to it."

"I'll put on some coffee." Jim looked over at where Matt was holding Griffin in a sleeper hold as the younger man flailed. "Haight, don't break him. I refuse to go through all this to find another model."

Matt dropped Griffin onto the floor. "Like… a model model? Someone taller, I assume."

"He likes young, but not children. They're all like eleven! Besides, I'm already house-trained," Griffin said, indignant, as he got up off the floor. "You're all insane. Except Evan. He's an adult."

"He's ninety-seven on the inside." Matt winked, then blew Evan an obnoxious kiss.

"I'm going to make coffee. Evan, you're in charge of these two."

As soon as Jim left the dining room, Matt and Griffin shared a look both mischievous and charming.

"Whatever it is, no."

"IT" TURNED out to be champagne, which Evan said yes to.

THEY SETTLED into the guest room since tomorrow was Sunday, no one had to work, and they really did put away a lot of red wine.

Matt couldn't wipe the ridiculous smile off his face. He stripped down to his boxers and bounced into bed, nearly upending a texting Evan in the process.

"Everything is fine at home. Danny set the alarm and locked the back door. He and Elizabeth have movie plans with friends tomorrow," Evan reported as he put his phone on the nightstand. "Jane's mother is driving them."

"Thanks for the report." Matt snuggled down next to him, moving his hands under the cover to tug Evan closer.

"You're in a mood." Evan let himself be pulled, which made Matt incredibly happy.

"A great mood, an amazing mood." His hands wandered to the band of Evan's boxers.

"We should have driven home," Evan murmured, but he didn't push Matt's hands away.

"I don't need to be home to do this." He shut Evan's further protestations off with a kiss—quick, dirty, and lots of tongue—sucking and biting until he could feel Evan's erection pressed against his hip as they rolled back onto the bed.

The kissing worked for a few minutes, but Matt wanted more. He wrenched his mouth away as long as it took to yank Evan's boxers down just enough to get a hand on his dick.

Evan snickered against his shoulder, punctuating it with a mild bite.

Matt's brain divided itself between jerking the hard length in his fist exactly the way Evan liked it, and a reminder to ask what kind of wine they had, because hell, he liked the results.

"You want…," Evan started to say, then arched his back as Matt got impatient, speeding up his strokes, tightening his grip as he went back to ravaging Evan's mouth. His palm grew slick as Evan began to rock up against him.

"I want this." Matt smirked, unrelenting as he jerked Evan off. Every twist and turn gave Matt the chance to rub his own hard-on against Evan's hip. Long and slow and thorough had its place, but right now Matt just wanted to see Evan lose his fucking mind.

"Oh shit," he muttered, eyes closing as he leaned forward. Matt wrapped his free arm around Evan's shoulders, stroking until his arm hurt and Evan spilled over with a long, low moan.

Matt licked up the side of Evan's neck, then dragged his wet hand over his *future husband's* stomach, taking full advantage of this rare pliability.

"Stop that," Evan said, falling back against the pillows, flushed and smirking.

"I don't want to mess up the fancy sheets." Matt instead used Evan's chest to wipe his hand off. He made it to right between his nipples before Evan grabbed his wrist.

"You're pushing your luck."

Matt waggled his eyebrows as he rubbed his as-yet-unrelieved dick against Evan's hip. "Are you going to scold me? Spank me a little?"

"I drank a lot of wine, I didn't suffer a head wound." Evan seemed to realize what he was smeared with, his face scrunching up.

"I love it when you talk dirty." Matt rolled over halfway to grab the tissue box off the nightstand. "Here, expensive tissues. They're probably made from angel wings."

Evan took half the box to clean himself off while Matt impatiently rutted against his side.

"If you throw these tissues away, I'll return the favor."

"If you return the favor with your mouth, we won't have to worry about more tissues," Matt volleyed back, wriggling out of his boxers in a second flat.

Matt waited for the ceremonial rolling of the eyes or Evan's veto, but the wicked grin he got in return made him want to invest in whatever winery produced that elixir.

Tossing the tissues on the floor, Evan rolled over on top of Matt with what might be called a growl.

"Very practical," he said. "I like practical."

Matt put his hands on Evan's shoulders, giving him a gentle push as he licked his lips. "I like it when you're sucking my dick."

"Romantic."

"So romantic." Matt choked on his words as Evan slid down between his legs, making sure every inch of their bodies touched.

"So romantic," Evan echoed, licking Matt root to tip.

God bless red wine.

HEAD STUFFED with cotton and mouth tasting like the floor of an old Chevy, Matt wandered out of the bedroom far too early for his liking. He'd woken up with a start and then couldn't get back to sleep. Didn't old people wake up super early? Was he old now?

"Put on pants, Daisy and Sadie will be here in five," Jim said as he walked by Matt in the hallway. Matt blinked at him blearily. Jim in tight black workout clothes, faintly smelling of sweat, appeared as if a mirage.

"What?"

"We do Sunday breakfast with Daisy and Sadie, so put on pants," he repeated slowly. "Pancakes and bacon, lots of coffee."

"I love you, even though you're a psycho who exercises on a Sunday morning," Matt muttered, ducking back into the bedroom. "You drank as much as we did!"

He debated a shower and settled for a quick wash before putting his clothes from last night back on. Evan snored loudly in the bed, worn out from their drinking and sexual escapades, which ended up including a hand job, a blowjob, and some pretty spectacular follow-up frottage. Maybe he wasn't old.

Matt stood up a little straighter. *Nice work there, Haight*, he thought.

The guest bathroom touches were clearly Daisy's influence: new toothbrushes that looked as if carved from wood, citrusy-smelling deodorant, shaving stuff, and towels that felt like clouds the color of café au lait. Classy aftershave he could never afford. He patted some on his face before whistling out the door in anticipation of coffee.

"Hey, Evan, wake up," he whispered loudly, shaking his future husband—future. *Husband*—on the shoulder. "Breakfast."

Evan grumbled, eyes still closed as he tried to tug the covers over his head. "Go away."

"You know they have expensive bacon," Matt said in a normal voice, then followed up with a loud smacking kiss against Evan's cheek.

"Where… what?" Evan came around slowly, blinking and licking his lips as if tasting the vague wine hangover.

"We're at Jim and Griffin's. There's food downstairs. Oh, and Daisy and Sadie." Matt got off the bed, slapping Evan on the ass for good measure. "Come on. I love you, but I'm not missing my coffee for much longer."

"Go. I'll be down in a few." Evan sat up slowly, grabbing his head as he moved. "Any chance they're also serving aspirin?"

"Probably fancy aspirin too. From France." Matt dropped another kiss onto Evan's head. "Don't be long."

Evan's response was just a moan as his face smacked back into the pillow.

HALFWAY DOWNSTAIRS, Matt started to smell breakfast. Heavenly, beautiful breakfast—coffee, frying pork, and who needed more than that?

He also heard squealing.

"My goodness, is that Miss Sadie?"

The auburn-haired toddler spotted him as he came around the corner and began to clap her hands together delightedly.

"I was hoping to get her fed before you showed up," Daisy said as she sat at the table with a bowl in one hand and a spoon of oatmeal in the other. Both she and Sadie were dressed in navy hoodies and pale blue sweatpants—though the baby's outfit was accessorized with a bib. "She's distracted by other children."

"This hangover is not kid-approved, believe me." He dropped a kiss on her cheek before doing the same to Sadie.

"You boys are terrible influences on each other."

"I happen to know you can drink Griffin under the table," Matt responded as he headed for the magnificent coffee maker chugging away on the counter. "You need a refill?"

"Always."

"Sadie could drink Griffin under the table," Jim said.

At the giant six-burner stove, Jim manned several sizzling frying pans, a spatula in each hand. The sweaty clothes were gone, replaced by jeans and a black sweater. *Ninja health nut*, Matt thought.

"Where's *my* kiss?" Jim asked.

"With your future husband, I'm guessing. I could slap your ass if you want."

"Language!" called Daisy.

"A-s-s."

"Yes, you are."

"This is fun. We should live on a commune together. You, me, our menfolk, Daisy and the wee child, our kids. Your kid." Matt grabbed the full carafe on the counter and one of the enormous white cups stacked next to it.

Jim side-eyed him so hard Matt only half-jokingly winced.

"No?"

Daisy hooted from the table.

"What say you, Daisy Mae? Wanna move to Queens and be my sister-wife?"

Griffin stumbled into the kitchen wearing Kermit the Frog pajamas, glasses, and hair askew. "What the hell did I walk into?"

"Matt's being chippy," Daisy said as she tried to tempt Sadie into eating more oatmeal, but the toddler shook her head, preferring to focus on the adults.

"Too loud," Griffin muttered as he plunked down into a chair. "Good morning, sweet Sadie."

"Niff," she said adoringly.

Matt refilled Daisy's cup, then sacrificed his own for Griffin.

NEWLY POURED cup of coffee in hand, Matt resumed his place leaning against the counter as the scene of domestic bliss played out before him. He basked in the pleasure of his extended family. The banter and the smiles. Wasn't too long ago when they were all in various states of sadness. Hopelessness. Separation, literal and figurative. He remembered hiding out here during the fights with Evan, Jim and Griffin's relationship full of tension with Daisy and Bennett's marriage going to shit.

Not everything was fixed, nothing was perfect, but Matt couldn't help but feel they'd passed some sort of test. Jim and Griffin's baby. Marrying Evan. The kids growing up. It was all coming together.

"What the hell is that look on your face?" Jim asked, reaching across the counter for an empty platter. "Do I have to throw out the sheets?"

"Hmmm? Yes. And I might have to buy you a new mattress." He sipped his coffee, batting his eyelashes at Jim over the rim. "I definitely recommend getting rid of the washcloth in the hamper."

"I'm going to have to hide my child from you people once she starts understanding innuendo," Daisy sighed.

EVAN TOOK a long hot shower in the guest bathroom. The rainfall fixtures, the towel heater—he'd been in less luxurious hotels.

"I have bathroom envy," he muttered to himself as he toweled himself off in front of the fogged-up mirror.

The threatening hangover abated by the shower, Evan brushed his teeth slowly, his thoughts drifting to last night. At some point he expected for sex to get boring, routine. Even the best sexual relationships had to dull at some point.

Right?

Then again—and he was loath to compare—he and Sherri didn't want for wanting. Slow spots could be blamed on children and work and stress, not a lack of desire. So maybe even someone like Evan, slow to rev up and incredibly selective as to who did the revving, could enjoy a robust sex life.

Maybe even a thorough rubbing off in their friends' guestroom led to feeling a little punch-drunk the next day.

Or maybe it was all that red wine.

Or maybe it was the thrill of their secret.

"TECHNICALLY THIS is a walk of shame" greeted him when he entered Jim and Griffin's enormous kitchen. Griffin sat at the table, a forkful of pancakes in one hand and a wicked grin on his face.

"How do you figure?" Evan asked, taking stock of Jim, Matt, and Daisy in the remaining chairs, all in various states of eating.

"Matt already tattled about your shenanigans," he said sweetly. "And you're wearing the same clothes!"

"That's a naughty sleepover," Daisy offered. She patted her mouth with a napkin, then stood up to give Evan a hug. "Not a walk of shame."

"Thank you." Evan patted her back, hoping it translated to *hope you're doing okay*.

She gave him a wink before sitting back down.

Griffin puckered up, but Evan just patted the nest on his head before circling over to sit down next to Matt, who gave him loving eyes in between bites of bacon.

"Morning." Jim waved the coffee carafe in Evan's direction. "I hope the facilities were to your liking."

"Your shower is a magical experience." Evan accepted the carafe from Jim, then poured himself a cup filled right to the brim.

"You don't want to know how much it cost." Griffin passed along a heaping platter of pancakes and scrambled eggs.

A gentle tug on his pants leg and Evan peered under the table—where Sadie sat, dancing a purple monkey over everyone's feet.

"Hey, Sadie."

She waved the monkey in his general direction.

When he came back up, he got a syrupy kiss on the cheek from Matt.

"I love our lives, but we might consider moving up here permanently."

"Only if you want to have endless conversations about weddings and babies," Griffin said, then froze, gaze darting to Daisy, who reached for the saltshaker.

"I can feel you looking at me with your cartoon eyes," she said calmly, focused on her plate of food. "I'm happy for you guys." She looked up, her perfectly poised face punctuating her tone. "Truly. I mean, life goes on, right? After the year we've had, this little group needs only good news from now on."

Evan felt Matt pressed against him, shoulder to shoulder, hip to hip. He watched Griffin's expression melt into goofy happiness, and even stoic Jim cast a smile across the table. Under the table, Sadie babbled to herself.

Only good news, even if it stayed between two lovers.

TEN DAYS later Matt sat at his desk, considering turning the furnace on as he sipped his morning coffee. Quiet house, a stack of work to go over before his lunchtime conference call with Jim. A dozen phone calls to make. Contentment settled over him as he reached for his phone.

A text appeared, from Evan.

What are you doing Thursday, week after next?

Matt glanced over at his wall calendar, then double-checked his laptop.

Nothing. Why?

The three little dots hovered for a few seconds.

Let's do it.

A sex joke came to mind first, but a second later, Matt got it. He dropped his phone on the desktop as a frisson of delightful nerves sparked him to sit up straight. He took a moment to move his coffee cup three inches and straighten his laptop, then picked up his phone.

Okay.

Another long pause with those dancing dots.

Great.

Matt stared at the screen, a ridiculous smile pulling at his cheeks. Great.

NOTHING HAD indicated today would birth a decision.

Evan woke up, showered, checked his email, drank coffee, briefly complained about the chill in the air to Matt, then negotiated the traffic into the city. A normal Wednesday.

His morning brief finished, Evan sat down at his desk with another cup of coffee, looked at the calendar, and thought, *We should get married the week after next.*

He froze for a second, the cup halfway to his lips.

The need for secrecy still felt right, the totem of "this is for us" lovingly curled inside his brain. All the pomp and circumstance around even his rushed wedding with Sherri amounted to pleasing her parents and her priest; at no point during the process did Evan think, *I love her more now.* He'd made his decision about her long before that moment, as he'd decided Matt was forever so long ago he couldn't even pinpoint the time and place.

Outside his office, Evan observed his precinct busy at work. Phones ringing, conversations and laughter, the serious expressions of men and women trying to protect. Serve. He tried to imagine the chaos that would descend if his and Matt's marriage became a PR stunt.

He put down the coffee, picked up the phone, and texted Matt.

PLANNING A secret wedding meant lists in code ("Gorilla glue, newspaper" meant "Suits at cleaner's and marriage license") and slickly creative lies they plotted in bed with the lights out ("Can Jane's mom drive you to soccer practice? I have a meeting downtown."). Matt said something vague to Jim about an appointment, which proved unnecessary as his best friend and business partner had other things to worry about.

"Jim's preoccupied with making sperm, so we're good there," Matt reported, whispering into Evan's ear as they were making dinner Sunday night. "They're going to try and knock up Griffin's sister that week."

Evan stopped stirring the Alfredo sauce, a grossed-out look on his face. Matt snickered.

"Day off procured?"

"Yeah." Evan indicated the boiling pot of water with a tilt of his head.

"We have the uh—newspaper to get this week."

Evan opened his mouth to answer, but Elizabeth strode into the kitchen, rubbing her hands together. "I am so hungry!" she declared.

Matt swatted her with the dish towel. "Feel free to help. Maybe find something green in the fridge?"

"A vegetable or just something you left in there too long?" Elizabeth said sweetly, getting another swat for her sass.

With a wink, Matt chased Elizabeth around the kitchen twice before Evan remembered the boiling pasta and saved dinner.

THE FIRST wrinkle in their plan came when Evan realized they needed a witness to get their license. Their procured two-hour block of time—to get to the Bronx courthouse, get the license, and get back to their respective jobs—left little time for debate. Who could they trust?

"With our lives? I could reel off a list. With a secret? Zero. Not one of them," Matt bitched as he got dressed, Evan on speakerphone as he drove to work.

"Not even Jim?"

Matt considered his best friend for a moment but dismissed it. Keeping a secret of that magnitude from Griffin would eat at his stomach lining, and while he might not say anything, the stern disapproving looks they'd get for eternity were not worth it.

Before Matt could answer, Evan was replying to himself. "No, that wouldn't be fair. I don't want to ask him to keep secrets from Griffin."

"Good point. What about...." He trailed off. If Vic weren't in Florida, he'd consider it, but they didn't have time to get him up there. "Abe! Abe Klein!" Matt yelled suddenly, his shirt half-unbuttoned.

"Your ex-partner?"

"Yeah. It's perfect. He doesn't socialize with our sprawling group of busybodies, never crosses paths with them. And if we ask him not to share with Vic, he would keep his mouth shut."

"Hmmm." Evan was quiet for a few seconds over the phone line. "Yeah, okay. That sounds perfect. Do you think he can make it on such short notice?"

"I'll call him, but generally speaking, he's either at a Yankees game or sitting in a bar three doors down from his apartment. He can probably squeeze us in."

ABE KLEIN did not, in fact, have plans.

"I'm glad to help you, Matthew, but you are playing chauffer if I'm keeping a secret."

The next day Matt picked him up, gunning the motor as his nerves kicked up and sweat began to form under his armpits. A dress shirt suddenly felt like a terrible idea. If this was his reaction to the license-getting, they'd have to hose him down for the actual marriage vows.

Abe, in what Matt recognized as his funeral suit, shuffled to the car, cane in one hand and a dapper hat with an owl feather in the other.

"We're not shaking down some bar owners," Matt said as a greeting when Abe settled into the passenger seat. "You look like an extra from *The Sopranos*."

"Hmph," Abe answered, struggling a bit to get the seat belt on, his hat and cane stowed on the floor.

Matt struggled himself—with not offering to help. Abe would probably shoot him.

"I figured I'd dress up for such a momentous occasion. Matthew Haight, legendary tomcat, officially taken off the market."

"I've been off the market for years. Where have you been?"

"The bleachers at Yankee Stadium."

THEY CHATTED about sports and the weather and the mayor being a bonehead. For a moment Matt felt like he was driving a time machine back to his homicide days with Abe.

"The more things change, the more they stay the same," Matt muttered, half to himself, earning a bark of laughter from Abe.

"You takin' my lines?"

"I thought I read that in a fortune cookie."

Just a few blocks away from the courthouse, Matt began swallowing repeatedly and tapping out a furious beat on the steering wheel. He felt Abe's amused gaze on him but kept staring straight ahead as a cop attempted to direct traffic around emergency manhole cover work. The road rage was palpable.

"You okay?"

"Yeah. Stupid traffic," he added.

"Evan meetin' us there?"

"Yeah."

"You okay?"

Matt turned his head enough to shoot Abe a look. "Asked and answered."

"Just trying to be a good witness," Abe said with a smirk. "Want to make sure you aren't having second thoughts about this."

Matt opened his mouth, then closed it. "I don't even have first thoughts on it," he said finally. "Never expected this—any of it. Now I'm... I'm freaking out a little."

The confession made him sweat even more.

"Hmmm," Abe murmured. His tone had definitely shifted. "Well, we got some time as it's clearly this guy's first day directing traffic." On cue, a truck driver leaned out of his white panel truck and began screaming. "You want to get married?"

"I thought I was already married. So what about a piece of paper makes things different?" The line from *Princess Bride* echoed in his head. *Marriage is what brings us together today.* A slightly hysterical laugh got stuck in his throat.

Together to do what?

Be together forever? Love each other? Raise the kids together? Pay bills, buy groceries, bitch about plumbing, and argue over who had to rake the leaves?

They'd been doing that, successfully, for years.

So why now? Why this?

He said as much to Abe, who hummed again in response.

"I've got two divorces under my belt, so take this with a shaker of salt," he said. "But what you're talking about is the everyday stuff. You make a commitment, you deal with the consequences. Not just in marriage—having kids, having a career, owning a house. All of it is saying, 'All right, I accept the responsibility for this.'" Abe looked out the window. "But... you don't want a car anymore, you sell it. You don't want to be married, you split up. Even kids—well, you know as well as I do how many of them get left behind."

"This is not helping my state of mind," Matt sighed, resting his head against the steering wheel. The background music of horns and cursing seemed apropos.

"The reason you stay," Abe plowed on, "is a higher reason for being there. You make a commitment for more than just responsibility. You make a... a vow. That even when the responsibility is too damn much, you take a breath and you keep going. Because you cherish it. Because you can't think of another place you'd rather be or another person you'd rather be doing it with."

Matt stewed in this for a moment, lifting his head to watch the first car at the head of their mini jam peeling out in the other oncoming lane at the wildly waving behest of the traffic cop.

"I've never felt about a car the way I feel about Evan," he said finally as Abe guffawed next to him. "And that speech would be a thing of beauty if it wasn't for the divorce rate."

"I know. I contributed twice. But then again, I didn't marry for the right reasons either time."

"So right person, right reasons. Commitment and responsibility and cherishing and the long haul," Matt read off, half-sarcastically. "A lot of balls in the air."

"A lot of balls to bother with," Abe laughed. "All I'm saying is— you two have a good thing. You proved you can push through a dozen or so walls of bullshit to be together. Now you're just putting a seal on it. A badge of honor."

Matt put the car back in Drive as the furious truck driver finally got his window to move, flipping off the cop as he did. He remembered another badge he cherished, one he lost. Taking another one felt like tempting fate.

But. This was Evan.

"I want to get married because I cherish my responsibility and there's no place I'd rather be. And Evan is not a car," Matt said quietly as he turned the steering wheel.

"Not tellin' you what to do, but those are some nice vows."

"Those are terrible vows."

Abe shrugged. "Two divorces."

EVAN HID in the bathroom of the Bronx courthouse, waiting for Matt's text that they had arrived.

He had no dealings up this far, but you never knew what cops or lawyers were making a special trip to testify or take a meeting. Clerks, messengers, secretaries—hell, in his worst nightmares, he'd run into Helena and Shane, who suddenly decided to have lunch up here.

Which was insane, but still.

His window of two hours felt as tight as his collar. He'd purposely come in over the weekend, clearly visible at his desk as he slogged through stacks of files. His second-in-command insisted he come in late on Monday morning, and Evan went through his usual routine of protest before giving in.

A pretty good acting job, if he did say so himself.

He stood in a stall for almost twenty minutes, praying no one spent much time in here or noticed a guy nervously tapping his foot.

Evan clung to that word—*mine*, because this was his, all his, and he didn't want to share—and tried to hush his practical side, which just had one question. *Why?*

All the subterfuge for what?

More than a quarter of a century ago, Evan and a pregnant Sherri had walked into city hall for a license with Ellie and Sherri's cousin Nina at their side—Ellie to cheer them on and Nina because Ellie was too young to be their witness. They were rushed, everyone taking a break from school and jobs, buried under the pressure of Sherri's mother's exhausting pace to get the wedding done before Sherri's belly started to show.

"We should have gone to Vegas," Sherri had bitched, eating saltines out of her purse to keep from throwing up while they waited.

"You should have used condoms," Nina said under her breath, which made Ellie break into giggles.

Evan pulled Sherri against him, rubbing her back as they watched throngs of couples line up to get their licenses. "I love you," he whispered in her ear. "That's the only thing that matters."

I love you. That's the only thing that matters.

Evan rested his head against the stall door, a smile breaking across his face.

Mine.

Finally a text pinged.

Meet us in the lobby.

Evan took a deep breath, exiting the stall. He washed his hands calmly, then shared a long stare in the mirror with his reflection.

ABE GAVE Evan a backslapping hug when they met up, with an extra whack of his cane as he pulled away.

"If you need a best man, I can be bought," he whispered, clearly delighted by the subterfuge.

Evan controlled his first impulse—to look around and see if anyone heard.

Matt reached down to squeeze Evan's hand, then moved to let go, but Evan held on tight. "We'll keep that in mind," he said. "But are we talking a bottle of scotch or a trip to Hawaii?"

"Yes," Abe deadpanned before cracking up at his own humor.

"As we are on a schedule," Matt interrupted, "let's get upstairs and do this. No clue what the line is like."

Abe smirked as he shuffled over to the elevator.

"Hey," Matt said as they followed. Evan knocked their shoulders together. "You doing all right?"

"I'm good. Just realizing I am out of practice being undercover. I just hid in a bathroom stall for twenty minutes."

"You're lucky no one thought you were trolling the men's room for sex."

Evan stepped into the elevator; he felt his eyes go wide with panic.

Abe continued to laugh, pressing their floor number with his cane.

THE SENSE of calm settling over Matt began to evaporate when the elevator doors opened, letting them out in the hallway with the clerk's office. He'd been so caught up in Evan's reactions, he completely missed his own concerns.

Matt knew a lot of people—and people knew him. He and Evan had just months before been in the local papers due to Tripp Ingersoll's splashy and dramatic arrest. Evan was the first out gay captain in the NYPD. Matt's infamy seemed to have run its course, but still. People were going to see them, the gossip train would start, and that would be the end of their secret.

Not to mention, when their friends and family found out they hid this? Hell. To. Pay.

He clutched Evan's hand a little tighter as they set off down the hallway—only to be blocked by Abe's cane.

"Other way," he directed, toward a private office at the opposite end.

"No, the clerk is—" Evan started, but Abe waved him off.

"Other way."

Abe went around them, a jerk of his head directing them to follow. Matt gave Evan a look. Evan shrugged.

"I'm not going to argue with him, are you? I have a feeling he knows how to use that cane."

ABE KLEIN worked for the NYPD for over thirty years.

Playing politics wasn't a skill he'd mastered, but a high arrest rate and good reputation made him a valuable asset to the department. It also earned him the respect of everyone from clerks to captains, who liked having him on their side.

He also never shat where he ate—which meant no one in the NYPD or court system could ever accuse him of sleeping with their wife, sister, or girlfriend.

In addition to his pension, Abe had retired with a pocketful of favors of the "you call me if you need anything" variety.

At the end of the hall sat the office of Miriam Burns Kelly, city clerk and the daughter of a dear friend of Abe's. A quick phone call last night to Buddy Burns, and after the bullshit session on the mayor being an idiot and a rundown of who died since last they talked, Abe had assurances that Miriam could help his friends "quietly," no questions asked.

As far as wedding gifts went, it wasn't china, but Abe knew the boys would appreciate it.

"MIRIAM!" ABE said, kissing her on the cheek after they were ushered into her small office.

Standing awkwardly—and still not knowing what was going on—Matt gave Abe the visitor chair and leaned against the closed door with Evan by his side.

"So nice to meet you," Miriam said, extending her hand to first Evan, then Matt. "I wasn't sure what the need for secrecy was for, but now I get it." Her dimples and warm smile were in contrast to the severe blonde bun and serious square glasses. "Gentlemen, it's a pleasure."

Matt felt a mild panic as he exchanged glances with Evan.

Abe turned in the worn beige chair to regard them with a smug smile. "I called in a favor. Miriam is going to take care of this personally so less eyes get a pass over your private business."

A lump formed in Matt's throat. Abe Klein was the man, just like he'd always known.

"Thank you," Evan said sincerely as Matt gave him a playful punch in the shoulder.

"And just so you know, I'm glad to arrange something private with Judge Wernicky. He does most of the weddings," Miriam said as she headed back to her desk. Piles of paper covered every surface, with memos and a large Marvel superhero calendar on the wall. A Thor bobblehead on her computer nodded as she sat down.

"You have all the paperwork? And the check?" Her tone went all efficient business.

Evan pulled an envelope from his inside jacket pocket as Matt went for his ID. They were prepared—overprepared, even, with documents that weren't even on the website.

Miriam pursed her lips as she worked, handing them each a clipboard with paperwork to fill out, including Abe. The scratching of pens filled the room.

To lighten his own overly emotional mood, Matt pretended to look at Evan's answers, like he was cheating on a test. Evan pulled the clipboard out of his line of sight before rolling his eyes.

"Trying to steal my Social Security number?" he asked in a whisper.

"I wanted to see what you put down for number seven."

"Stop it."

"Wanna play naughty student and stern headmaster?"

Evan hit him with the clipboard.

"Okay, looks like everything is in order," Miriam said as she read over everyone's forms. "Give me a few minutes to process everything."

Abe shifted in his chair, regaling Evan and Matt with a twinkle in his eye. "You two should have thought of this. Nobody owes you nothing?"

"Most of the favors I could call in are from, uh… former associates with whom I shared some personal time. And that seemed, you know, weird," Matt demurred, avoiding Evan's gaze, which burned into the side of his head.

Miriam snorted from behind her pile of paper.

"I didn't want to put anyone in an awkward position," Evan said with a shrug. "If no one knows to ask Miriam if she processed a marriage license for us, then she never has to lie."

"Such a Boy Scout," Matt said under his breath, petting Evan's knee.

"As for me, I probably can't be bought," Abe said, tapping his cane against the floor. "I mean, I'd like to think I'm unimpeachable, but who the hell knows."

"Tickets to Hawaii or scotch?" asked Matt.

"Both."

At her desk, Miriam clicked and clacked on her computer until the next sound was the soft whirr of the printer. "Okay, we are almost done." She handed them back their IDs and paperwork. "Your license is almost ready."

Matt relaxed slightly. "That was easy."

"Well, yes." Miriam smiled brightly. "Now we just have to set something on the judge's schedule."

Nerves rushed back as Matt attempted to look casual in the awkward office chair. He crossed, uncrossed, and recrossed his legs in a matter of ten seconds, which left Evan staring at him like he'd burped in church.

"We've sort of set things up for Thursday…," Evan said, calm and collected as Matt jittered.

"Hmmm." Miriam clicked and clacked a bit more on her computer, pulling up a calendar program as Matt watched—studiously ignoring Evan's sideways glancing. "I can do first thing in the morning or three thirty."

Evan put his hand on Matt's arm, forcing him to look Evan in the eye. "Three thirty on Thursday work for you?"

"Alliteration-wise, yes," Matt cracked—because that's what he did when he was freaking out—then swallowed a few times. He gave himself a moment to pause, and think, and stare at Evan's stupidly handsome face. For whatever reason, his clearest memory at that moment was the first time they met.

Abe's retirement party, when they were both residents of rock bottom, feeling alone in a crowd. Evan smiling at him from across the table.

"You sure?" Anxiety and scrutiny managed to coexist in Evan's expression.

The breathless and terrifying realization of being in love with Evan disrupted Matt's… everything. Before Evan and After Evan were measured from bitterly getting by to living his best life. It went without saying that this man had changed his life. No other combination of events would have resulted in a better outcome.

Cherish it. Pin that badge on his chest—he'd wear it proudly.

Matt took a deep breath. "Positive."

THEY DUCKED out an employee entrance out back, coming through some scaffolding onto the street. Dozens of people hurried by, paying no notice to the three men standing off to one side, but that didn't stop Evan from keeping alert.

His palms were sweaty, his heart beating against his rib cage, and he needed to get this stupid smile off his face before he got back to the office.

"So I'll see you boys on Thursday?" Abe asked, looking pleased as punch as he rocked back on his heels, hat perched on his head. "Haight? You're picking me up."

Matt's hand tucked into Evan's; his grip tightened as he reflected back his own dumb grin.

"Three o'clock. You got anything besides a funeral suit?" Matt teased.

"My dress blues haven't fit in twenty years." Abe poked him with his cane, rapping his lower leg. "Your choices are a white shirt and a light blue shirt. Same suit, same tie, same shoes."

Evan covered his laughter with a faked cough.

"You at least got a better hat?"

Abe looked affronted but nodded anyway. "Fine. But let me tell you, there better be a bottle of Johnnie Walker Double Black in the car."

"With a red bow on top?"

"I should think so. Now kiss Evan so we can get me home. I got plans." Abe turned to give them some privacy, arms crossed over his chest.

"The man's a decorated police officer, I need to follow his directions," Matt murmured, pulling Evan deeper into the shadows of the scaffolding.

Evan searched Matt's face one more time—looking for nerves or regrets or anything—but only found his ever-present smirk and adoration shining from his eyes.

"I love you," Evan murmured as Matt brushed his fingers along Evan's jaw, an intimate touch that seemed out of place on a busy Bronx street.

"You better," Matt whispered back, moving close enough to kiss. "We're getting married day after tomorrow."

Evan closed the distance between them, eyes shut as he slanted his lips against Matt's.

THEY PARTED at the corner, Matt and Abe moving slowly in one direction as Evan hurried to his car. The marriage license sat in his left jacket pocket, and he could swear it was glowing radioactively.

He checked his phone, answering messages and emails as he waited for the light to change. Nothing was blowing up—thankfully, which meant he didn't have to feel guilty about taking this time off. And taking time off Thursday to get married.

Married.

Evan slowed down, people rushing past him, elbows and shopping bags and purses slamming into him. He didn't notice. The sounds of traffic died around him; his legs kept moving as the wave of humanity pushed him to the other side of the street.

He blinked as he tripped over the curb, nearly dropping his phone.

Gathering his wits, Evan continued the trek to his car.

THE DRIVE back to the city proved uneventful. Evan listened to the radio, prioritized his schedule for the rest of the day, and thought about dinner. Every few minutes, however, he found himself laughing out loud or just smiling so much his face hurt.

Married.

This unexpected giddiness plagued his logical side all the way to the parking garage, following him into the precinct. How could something that made him want to shout from the rooftops and hide it away at the same time exist?

Abe's safely tucked into his barstool. On my way home, Matt texted a few minutes after he arrived at his desk. He included a few emojis that made no sense, like a postal worker, a squirrel, and sushi. If that was wedding code, Evan was at a loss to translate.

See you later, Evan responded, because all his other words were tied up in the glowing paper in his pocket. He didn't even dare take it out lest it fall to the floor and get discovered, because surely his life had turned into a sitcom.

Work called and Evan threw himself into the papers on his desk with gusto, welcoming the distraction.

THEY SURVIVED the next forty-eight hours through sheer determination, some raucous sex, and stress eating. The latter was mostly Matt, who found himself ravenous. Or maybe putting food in his mouth meant keeping quiet, something he was having trouble doing.

It wasn't even a fear he'd blurt out they were getting married. No, it was more that he couldn't stop telling Evan he loved him.

The twins gave him strange looks through dinner as he stuffed another roll in his mouth.

"Matt, you need to drink less coffee during the day," Elizabeth said, pouring him a glass of water and pushing it toward him with a concerned look. "You're, like, about to explode."

Danny made a helpful exploding sound.

"Yes, Matt, less coffee sounds like a plan." Evan kicked him under the table. "Or maybe go to bed early. You need to sleep."

"Ew," Danny muttered, sharing a face with Elizabeth. "Remind me to put my Beats on tonight."

Matt stared at the teens before bursting into snorting laughter. His eyes watered as he helplessly gave in to the nerves that had been plaguing him; he put his hands over his face to try to stem his mirth.

"Is Matt losing it?" Elizabeth whispered across the table.

"No, he's just… tired. And that isn't code for anything." Matt could only hear Evan—and the contained humor in his tone was unmistakable. It was only a matter of time before Evan lost it as well. "I'm going to put him to bed."

Danny coughed.

"Stop making that face, Daniel." Evan's voice broke slightly as Matt felt his whole body shaking.

Matt wiped his eyes, trying to bring himself under control. He grabbed a handful of napkins, taking deep, shuddering breaths until the laughter slowed down to a few snorts. "I'm… fine," he choked out. "Just… tired."

Elizabeth snickered, then gave a snort of her own. "It's like sneezing! I want to laugh now too."

"Oh my God." Danny threw his hands up. "Is there a gas leak in here?"

"Laughing gas?" Elizabeth giggled.

"Not you too," he accused before gathering up his silverware, plate, and glass. "I'm going to eat in the living room where it's quiet."

Elizabeth's eyes twinkled. "Wait for me!" She grabbed her stuff, ignoring her brother's grumbles.

"Defeats the purpose if you follow me!" he yelled over his shoulder.

Matt continued to wipe his eyes, watching as she ran off to bug her brother in front of the television. "God, their future spouses need to be warned about the need they have to bug each other."

"Are you finished with your little...." Evan hand-waved. "What was that?"

"I'm tired," Matt articulated, punctuated with an eye roll.

"You're nuts. Go to bed."

Matt waggled his eyebrows.

Evan's expression threatened to break, but he took a deep breath and settled down into his best captain face. "Mr. Haight, go to bed. That's an order."

Licking his lips, Matt leaned over and kissed Evan's cheek. "Starting the honeymoon early?" He could almost taste the delicious heated flush on his future husband's face; Evan's lips twitched, so Matt stole another peck.

"Maybe." Evan kissed him back, then followed up with a little push against his shoulders. "Go now."

"I love it when you take charge," Matt said as he stood up.

From the living room, he heard Danny groan.

MUCH LIKE their license escapade a few days earlier, they drove separately to the Bronx courthouse. With his good suit tucked in the trunk, Evan had gone off to work, waving goodbye to the twins and Matt like he wasn't holding the biggest secret of the century in his pocket.

Matt waited until the house was empty to put his good duds on, then casually drove to pick up their best man and witness.

Abe, as promised, wore the same outfit he had two days previously, but this time with a blue shirt and a fedora with a peacock feather. He shuffled into the front seat, a delighted grin on his face, and shut the car door with a healthy slam.

"It's the big day, Haight! How're your feet? Cold as ice?"

"Like I'm wearing penguins as shoes," Matt deadpanned.

Hooting, Abe banged on the dashboard. "Let's go, then."

"Your Johnnie Walker's in the back seat. Couldn't find a red bow, so you're settling for green Christmas ribbon I found in the junk drawer."

"I'm going to be honest, I thought gay weddings were a bit classier." Abe shook his head as Matt pulled out of his parking spot. "I seen stuff on the television, and it's always fancy. In a field or something."

"Oddly enough, being in a relationship with Evan did not improve my wedding-planning skills. Weird," Matt said drily. "Then again, my best friend is marrying his boyfriend soon, and I can guarantee... fanciness."

Abe turned on the radio. "Maybe I can get an invite to that wedding."

WITH ABE waiting in the car, restless energy propelled Matt onto the sidewalk for some pacing. Fifteen minutes early, Evan on his way—crisp weather might keep him from sweating through his suit.

Then he saw it. Parked on the corner in front of the Bronx courthouse sat a cart piled with wedding accoutrements. Boutonnières, bouquets, veils, and commemorative picture frames sat alongside tiny plastic bags of confetti. It was an eloping couple's one-stop shop for wedding gear.

Matt contemplated the monstrosity, which hadn't been there when they came for the license, awed at the insidious nature that was the wedding business, taking over this former newsstand in front of the courthouse. Everything they'd tried to avoid, as accessible as halal during lunchtime. He peeked around the back to see if there was a rack of dresses and tuxes tucked behind as well.

No.

"That might actually be a good business plan," he muttered to himself, checking his watch for the tenth time, then felt his pocket to make sure everything was still there.

In Matt's pocket under his vigilant protection? The license, retrieved from their closet, conveniently hidden behind some old snow boots. They'd debated a bit about rings—which neither would wear so what was the point—and decided against them. Matt and Evan were getting married today, playing by their own rules.

He was still wondering why not rings as he debated buying flowers for their lapels.

Abe's pep talk continued to resonate. This wedding felt like a badge he would pin to his chest—we do this because we love each other, and we cherish each other. For no one else but the two of them. When they met, at the bottom of that metaphorical well, the climb out built on their mutual dependence and support. They stood on each other's shoulders until fresh air and light found them again—and this moment felt like putting a flag atop Mount Everest.

He squinted behind his sunglasses, then pulled out his wallet.

"Those two," he said to the young man scrolling through his phone in utter boredom. White roses with those little weed-looking things that always reminded Matt of weddings anyway. "I didn't see this portable wedding mart the other day."

"Twenty-two," the young man said, pocketing his phone to grab the two plastic-bagged flowers. "Sometimes even I need a day off, man. The day before was like, every single person in the Bronx just had to get married. Brutal."

"Jesus Christ," Matt muttered. "Do I even want to know what the bouquets cost?" He dug around his wallet for singles.

"Depends. Cheaper than having your new wife pissed because you forgot." The kid laughed at his own joke.

"Fortunately I'm marrying a man who hates flowers." Matt handed over the bills.

Sign of the times, Matt supposed, because the kid didn't even blink. "No refunds," he warned, eyeing Matt suspiciously. "So why are you bothering?"

Matt sighed as he took the flowers in hand. "The wedding industry is a juggernaut that cannot be stopped, and I just became its latest victim."

EVAN DROVE down the narrow streets surrounding the courthouse, searching for a spot. He'd hoped coming later in the day, at the end of the court's business hours, would afford him something a bit closer, but finally, in desperation, he squeezed the car into a space near the end of the park—which meant a bit of a hike to where Matt waited.

He'd changed into his best suit in a McDonald's bathroom before leaving the city, a flurry of nerves and excitement. Everything seemed to be falling into place, a phenomenon Evan wasn't intimately acquainted with as he walked past throngs of schoolchildren and mothers with baby carriages and old men playing chess. Every step, every clack of his dress shoes on the pavement, brought him closer to Matt and this dip into… un-Evan-like behavior.

His palms began to sweat.

Fumbling, Evan got his phone out to text Matt.

Where are you?

Look for the giant wedding mall on the corner.

What?

You cannot miss it. Believe me.

A few more blocks and Evan spotted Matt pacing in front of a newsstand, except as he got closer, he realized what Matt meant. A woman tried on a veil as someone he presumed to be her mother held an ornate picture frame in each hand as if trying to decide between them.

Matt spotted him when he reached the other side of the street; Evan waved nervously as he waited for the light to change.

"Hey," he said as he jogged over to Matt's side, heart fluttering. "Wow, you look great."

Matt's best suit—the navy rich client suit, the one Bennett and Daisy had given him two Christmases ago—fit him perfectly, so much so that Evan gave him a lingering once-over.

"You always give me that look when I wear this," Matt said delightedly. He waved two small plastic containers under Evan's nose. "Here, have a rose."

"Oh." Evan hadn't thought of flowers, but the little white rose, already halfway to wilted, made him smile. "Perfect."

"You ready to do this?" Matt handed him one container, then opened the one he kept. When he moved to pin it on Evan, Evan got light-headed with what felt strangely like lust.

"Huh?"

Matt fussed with the giant pin and Evan's lapel. "Are you ready to get hitched? And why is this so hard? I did this for prom, why can't I remember?"

Evan tried not to flinch when Matt stuck him. "Prom for you was like, forty-seven years ago," he said.

Indignant, Matt stuck him again, this time clearly on purpose.

"Yes, by the way. I'm ready to get married," Evan said finally. Matt grinned as he managed to attach the rose to Evan's jacket.

"Excellent. Because I'm really looking forward to the honeymoon."

Evan returned the favor, attaching the boutonnière onto Matt's jacket. And maybe he copped a feel of the chest beneath that fancy blue suit.

"You are quite the randy groom," Matt muttered, leaning over to smack a quick kiss on Evan's lips.

"Who knew?" Evan cleared his throat as Matt walked over to drop the empty plastic containers into the garbage can on the corner. He felt a little drunk as he stared at Matt, his brain shorting out.

Mine.

Matt detoured on his way back to go to his car, which Evan realized was parked near the corner. A second later the door opened and Abe's fedoraed head appeared.

He waved wildly at Evan as Matt helped him out of the car.

This was it, Evan thought. This was really it.

"This is very exciting," Abe said as he reached Evan's side. He noticed the flower on Evan, then Matt, and then looked at Evan again. "What? The best man doesn't get one?"

"I got you Johnnie Walker Double Black!" Matt reached for his wallet, mumbling as he walked back over to the Marriage Mart on the corner.

Abe poked Evan in the ribs. "You okay? Haight's vibrating like his On button is stuck. You look dazed."

Evan blinked a few times; fully aware he was still staring at Matt. "I'm great, actually. Surprisingly." Because truth be told, he'd expected a certain amount of freaking out by now. Not the fluttering joy in his chest. Not the lustful gaze. "It's going to be nice to bust his balls later for being the nervous groom."

"You crazy kids," Abe chuckled.

Matt returned with a carnation spray-painted a sickly bright blue. "I think this matches the bird attached to your hat."

"It does, actually." Sticking out his chest, Abe smiled brightly as Matt attached it—this time without much groping.

"You're getting good at that," Evan said.

"I'm ready for prom."

Evan checked his watch. "I hope you're also ready to get married, because we have to get upstairs."

THEY MET Miriam at the employees' entrance again. She sparkled with delight at their suits and cooed over the flowers. "I have some rice at my desk if you think it'll help the mood, and I'm available for flower girl duties." Her floral dress fit the offer perfectly.

The trek through the hallways went much quicker and much less anxiously; Evan knew at the end of the workday no one would notice the weird little party hoofing it toward the judge's chambers.

"Hi, Darrell!" Miriam greeted the bailiff and then knocked on the judge's door.

"Come," a stern voice echoed from the other side.

"Wernicky," Matt muttered. "Anyone know him?"

Evan shrugged. The name didn't ring a bell. Abe responded in kind.

"He's super nice," Miriam chimed in as she opened the door. "And he's promised this is totally a private thing."

In Judge Wernicky's chambers, a blast of air-conditioning greeted them. Behind the large wood desk—freshly shined—sat an enormous man, like a Jets linebacker had been thrown into a robe and arranged to look official.

Evan guessed him to be about fifty, with a Marine's haircut and ruddy complexion. He stood up and Evan felt his head tilt back. Not a football player—maybe basketball. His head was the size of a car engine.

"Gentlemen," he said gruffly. He approached them with his hand outstretched. "Congratulations."

"We appreciate your discretion, sir." Evan tried not to wince as the judge crushed his hand.

"Miriam explained things to me." Judge Wernicky's broad face broke into a lighthearted grin, and his voice rose about two octaves. "Just so you know, this is my thing. I'm kind of known as the judge to the stars. Lots of private ceremonies, lots of stuff done on the QT." He chuckled. "You should see all the pictures I can't show people!"

"That sounds dirty," Matt whispered for Evan's ears only.

Judge Wernicky clapped his hands. "Shall we, gentlemen?"

THERE WAS certain poetry to a jovial giant marrying them. A judge that could bench-press all three of them with one hand while scrolling through his phone to show them a photo of "that guy from the TV show and the model."

To break up the sausage fest, Miriam stood to one side, holding the judge's cactus like a demented flower girl. Abe planted himself next to Matt, surreptitiously tucking a handkerchief that Matt pretended not to notice in his pocket.

"You want some pictures to commemorate the occasion? Maybe a video?" the judge asked, indicating Miriam.

Evan froze for a second, and Matt scanned his face for some sort of assistance in answering.

"Actually," Evan said, "yes. That would be great."

Matt felt his face folding into confusion. "Really?"

"I'll hide it in the tax file," he said, shrugging. "No one will find it there." He handed his phone to Miriam, who put the cactus back on the windowsill. "It might be nice to, you know, have."

"Okay. That's weird coming from you." Matt wiped his damp palms on his pants. He turned to the judge, then a wildly grinning Abe. "Okay. Here we go."

"You want the quick version? Because if not, I have a really nice thing I do for people in love," the judge said.

"Do the love thing," Abe spoke up. "Nice and mushy."

Wernicky looked delighted. "Outstanding. Mentions of God?"

"No, thanks," Matt said with confidence.

"Any readings at all? I'm sure we can find something that suits."

"Well…," Evan started to say, but Miriam piped up.

"Can I make a case for some Brontë?"

Evan and Matt shared a look, and Evan swore he heard Matt's voice in his head.

"Miriam, you've been so sweet to us. We would love whatever you pick. Would you mind reading it?"

"Oh, of course!"

"Very nice." The judge clearly approved. "Rings?"

"No, actually. We can skip that part," Evan said as Matt squeezed his hand. "Is that okay?"

"Sure, sure." The judge went to his desk and collected a piece of paper from the blotter. "I think that's everything, folks. Let's get this going."

"DEARLY BELOVED, we are gathered today to join Evan Cerelli and Matthew Haight in matrimony." The judge loomed over them, the piece of paper in hand seemingly dwarfed by his size. "While some may think a courthouse wedding isn't romantic, I think it says, 'Screw all the fancy stuff, we just want to get hitched.'"

Evan's mouth wobbled in amusement as he clutched Matt's hands.

"You two have come before me today with the intention to seal your union. Making a life together doesn't have much use for a piece of paper, but tradition and the law have made this ceremony something of importance. Solemn but joyful. Symbolic but binding.

"Evan and Matthew, today you celebrate one of life's greatest moments and give recognition to the worth and beauty of love, as you join together in vows of marriage." He winked. "Just to get this out of the way, anyone have any reason to object?"

Abe snickered.

"Good. Miriam, you okay over there?"

Miriam chuckled behind the phone as she recorded the moment for posterity.

"Excellent." Judge Wernicky cleared his throat and ruffled the paper. "Here we go.

"Evan, do you take Matthew to be your husband?"

"I do," Evan said, loudly and clearly, even as his throat went rough.

"Do you promise to love, honor, cherish, and protect him, forsaking all others and holding only unto him?"

"Yes, I do." Matt squeezed his hands tightly as Evan spoke the words directly to him.

"Matthew, do you take Evan to be your husband?"

"Hell yes."

"Do you promise to love, honor, cherish, and protect him, forsaking all others and holding only unto him?"

"I do."

Judge Wernicky beamed at them.

"Almost there, gentlemen. Evan, repeat after me…."

Evan took a deep breath, ready to recite the familiar vows. "I, Evan, take you, Matthew, to be my husband. To have and to hold, in sickness and in health, for richer or for poorer, and I promise my love to you." Evan exhaled slowly. "Always. Even when you live only to drive me crazy."

Matt sniffled loudly, which set off Abe, and Evan coughed in an attempt not to break into nervous laughter.

"I, Matthew, take you, Evan, to be my husband. To have and to hold, in sickness and in health, for richer or for poorer, and I promise my love to you." Matt nodded as he said the words. "Even when you get all… Evan," he added softly.

Abe snickered, then blew his nose loudly.

"Miriam?"

She'd arranged the phone on its stand, sitting on the judge's file cabinet. Ducking into the shot, Miriam took her own phone out of her dress pocket and began to read.

"I have two things to share." She cleared her throat. "Emily Brontë wrote, 'Whatever our souls are made of, his and mine are the same.'" Miriam looked up, giving them a delighted smile.

"And then I turn to her sister Charlotte to add, 'I ask you to pass through life at my side—to be my second self, and best earthly companion,'" she said with a sigh.

"Oh man," Matt said wetly, and Evan broke into a damp laugh of his own. Miriam couldn't have chosen a better set of quotes to grace their ceremony with.

"Perfect." The judge continued. "Evan and Matthew, just as two very different threads woven in opposite directions can form a beautiful tapestry, so can your two lives merge together to form a very beautiful marriage. To make your marriage work will take love. That is the core of your marriage, as it's the reason you are here. But it also will take trust—to know in your hearts you want the best for each other. It will take dedication—to stay open to one another, to learn and to grow together even when this is not always so easy to do. It will take faith—to always be willing to go forward to tomorrow, never really knowing what tomorrow will bring. And it will take commitment—to hold true to the journey you both now pledge to share together."

Evan couldn't look away from Matt's face, but the sound of Abe's breath hitching was unmistakable.

"Evan and Matthew, insomuch as the two of you have agreed to live together in matrimony and have promised your love for each other by these vows, I now declare you to be husband and husband."

Time seemed to suspend for a moment. Evan swallowed back a burst of intense emotion as he stared into his husband's face. To know such love twice in a lifetime was unexpected; he'd never felt so humble.

"Congratulations, gentlemen, you may seal your union with a kiss."

"Now the part I can really get behind," Matt choked out, grabbing Evan's face with both hands. "This was an excellent idea."

Evan was still laughing when Matt pressed their lips together with exuberance.

"MAZEL TOV," Abe Klein said, clapping his hands together. Miriam cheered and clapped along with Judge Wernicky. Matt heard all this from a distance as he kissed Evan until he pulled back in need of air.

"That," he said, still holding on to Evan, "was weirdly awesome. And I'm glad no one was here to watch me be the sap."

Evan pulled away just enough to wipe his eyes with his fist. "I'm keeping that video for blackmail purposes."

Abe pounded Matt on the back; they turned to find the older man dabbing at his face with his handkerchief. "Congratulations, boys."

Feeling wildly emotional, Matt disengaged from Evan long enough to give Abe a tight hug. "Thanks for everything, Abe."

"This is a good day, a very good day," he muttered before wiggling out of Matt's grasp. He coughed, not making eye contact with anyone for a moment. "Evan? You keep this idiot in line."

"I just promised to do that. The 'idiot' was understood." Evan patted Abe's arm. "We appreciate everything you've done for us."

"Eh. I just wanted to get out a little bit." Abe put his gruff exterior on, stepping back from their little circle. "And you know, the scotch."

Matt sniffled, giving Abe his space. "Should have brought it in. I could use a belt."

"We have a few pieces of paper to sign, gentlemen, and then I'll let you get on your way," Judge Wernicky said gently, interrupting their conversation. "Miriam?"

She shut off the phone, fiddling with it for a second. "All saved." She handed it back to Evan. "I labeled it 'tax videos.'"

"Perfect." Evan tucked the phone into his jacket pocket. Matt grabbed his other hand, holding tight. "Thank you so much."

"My pleasure. Now let me get clerking!"

Miriam fussed at the judge's desk for a few moments. Matt felt like the ground was moving underneath him; Evan's hand kept him steady as he tried to reconcile what just happened. He didn't expect the flood of emotions, didn't expect to feel so freaking happy at this moment. From the dazed look on his face, Evan wasn't all that prepared either.

When Matt's phone buzzed in his pocket, he jumped with surprise.

He pulled it out, checking the screen. "Danny's having dinner at Ollie's house," he said. "Elizabeth is going to the gym with Jane." Matt gave Evan his best waggling eyebrows. "We have the house to ourselves until at least eight."

Evan's eyes got wide. "I hope we don't hit any traffic."

JUDGE WERNICKY slapped them both on the back and insisted on taking a picture, after swearing on an actual Bible that he'd never show anyone. Miriam hugged them repeatedly, then Abe, then Evan and Matt again.

"Tell Buddy I said thank you," Abe said, kissing her cheek before they left.

"I'll send the marriage certificate to Abe's place," Miriam promised. "Your secret is safe with me."

"We need to buy her a pony," Matt said as they walked down the hall toward the now familiar back exit.

"Flowers at least." Evan squeezed his hand as they kept the pace slow so Abe could keep up.

When they reached the corner, the wedding accoutrements cart was closed down, and the entire bustle associated with the courthouse dissipated. A chilly wind blew as the sun started to go down, and Evan took the moment in, a mental picture to keep tucked away.

"I'll drop Abe off, then meet you at home?" Matt asked, pulling him into a hug.

"Yeah. Give me a chance to, uh, set things up." Evan hoped his husband—*husband*—got the message.

He shouldn't have doubted it for a second, because Matt's grin could be seen from space.

"Perfect. And I hid a bottle of champagne behind the basement freezer." He somehow made that sound dirty. Evan's body responded in a borderline embarrassing way.

Made more embarrassing when Abe Klein coughed like he'd caught the plague.

"I am an open-minded person, but if you start making out on this street corner, I'm going to hit you with my cane," he announced, just loud enough to make Evan jump back. "Call me old-fashioned."

"Maybe if you'd kissed your wives in public you'd still be married, twice," Matt deadpanned as he kissed Evan on the cheek before letting him go.

"I'll have you know there were no complaints in that department." Abe drew himself up to full height. "If you need some pointers for your wedding night, I have some moves that'll blow your—"

"And I'm going to my car now," Evan interrupted. "Walking away quickly, pretending I don't know you people." He gave Abe a salute. "Thank you again."

"I'd say anytime, but you two better not split up." He gave a serious scowl in Evan's direction. "You hear me?"

"This is it," Evan said, finding Matt's gaze in the dimming light. Even if, God forbid, he found himself alone again....

"Good. Now take me home, Matthew. I have some Johnnie Walker Double Black to enjoy."

"I MEANT it," Abe said as Matt pulled down his block, looking for a spot to double-park so he could let his friend out. "Don't let me down."

Matt laughed, finding a partially open space near a fire hydrant. "Abe, this was just a thing... a wonderful thing, it turns out, but it doesn't change a thing. I'm not going anywhere. If he kicks me out, I'll camp out in the backyard until I can charm my way back through the front door."

"Don't let it come to that." Abe was being disturbingly serious, and Matt put the car into Park when he angled into the spot. He hit the flashers just in case.

"Why are you worried all of a sudden? I thought you were happy for us."

Abe looked out the passenger window, his face obscured by the shadows and his hat. "I just want what's best for you, Matty," he said, calling up his old nickname. "You haven't had it easy."

Matt reached out to touch Abe's shoulder, giving it a squeeze until his friend turned to face him. "I appreciate that. Hasn't been a smooth ride, but the last few years… I don't know. Maybe it makes up for all that shit."

Truth was, he almost never thought about it. The job, the disgrace, the unfair decisions made by people in power. When he lost his badge, he thought his life was over, but in retrospect, it was gearing up to begin.

"I'm proof positive when it comes to second chances. So don't worry, okay?"

Abe nodded, then patted Matt's hand. "I'll drink my worries away."

"That's the spirit."

MATT GOT Abe into his apartment with his cane and his fancy hat and his bottle of scotch. "I'll call you in a few days. We'll have lunch."

"You know where to find me." Abe shrugged out of his suit jacket as he waved Matt away. "Don't forget to take your flower off."

"Damn." Matt put his hand on his lapel. "You really earned that liquor."

Another quick hug and then Matt was running for the front door of the building, pressing the key fob to open the doors of his car. If he blessedly missed some traffic, he might be home in time to enjoy both the champagne and his new husband.

EVAN CALLED the precinct from the car as he drove home. Everything was fine, no need for him to come in, but he should be advised that his meeting calendar for tomorrow had filled in his absence. Of course.

"See you tomorrow," he said, ending the call with a shrug. And he would be worrying about it tomorrow, because right now, he had plans.

Sexual plans, which made his face burn. He expected to feel a little emotional today, but horny? So not his usual style.

If things went the way he wanted, Matt was going to insist they get married every other month.

He removed the boutonnière at a traffic light a few blocks from home and dropped it into his jacket pocket.

EVAN FOUND the ice bucket in the bottom of the china closet, filled with New Year's Eve themed napkins and a handful of blackout candles. He dumped everything out, then walked to the kitchen. Ice, check. Champagne he'd brought up from the basement, check. Other supplies necessary—already in the bedroom. Evan himself?

Thoroughly and completely ready to go.

He kept one eye on the microwave clock as he gathered what he needed, then climbed the stairs. New ETAs for the twins put them in at nine, as per the flood of texts on his phone a few minutes ago, and he was loath to act out of character by telling them to stay out later on a school night.

Come on, Evan, he thought to himself, *you deserve to get laid tonight*.

"What's gotten into me?" he asked aloud at the top of the stairs, then heard Matt's voice answering.

Blushing, he hurried into the bedroom.

THE CLEAN sheets Evan left next to the bed because they'd probably need them afterward. He grabbed two towels he privately referred to as the sex towels from the closet, laying them on the nightstand. Candle ready to be lit—oh God, was that too cheesy? He checked his phone again.

Five minutes. Matt's last text put him about two minutes away, and Evan debated stripping out of his shorts and T-shirt for a full thirty seconds.

Well, that would appear overanxious.

He turned back the sheets when he heard the front door open, then lit the candle. What the hell, you only live once.

MATT WAS halfway out of his suit jacket by the time he hit the stairs. His brain ran a nonstop blur of things he wanted to do when he made it to the bedroom, but he forced himself to slow down just a touch.

Not a booty call—his wedding night. Evening. They had about ninety minutes, according to Evan's last text.

Breathing deeply, Matt got to the bedroom door and… knocked.

"Idiot," he said.

The door opened, with a confused—and barely dressed—Evan on the other side. "Why did you knock?"

Matt gestured with both hands. "I have literally no idea."

Evan smirked as he grabbed Matt's tie. "You have been a revelation today."

"So have you." Matt let himself be dragged into the bedroom, throwing his best sultry eyes. "I'm a sap and you're a fucking horndog. If I'd known that, I'd have married you sooner."

"I knew you'd say that."

Matt tried to lean in for a kiss, but Evan dodged him, maneuvering Matt into the bedroom, then turned him around. "Come here," Matt growled, but Evan surprised him by letting go of his tie, then shoving him onto the bed.

Barely having time to react, Matt found himself with a lapful of Evan, who straddled him with a forcefulness that had him hard and panting in a split second. He ran his hands down to grab Evan's ass, grinding up as he did.

Matt's eyes rolled back into his head with pleasure as Evan smirked down at him.

"You still want that kiss?" he murmured, cupping his hands around the back of Matt's head.

"I can think of a few other places for your mouth," Matt answered before yanking at the waistband of Evan's boxers.

"I was thinking the same thing." Evan leaned down, teasing Matt by darting down, then pulling back before he could catch a kiss. He pushed his dick against Matt's stomach, grinding down with a clear message.

"Tell me we are ready to go," Matt gasped, getting a little more focused on separating Evan from his shorts. "Because I can't wait."

"You're wearing too many clothes." When Evan slid off his lap, Matt made a grab to keep him close.

The tented boxers didn't stay on Evan for very long—he stripped them off, then followed with his T-shirt. Matt put his hand on his dick with a laugh. "Killing me."

"We've got all night," Evan murmured.

"Ninety minutes."

"I have faith in you."

Matt attacked his shirt buttons as Evan walked around to the other side of the bed to stand behind him. He crawled behind him, hands stroking up his now bare arms to his shoulders.

"Let me help you with that." He reached down to grab the hem of Matt's undershirt, pulling it over his head in one quick move. He backed away, giving Matt room to move. "Lie back."

In a hot second, Matt twisted slightly, falling back onto the bed, looking up at Evan with a smug expression. "Oh, perfect view," he murmured, reaching over his head to wrap his arms around Evan's hips. "Come here."

"I thought you were fucking me," Evan said boldly, allowing himself to be positioned over Matt's mouth.

"Hmmm," Matt responded, then lifted his head to slowly suck the head of Evan's dick.

EVAN BEGAN to shake. Matt teased him with licks, then drew him back in just shallow enough to drive Evan out of his mind. Sweat trickled down the back of his neck as he angled his body forward, balancing on one hand while the other attempted to unhook Matt's belt.

Not easy, particularly when Matt gripped his fingers into Evan's hips, shoving him deeper into his mouth.

"Unfair," Evan choked, losing himself in the sensation of Matt's mouth and Matt's fingers holding him in place and Matt's unerring ability to blow his freaking mind.

Among other things.

"Matt, Matt." Panting, Evan got the belt and top button open; the zipper proved difficult when one of Matt's palms came down hard on his ass. Stars—he saw actual stars, both elbows giving out as he collapsed on Matt's body.

"Two can play at that game," he muttered, drawing the impressive hard-on currently under him into his hand.

MATT'S THROAT burned as Evan sprawled over him, taking him deeper than he'd been expecting, but no complaints, not a one as he brought his hand down again on Evan's ass. The feel of his husband—husband!—stroking broke the rhythm for a second; he choked a bit, then angled his hips up with encouragement.

For a moment, at least. Until his self-control started to slip as Evan started to thrust and he started to thrust and the goal… mission started to fade.

Matt pushed Evan's hips up far enough to pull off with a loud slurp.

"Easy, killer, I have plans," he rasped.

"You started it." Evan licked the head of Matt's dick in clear defiance.

Laughing, Matt gave Evan a shove, knocking him over onto the mattress.

"How much work do I have to do here?"

Evan didn't say anything, but the smirk was delightful. Delicious. He seemed to consider Matt's question, then slowly rolled over onto his stomach.

"Where's the…." Matt didn't get the whole question out because Evan's hand was sliding under the pillow as soon as he opened his mouth. The bottle landed on his stomach a second later.

"Damn."

"Ninety minutes," Evan reminded, folding his arms and laying his head down.

"Goddamn." Matt sat up, stripping out of his pants and boxers so fast he heard a sonic boom. He shifted on the bed, moving until he could straddle Evan's lower legs—a perfect view of the muscled back and supremely enjoyable ass Matt would be coming home to for the rest of his natural life.

Yeah, there was a reason Evan didn't let him write his own vows. He'd have absolutely included that ass.

"Ninety—" Evan began, but Matt interrupted him with a sucking kiss at the middle of his shoulder blades.

"Shut up, please."

He slid back a little more until he could push Evan's legs apart just enough to reach his goal. A stretch of his hand got the lube, and he resumed his journey as he flicked the top open, licking down to the base of his spine, enjoying every moan and mutter from above.

He smirked as Evan struggled to open his legs a bit wider—desperate, okay, yes, Matt thought as he swiped his tongue just enough to tease. At the loud groan, Matt sat up and squeezed the lube onto his fingers. The wedding ceremony had clearly been foreplay, because he couldn't wait, and from the way Evan writhed underneath him, he wasn't going to complain about fast and hard.

"How much?" Matt asked, teasing gently before sliding a finger inside Evan.

"Hurry up." Evan squirmed, shoving back urgently. He pushed up on his knees, nearly knocking Matt off the bed, disengaging their bodies. "Don't need… before you got here," he huffed.

Matt almost swallowed his tongue as he admired the gorgeous slope of Evan's body, the way he opened himself up. Dizzy with want, Matt grabbed Evan's hips again, lining up, almost breathless with how much he wanted this.

When he pushed in—slowly, because otherwise he feared hurting Evan—Matt saw spots. His whole body burned with want.

Evan moaned beneath him, part pain and part pleasure. The familiar soundtrack to their intimacy signaled Matt to press in, a little bit harder, a little bit faster. He thrust gently, pushing and then pulling, spurred on by each sound drawn out of Evan's throat. Leaning down, Matt wrapped an arm around Evan's neck, anchoring them together front to back, sweat slicking each movement.

"Okay?" Matt muttered, trying to catch his breath as his hips began to shift sharply and Evan shoved backward.

Evan didn't say anything; he angled his elbows against the mattress, then began an almost relentless movement against Matt.

"Oh" was all Matt managed before responding in kind. The bed shook beneath them, rattling the nightstands and jerking the headboard into the wall. Matt thought the whole room was going to collapse around them as he held on for dear life while Evan went crazy beneath him.

His orgasm began to rush up suddenly; one second he lost himself in every rough stroke, the next he felt everything seize up, his thrusts going frantic. Enough sense reminded him to reach around to hurry Evan up, but his fingers encountered proof Evan was taking care of that himself.

"Holy shit," Matt babbled as Evan's free hand gripped the sheets.

"Oh fuck," Evan gasped. "Oh fuck."

Everything went nuclear after that; Matt's orgasm couldn't be denied as he tightened his forearm around Evan's neck and let his body go. Everything stuttered, then stopped; then Evan frantically moved beneath him until he came with a shout.

THE FIRST thing Evan heard as he came back from whatever sexual deviancy just occurred was Matt murmuring, "We still have forty minutes" against his ear.

"It's going to take me that long to clean up," Evan said into the mattress, where his face was currently pressed.

Matt pulled out gently, and Evan didn't even flinch. Oh how he was going to pay for this tomorrow, during his full meeting schedule.

He smiled as Matt began kissing his back and shoulders.

"How about a shower?" Evan asked, turning his head to one side.

Snickering, Matt pinched his ass.

SHOWERED—AND WITH a slightly sore throat given his performance on his knees—Evan jogged downstairs in his boxers and T-shirt, leaving Matt snoring under the covers.

"I did a lot of work tonight," Matt said before he faded out.

The lights were out, including the outside light, which meant the kids were home. In the kitchen, he found half a pizza in the fridge with a Post-it Note stuck on the box. A smiley face and two hearts meant Elizabeth.

Evan put the note on the fridge under a magnet.

Their wedding dinner would consist of half a sausage and mushroom pizza, a crumb cake they kept "in case of company," and a box of cheese breadsticks he found in the cabinet. He tried to class it up a bit, put everything on a tray with a handful of napkins, all the while musing over the day.

He'd spent most of his life as a married man—far longer than he hadn't, between living with Matt and being with Sherri. Once again Evan Cerelli was someone's husband. Wasn't always good at it—sometimes he was fucking terrible. Sometimes he hadn't a clue what he'd done to deserve both Sherri and Matt in his life, to have them both be such amazing people who loved him despite his flaws.

His hands paused as he arranged the plates. No ring on his finger, but a peace settled into every molecule of his body.

WAKING FROM his catnap, Matt rolled over, arm hitting the empty pillow beside him.

He registered every delicious burn in his body, then stretched with a smile. Oh hell yes, quite a kickoff to their night of nuptial celebration. Rounds one and two, impressive. Round three would be a stretch, because he wasn't as young as he used to be....

The door creaked open. Evan ducked in, hands full of a tray laden with food. Matt smelled pizza and sat up with interest. "How did you magic up sausage?"

"Elizabeth loves us." Evan kicked the door closed behind him.

"Don't tell Katie, but she's my favorite tonight."

"Hey."

He laid the tray on the end of the bed, a look of suggestive indignation on his face.

Matt plumped the pillows up behind him, then leaned over to grab the half bottle of champagne. "Favorite child. You're my favorite… everything else," he said, waving the bottle in Evan's direction.

"That's better." Evan handed him a plate of pizza.

THEY SAT shoulder to shoulder, hip to hip, eating their pizza, then the breadsticks, then the cake, and sharing the bottle of champagne. Matt considered this the height of hedonistic behavior from Evan, and sighed with the pleasure of it. He knew Evan's true nature would correct course at some point, but he was milking every last drop.

"This isn't the smartest thing I've ever done," Evan said, indicating the bottle, then gesturing toward his ass. "I have about sixty-four meetings tomorrow."

"I'm sorry. You might want to bring a cushion to sit on. The only thing on my to-do list is I have to make fun of Jim impregnating Griffin's sister and order groceries online."

"Well, now you have to blow me to make up for it."

"Yes, dear." Matt kissed Evan on the cheek.

They ate the last of the crumb cake in silence.

"But tomorrow, because I'm tired."

Matt sighed dramatically as he drained the last of the champagne. "That didn't last long."

"What?"

"The newlywed bliss."

Evan elbowed him, then stole his last bit of cake. Silly and carefree Evan—he wanted to bottle it and keep it forever, like the wedding video file tucked away in the tax folder on Evan's phone.

Matt laid his head against the headboard, studying Evan's profile. "We're still not uh… telling people, are we?" he asked cautiously.

Evan turned his head. "No. Aren't we?"

"Yes." Matt wiped his hands and face with a napkin. "I'm sure about it."

"Are you?"

"Yes."

Matt crumpled the napkin into a ball and threw it at Evan's face. "Who's on first?"

"I CAN'T believe no one has figured this out," Evan murmured into Matt's ear as they twirled around the dance floor.

Matt tightened his arms around Evan's waist, slotting them close together in a way that bordered on dirty.

Evan didn't care.

"Especially since they're such nosy sons of bitches."

They moved slowly, trading off who was leading like it was second nature. They were getting good at this, the give and take, letting instinct be their guide instead of thinking too hard.

Evan knew, in the quiet of the moment, that this was their real secret. How they made this work—made them work.

Trust.

Letting go.

"Stop thinking so loud. This is romantic," Matt whispered, ending his words with a kiss against the curve of Evan's ear.

It was romantic, cradled in Matt's arms, the whirling dervish of the night settling around them.

"We could make an announcement," he said, thinking of the kids' excitement, Jim and Griffin's support, Helena and Shane's enthusiasm.

"Or we could keep a secret like we agreed." Matt moved his head just enough to give Evan a look.

"Fine." Evan laid his head back on Matt's shoulder. A secret just for them. Yes, that seemed right.

The DJ switched songs but not tempos: an old Motown song that invited more couples to the dance floor. Evan saw love in every stage— blushing teens to folks just grateful to have an intimate moment away from the kids to the smooth dancing moves of those who'd been doing this for decades.

This wasn't the way his life was supposed to go, but this was exactly where he was meant to be.

2
A CHRISTMAS WEDDING:
MATT'S FAVORITE CHILD GETS MARRIED

MATT KNEW it was coming. His stepparent antenna triggered and twitched as the calendar years passed. Danny got taller and taller; Elizabeth became less and less recognizable. As Miranda and Kent settled into an adult relationship, Matt felt the hands of time moving as obviously as his hairline.

He tried not to see the kids as they were that first snowy day, when he showed up and faced two teenagers and two cherub-faced little ones who invited him for breakfast and never let him leave.

They were the ones leaving now. Soon.

Growing up.

Going to school.

Picking careers.

Falling in love.

Fashioning lives of their own.

Dealing with these emotions, these logistics, didn't come naturally to Matt. Every step for each of the kids was like the world's worst surprise party. You didn't want it, you refused to participate, but everyone jumped out from behind the sofa anyway.

Or something like that.

He tried to prepare, even going so far as googling—the only thing less embarrassing than going to the bookstore and wandering through the self-help section. He went to a Barnes & Noble on Long Island, for God's sake, just to make sure no one recognized him.

Jim and Griffin were dealing with potty training—zero help. Same with Bennett and Daisy. Helena just blinked, and Shane threatened to write a play based on "Matt's beautiful pain." His friend Liz the Shrink had moved to California in another fit of geographical betrayal.

He hated them all.

Bringing it up to Evan seemed cruel, because if Matt felt himself missing piles of laundry, who knew what could trigger Evan?

WHEN MIRANDA and Kent had gotten married two years ago, it was expected and executed appropriately for the longtime couple. Matt and Evan sat down with Blake and Cornelia—Kent's parents—and the kids, and with the aid of savings accounts, a calculator, and six pens and legal pads, they'd put a small yet classy affair together. A wedding hall in Brooklyn, her mother's remade gown, a college friend turned DJ, and a host of tears—it was lovely.

The long courtship gave Evan time to adjust—mostly. Kent was a great kid from a good family, and Miranda's turbulent teen years and young adulthood had given way to a measured and responsible woman with goals and plans, like she'd taken Evan's neurotic streak and refined and aimed it toward whatever she decided to do next. When she and Kent felt bored by the prospect of international banking (and who could blame them), they turned their attention to technical writing, opening up a small and lucrative company of their own out of their Brooklyn apartment.

He was proud of how little he cried. In public, that was. No one blamed him for needing two tissues when Miranda asked Matt to dance at the reception.

Time marched on, but at least it seemed to be going in a good direction.

Six months after the wedding, Katie, their second-oldest, came home from Boston for the holidays with a boy.

Which was not unusual. Katie always seem to have a swarm of them around her; Matt and Evan had met a few here or there over the years, during college visits and then later when she'd made the permanent move to Boston to work for the Celtics front office.

"The Celtics!"

"Matt, calm down. At least it's not the Red Sox."

"I know, I just… I feel so betrayed. We raised her better than that."

But this time the boy was a man named Austin, and he looked like a male model doing a photo shoot as a college professor. Warm brown skin and artfully braided hair that fell down to his shoulders, tall and slight—and blinking adoring eyes behind thick nerd glasses that weren't just for show. A true genius, apparently, studying a mishmash of words that Evan didn't understand at MIT. A true genius who apparently didn't realize he looked like he fell out of the pages of *Vogue for Dudes*.

"That isn't what it's called, Matt."

"Why do you know that?"

"I don't know the exact name, I'm just saying it's probably not Vogue for Dudes.*"*

Austin brought a lot of things into the relationship, one of which was a four-year-old boy named Josiah who lived with his father full-time. A ready-made family, which caused the entire relationship to bypass "dating and casual" for "serious as hell" in a hot second.

From the outside, one might imagine Matt's reluctance stemmed from the difficulties they might face together: Austin's potential career demands and travel, being an interracial couple, having a small child to raise right off the bat. They were both still in their twenties—even smart people needed life experience, and they were starting low in that department.

But everyone who knew Matt knew it wasn't any of those things.

On the other hand, Austin's youth and his fatherhood were the biggest icebreaker for Evan, because he knew the struggle of being a single father, and he admired Austin's parenting more than anything on his résumé. Josiah was a sweet and charming little boy who had him and Matt in his pocket by the end of their first visit.

Evan monitored the situation like he was on a case: new information was carefully cataloged; assessments were made. He talked to Katie, assuring her that Matt would come around. He talked to Matt to remind him that he needed to get over himself.

"It's too soon."

"For what? Her to fall in love?"

"Ugh, shut up. Stop saying those words."

"You know they're living together...."

"You're her father! Why aren't you more...."

"More what? Anxious? Twitchy? We have two more to go after this, Matt. I'd like to have a stomach lining when I retire."

One night a knock at the door revealed Austin nervously clutching an overnight bag. As soon as Evan opened the door, he knew exactly what this visit was about.

"Katie thinks this is a misogynistic ritual and I'm caving to archaic societal expectations," Austin began once they installed him at the dining room table with a beer.

Matt took two.

"And yet you're here," Matt said.

"Well, I respect Katie's thoughts on this—honestly, I feel the same way. Katie isn't property, and we are absolutely equals in every respect to our relationship," he said, slowly peeling the wrapper off the bottle.

"But?" Evan prompted.

"My parents told me to get my ass down here and do this right."

"Or else?"

Austin finally cracked a smile. "You know my parents?"

"It's in the old-school handbook." Evan put a soothing hand on Matt's shaking leg, which was currently rattling the table. "I'm looking forward to meeting them."

Austin's smile brightened.

"And I know," Evan continued, "that you have the utmost respect for my daughter and have no crazy ideas of including the word *obey* in any sort of, uh… ceremony… you might be planning."

"She'd kill me."

"I'd hold you down," Matt muttered.

Evan squeezed his knee. "It's nice to hear you say it, though, just like it's appreciated, you coming down to talk to us."

The young man swallowed, then sat up a bit straighter. With his dress shirt and tie, he looked like he was about to sell them insurance. "Well, sir. Sirs. I'd like to make it official. Katie is—Katie is everything I could have imagined in a partner. I'm a logical person, a scientist, I like order and reason, and for all the lists I could make you of why I love her, there's just a whole lot of…" He paused to take a deep breath. "…stuff I can't explain. And that's the best part." Austin took another, deeper breath. "The way she's taken to my son is a gift, and he loves her back, so much. I feel so fortunate to have found her." He paused again, appearing to collect himself. "I'm going to ask Katie to marry me when I get back to Boston. And I'd like to take your blessing back with me."

Evan could see Austin's earnest and honest feelings for his daughter written all over his face. He was sure. He knew Katie was sure. He knew that without his blessing, they would be getting married anyway—but he didn't want that moment to have any shadows hanging over it.

"Absolutely," Evan said, trying to keep Austin from passing out. Holding your breath that long wasn't healthy. "We're glad to have you and Josiah as part of the family."

Austin's gaze went to Matt; he and Katie had clearly discussed the most important part of this conversation, and Evan only felt a twinge of slight.

The leg jiggling stopped and the table went still. Now it was Evan's turn to take a deep breath before turning to Matt.

"Be good to her," Matt said finally, extending his hand across the table.

The "or else" was implied as Austin broken into a relieved grin.

"Thank you."

Sincere handshakes all around.

Beers consumed.

Austin slept on the couch while Matt and Evan held each other upstairs.

"A CHRISTMAS wedding and white tuxes—how could this day get any better?" Matt grumbled, readjusting his holly-green velvet bow tie in the hotel room mirror. The sprig of holly and berries on his lapel jiggled ominously and threatened to end up on the floor.

Evan's own butterflies—his joy, his tinge of sadness that Sherri wasn't here to see Katie walk down the aisle, the fact that he was now technically a grandparent—propelled him across the room. He wound his arms around Matt's middle, resting his chin on his shoulder.

They made a striking couple if he did say so himself. Fathers of the bride. He thought back to their secret city hall wedding, remembering their giddy joy.

Except right now Matt's eyes were watery and Evan's mouth couldn't quite find a smile without the wobble of his lower lip.

"It'll be okay," Evan said gently, for both of them. "She's making the right decision for her."

Matt hmphed, sliding his hands over Evan's. "He's got her dazzled."

"She's pretty dazzling herself."

Matt gave him a pointed look. "No kidding. I just don't want them to make a mistake."

Neither did Evan, but then again, he'd made his own decisions over the years that others had scoffed at. And they'd all turned out to be right in the end. "Whatever happens, we'll be here for her."

Matt sighed as he squeezed Evan's hand.

"You know, we're far too young to be grandfathers...."

"Shut up, please." Matt shuddered. "I don't want to talk about that part."

"Josiah's a great kid. And besides, it probably won't be long before either Miranda or Katie gets pregnant." Evan felt himself rambling as nerves pinched his insides. "We need to get used to it."

"What the hell do I know about little kids and babies?"

Evan made a face at Matt's reflection. "You helped me raise my four. You've been around the girls since they were born. How have you not noticed you're the child whisperer?"

"That sounds weird, like I shouldn't be able to go to the playground," Matt grumbled. He turned into Evan's arms until they were nose to nose.

"You are more of a mess than I am. How is that even possible?" Evan said, a tease in his voice.

"She's just…."

"She's not too young. Older than I was when I became a father for the first time." Evan rubbed circles onto Matt's back. "She's so mature and smart and capable—we did a great job with her."

Matt let out a soft puff of laughter and then pressed their lips together for a gentle moment. "Maybe you and…."

Evan was already shaking his head. "You and me and Sherri did a great job with those kids," he said firmly. "And Katie is going to be the best mom."

EVAN MANAGED to drag Matt out of their hotel room and down to the lobby where they would meet the rest of the wedding party. Katie and her bridesmaids, including both of her sisters, were already on their way, as were Austin and his group of MIT friends (none of whom looked like a model, which Matt found suspicious for no reason other than "it's weird. Is he the only hot guy who goes to school there?").

Their limo would take them to the church for their first view of Katie in her dress, something that Evan was dreading only because one handkerchief wasn't going to be nearly enough to stem his emotions.

They rode the elevator down in silence, hands clasped between them. Evan tried not to fixate on white tuxes and the general dirt level of New York City in December. Then he started thinking about Katie getting married and how the twins were going off to college… and went back to the condition of his cuffs by the time the reception rolled around.

In the lobby, among the sleek modern furniture and entering/ exiting tourists, Evan spotted the mop of brown hair belonging to his son, Danny. Next to him were the flower girls, chattering to each other as the teenager ignored his surroundings to play on his phone.

They were in charge of Sadie Ames and Caroline Drake-Shea until the church, while their parents enjoyed a rare morning out for brunch and mimosas without having to cut anyone's food or ask the waiter for chicken fingers.

Bliss.

Evan dragged Matt to the seating area and sent him to the couch to sit with Sadie and Caroline, both of whom wore matching holly-green velvet dresses with wreaths of white roses and holly on their heads. While he'd kept his mouth shut through the entire process of "swatches" and "concept boards," Evan continuously marveled that in the end, they all looked like tiny desserts at a holiday party.

Within seconds the girls were swarming Matt, asking him questions about the limo and the reception and when did they get cake?

The tiny smile creeping onto Matt's face told Evan he'd made the right decision.

"Where's Kent?"

Danny didn't even look up from his phone. "He went outside to tell the limo to go around the block once until you got down here."

"Why didn't you call us?" Evan felt the nerves start to creep up. His daughter was getting married. They were in Manhattan, home to traffic and all sorts of potential emergencies that might delay them getting to the church and that would throw the timing of everything off, and what if—

"Dad," Danny said loudly. He leaned his head back so he could give his father that exasperated stare he had perfected over the years. "We're still a half hour ahead of schedule. Katie built in worry time." Smirking, Danny went back to the starburst explosions and fast-moving ships on his phone.

Evan reined in his worries, ruffling his son's hair as he walked past. No force on earth—not even Miranda—could get the teen to cut his mop before the big day. He'd brushed it and put a little product in it, all the concession they were getting. Sadie and Caroline were perched on Matt's lap, their twin adoring gazes focused on his better half.

He smothered the urge to point out green fuzzies on white pants.

As he listened to Sadie and Caroline ping-pong storytell him about their trip to the hair salon with Sadie's mommy, Daisy, Matt reflected that one day he'd watch these two little cupcakes get married, and inexplicably, that made him feel better.

Someday he'd be kicking back some champagne and chilling as he watched two sets of his dearest friends—Jim giving Caro away? They'd have to buy elephant tranquilizers—run around, weeping and bleeding money, as they turned their precious children over to strangers.

Well, not strangers.

But still, people outside the family and their chosen circle of beloveds.

Was it wrong to hope Sadie and Caroline fell in love with each other once they reached a proper age? Like thirty?

"There was spray," Sadie was saying, her delicate features animated and auburn hair perfectly coiffed and maintained in dramatic looping curls. "And I had to close my eyes and hold my breath because the lady said it was bad for me! Why would they use something bad for me?"

"The price of beauty is steep," Matt said gravely.

Sadie blinked at him.

"Next time tell them you don't need the bad spray, okay? Your hair is allowed to move. It's a free country."

Caroline watched her with blue eyes so round and amazed she looked like a cartoon character. Her neat little black braids were tightly wound to her head, no doubt in the vain hope it would stay cute until pictures were over.

Her dads knew her well.

"Anyway, you both look perfect," he said, a hand at each of their backs, protective and steadying. "And you're going to do great during the ceremony."

Sadie nodded sagely. "I've done this before, at Mommy and Daddy's remarrying. I'm good at it."

Matt stifled a laugh. When he looked at Caroline, though, he caught the lower lip wobble. "What's up, Caro? You were so good at practice last night!" Matt slid an arm around the little girl's waist. "You just have to carry the flowers down the aisle. Then you go sit with your dads."

Caroline leaned against her godfather's chest. Matt felt his holly getting squished, but the hell with it. Sniffling little girls beat perfect garnish any day.

"What if I trip?" she mumbled.

"Hmmm." Matt rubbed Caroline's back. "I doubt that'll happen. But if you do, I'll trip too."

Sadie gasped. "Uncle Matt! You can't!"

"If Caroline trips, then I'm going to do it too," Matt said. He looked up to see Evan watching him with a smile on his face. "Evan?"

Evan started, as if unaware he was staring. He sat down on the coffee table across from Matt, his face serious. "Hmmm... I think that's a good idea. Then everyone will think it's part of the wedding. I'll fall too."

Matt nodded. "Good, good. Sadie, what do you think?"

The little girl looked torn. She bit her lip, looking at each of them in turn. Finally she set her gaze on Caroline, still tucked under Matt's arm.

Shoulders back, Sadie nodded. "I'll trip too," she told Caroline gravely. "Because you are my favorite friend."

"Me too," Danny called; the four of them looked in near unison in his direction. "I'm taking a dive if Caroline does."

The little girl smiled, ducking her head in embarrassment at all the attention.

"It would be better if you didn't," Sadie leaned forward and whispered. "Because that's a lot of people on the floor."

KENT RETURNED, red-cheeked and flushed from the cold, to gather everyone up for the limo. Evan helped the little girls into their coats while Matt sent texts to all the appropriate adults that they were on their way.

A few feet toward the door, Matt's phone buzzed with Katie's ringtone—"Sweet Caroline" by Neil Diamond, and she was just lucky he loved her so much.

"Hey, hang on."

Matt paused, then pulled his phone out.

"What's up? Everything okay?" Matt asked worriedly. Second thoughts? Feeling ill? Did she discover something his and Jim's background checks on Austin had not?

Katie laughed. "I'm fine. Everything's great." She sounded lighthearted and bubbly, but Matt knew that undercurrent in her tone. "I just.... I wanted to hear your voice."

"My voice? You need me to sing or something? That night at karaoke didn't happen—we've discussed this." Matt tucked himself into a corner as he watched Evan herd Caroline and Sadie out the door.

"I'm just—I'm so excited and happy, but like, whoa. I'm getting married! And a family that I'm becoming a part of, and I just…. Am I going to be able to do this? I'm not Josiah's mom."

Matt felt her worries because he'd lived them. As much as he loved the Cerelli kids, he wasn't their parent—not in a traditional sense of the word. He was their friend, their confidant, and their protector. He would lie down in front of a tank for them, step in front of a bullet without hesitation.

What he was, maybe there wasn't a word for it. But he knew Katie could do it.

"I'm not your mom," Matt said finally, his voice pitched soft. "Or your dad. But Katie, do you know how I feel about you? In your heart? Do you know?"

Katie sniffled through the line. "Of course I do. That's why you and Dad are walking me down the aisle today together."

Matt's heart pulsed in his chest. The honor was almost more than he could comprehend. "Don't try to take anyone's place, Katie. Make your own space in that kid's life and love him without expectation. You'll figure out what you mean to each other."

They breathed at each other for a few minutes; Matt knew Katie was crying, and he wasn't feeling all that steady himself.

"Maybe he'll become my favorite," she said finally, a damp laugh following her words. "Like I'm yours."

"Shhhh, that's our secret."

The door opened and Evan slipped through, his expression questioning. He came to stand next to Matt, who reached out his hand, tangling their fingers together.

"Miranda says my makeup is ruined, so I have to go get it fixed," Katie murmured. "But thank you. And I love you."

"Love you too. See you in a bit, okay? I'm the guy who looks like the ghost of Christmas Marshmallows Past."

Katie was giggling when she hung up, and that was all Matt cared about.

Evan handed him a handkerchief as soon as the phone was back in his pocket.

"I hope you have more of these," Matt sighed, wiping his eyes.

Linking their arms together, Evan pulled Matt close. "Let's go see our girl get married."

3
FELICITOUS
(SOUNDS LIKE A HOLIDAY WORD)

EVAN GOT home from the precinct at half past eight, shaking icy rain droplets off his overcoat before he went inside. December seemed determined to be as shitty as possible, weather-wise—and otherwise—and the silence of the house told him that Matt's moping hadn't improved.

T minus two days until Christmas, and the only indication in the Cerelli-Haight (Haight-Cerelli) household was a currently unplugged tree sitting forlornly in the front window. A few dozen Christmas cards sat on the dining room table, mostly unopened. The lack of presents—already shipped to their far-flung family—completed the depressing picture.

There would be no Christmas around these parts, at least not for Matt and Evan.

Matt's version of handling this development included brooding, splitting more wood than they could possibly use in a year, going to bed at nine every night, and saying things like "They have their own lives now—it's fiiiiine."

It didn't seem fine.

Truth be told, Evan existed in that dark well of bah humbug right next to him. He'd always struggled a bit with holidays, as they were so tied to being married to Sherri, but right from the beginning, Matt had worked to change that. He was their Santa, their head elf, their Director of Holiday Activities. But right now? He was Scrooge McGrinch, and Evan didn't blame him one bit.

The kids would not be home for Christmas.

His eldest, Miranda, and her husband, Kent, were spending a few months in London, where Kent was researching a book about royal gardens. Katie, her husband, Austin, and their son, Josiah, were in Boston, unable to travel down to New York, as Katie had to work the Celtics Christmas Day game.

Matt wore his Knicks jersey for four straight days in silent protest.

Twins Elizabeth and Danny, the youngest of the brood, were both studying abroad; Elizabeth in Paris and Danny in Spain. At least they would be spending the holidays with Miranda and Kent, which made Evan feel somewhat better.

Or it should have.

The entire crap scenario might have been bearable, he thought, leaving behind wet shoes and a soaking coat to wander into the kitchen for a beer. It might have been salvageable if their closest friends, Jim and Griffin, and their little girl, Caroline, could join them. At the very least they'd have had a child to spoil and a reason to celebrate.

Except this was their year to host Griffin's enormous family at their home upstate, and despite the invitation, Matt nixed the idea of spending Christmas with fifty people he wasn't related to and couldn't even begin to remember the names of.

Evan hadn't asked for elaboration because he already knew the answer—watching other families celebrate with their kids when his and Matt's were missing? No. Not enough beer in the world to medicate that ache.

On the refrigerator door, an invitation—actually a Post-it Note shaped like a wedge of swiss cheese with Helena's chicken scratch across it. She and Shane had purchased a new town house in the Village and, in the middle of renovation, didn't make plans for Christmas.

"Come over, bring liquor. No wait—we have liquor, bring food" was her invite as she left the precinct the day before. She gave him the note with the address and made him promise to at least consider it. Eight o'clock Christmas Eve.

Evan leaned against the counter and drank his beer.

He could cajole Matt into going—a little wine, a little sex; not his first rodeo in terms of getting Matt to do something. They'd have fun with their freewheeling friends. Eat too much, drink too much, and laugh inappropriately. Pass the night trying not to miss the kids. But Evan's heart just wasn't in it.

A tiny part of him knew he could have guilted the kids into coming home, laid out the money to get them all back to New York. The first holiday where none of them would be around? The first holiday ever spent apart? Hell, if he didn't want blood on his own hands, he could have unleashed the full impact of Matt Haight on the four of them and had them dutifully on the doorstep singing carols like a Hallmark commercial.

"I'm better than that," he said aloud in the silent kitchen of his dark, quiet house, and then he got himself a second beer. "It was their decision."

Or maybe he didn't want to face the fact that his beautiful, beloved children were all grown up and didn't need to be home for the holidays.

HE FOUND Matt upstairs in their rumpled bed, watching the Rangers destroy the Bruins.

"How was your day?" Matt mumbled as Evan began to strip out of his suit. "I forgot to make dinner."

"Shitty. It's fine—I ate peanut butter crackers out of the vending machine. And had two beers." He hung up his suit, wishing he had the gene that would allow him to throw his clothes on the floor. Like Matt. Whose clothes were on the floor, piled around Evan's feet.

"I had pork rinds and a Diet Mountain Dew." Matt rolled over, his hair sticking up every which way. "We're a special sort of pathetic."

Evan draped his tie on the rack, noting it was Elizabeth's gift to him last year. It crossed his mind to protest Matt's assessment, but really—he wasn't wrong.

The rest of his nightly routine went out the window. Suddenly the long, cold day and the crushing bleh of everything knocked Evan's legs out from under him. He shut the closet door in something resembling a slam, then turned toward the bed, where Matt already had the covers pulled back for him.

"Come on, I'll give you a blowjob," Matt said, at least throwing a growl into it.

Evan appreciated the effort.

AT FIVE forty-five, Evan's alarm went off, immediately followed by Matt's cell phone.

Playing "Too Shy" by Kajagoogoo.

Matt shot out his hand to grab the phone, death-gripping it until he got it to his ear, which was still tucked under the covers. "I swear to God—"

"Good morning, Matt!" Helena chirped, followed by some heavy breathing through the line. He knew she was calling from the treadmill, which made him hate her even more.

"Not Evan" was all he managed as Evan mumbled next to him, still half asleep as he rolled out of bed.

"I know."

"Then whyyyyyy?"

"Because I'll see Evan in about an hour, but I needed to talk to you. Now. You should be getting up too."

"Whyyyyyy?"

Helena sighed dramatically. He could imagine her in her swanky gym gear and pixie hair, smiling as she harassed him over the speaker in the NYPD gym. "Because Shane is picking you up at six thirty. You're going with him to pick up a piece of sculpture he bought. In Massapequa."

Matt dragged the phone away, pushing it toward where Evan stretched and creaked next to the bed. "I think Helena has been kidnapped and she's trying to give me a message about her captors."

Evan—because clearly he loved Matt and didn't want him to go to jail for killing an NYPD spokesperson/ex-detective—took the phone. "Helena…."

The rest of the conversation consisted of Evan saying "okay, but" and then pausing. With each passing second, Matt felt dread rising, stomach churning with dread. His day of lying around feeling sorry for himself and hoping the flu had descended on him was clearly about to be interrupted by an unrelentingly cheerful Shane and some crazyass errand.

"Uh… yeah," Evan said finally when the call ended, then dropped Matt's phone into the tangle of covers.

Even in the shadows, Matt could see the guilt.

"Shane is, like, made of money—they can hire someone," Matt bitched, even as he rolled out of bed. He tried to think if he had a T-shirt with a rude saying he could wear on this little adventure.

"She's being nice." Matt felt the bed shift. "She's worried about you." Evan's arms went around Matt's shoulders, and some of the tension seeped out of Matt's bones. "She's worried about me. I suspect there'll be a strong-armed lunch."

"Get a steak. And make her pay." Matt turned his head enough to find Evan's mouth; the familiar twist of lips, the way everything slotted together with practiced ease, knocked a bit more of the fog away.

When the kiss broke, Matt managed something resembling a smile in the face of Evan's concern. "I love you, and I'm glad I married you… even if your friends are psychotic."

WHEN MATT stomped out into the cold December morning—dressed like a ninja lumberjack—Shane was already in the driveway, behind the wheel of what could only be described as a gleaming red metrosexual monster truck.

"That's not a thing," Evan said, kissing Matt on the cheek before hightailing it to his own car, dwarfed by the vehicle behind it.

Shane honked and waved, then began gesturing an obscenely large cup of Starbucks through the window.

Matt grumbled, kicking through the frostbitten ground and what remained of their walkway plants. He walked slowly so as not to let Shane believe he could be compelled by Helena's demands and a vat of fancy coffee.

When he opened the door, a rush of warm air and the sounds of Chipmunks singing "O Holy Night" greeted him, along with Shane's giant grin.

"Happy holidays, Matt! Ready for our adventure?"

Matt stepped up and into the cab, then sank into the posh leather seats. He tried not to make a sound of delight at the heated-cushioned comfort as he slammed the door.

"It's a chestnut praline latte," Shane cajoled as he handed over the cup.

In front of the truck, Evan passive-aggressively gunned the motor.

"Whoops, don't want to piss off the cop." Shane threw the truck into Reverse, oddly at home behind the wheel. "Unless I have an ulterior motive."

Matt hunched down, taking a sip of his latte. "I didn't realize hipster types knew how to maneuver something this big."

Shane waggled his perfectly groomed eyebrows as he expertly pulled out of the driveway and then headed down the street. "That sounds dirty."

"You're actually a ridiculous human being."

They cruised through Matt and Evan's empty neighborhood, as all the sane people and schoolchildren were still in their warm houses. Matt felt warm and sleepy by the time they reached the Cross Bronx, avoiding conversation, as Shane seemed far more interested in harmonizing with the furry songsters on "Holly Jolly Christmas."

Finally Matt sucked down the last of his latte and cleared his throat. "So, this charity kidnapping—what's the object? If you're trying to cheer me up, please know it's completely impossible to get me to change my mind about being miserable."

"Charity…." Shane shook his head, his pom-pommed hat waggling on his head. "Nope. I need help moving this rad piece of sculpture, and you're around."

"Why didn't you ask Bennett? Or ask him to hire someone. Or hire someone yourself."

Shane snorted. "Have you seen him lift anything? He threw out his back last month moving Sadie's plastic dollhouse upstairs."

"So I'm brute strength and you're too cheap to pay someone?"

"More I don't trust just anyone with this piece." Shane's voice got all hushed and excited, like he was talking about Helena; it was almost sweet. "It's really special. And it's a secret."

Matt shifted, unwinding the scarf from around his neck. The heat inside the truck and his fancyassed coffee were starting to make him feel cooked. "From who? Helena knows."

Shane cackled, switching lanes like he was zipping around in a sports car. "Nope. She thinks she knows. The guy who's making it—we faked the whole thing. She picked out something for the backyard, but ha, I switched it out for something else. She's going to freak out. The goddess Helena, looking fierce, done in copper. It's stunning."

"Ahhhh." That made a bit more sense, and Matt released a bit of his cranky resentment. He was still mad at the world, but he couldn't deny his friend's enthusiasm in getting a wonderful gift for his wife.

"What did you get Evan, by the way?"

Matt knew his next words would result in him spending time at a mall at some point today, but he also knew Shane, and unless he wanted to be asked the same question for twenty miles…. "Nothing. We decide not to exch—"

He got no farther. Shane gasped, then hit a button on the NASA-level dashboard. "Siri, call Wifey."

"Oh, gross."

HELENA SHOWED up in Evan's office with a bag from the local bakery and a take-out tray of coffees, her face folded into a judgey frown. "Soooo…."

"Any word on the mission of holiday mercy?" Evan signed his name on another piece of paper—the first of many—and then gestured toward his visitor chair.

"They're on their way." She dropped the goodies on his desk. "Shane is going all out to cheer Matt up."

"And I'm your project?"

"Duh. We did rock, paper, scissors and I lost," Helena said, dry as the Sahara.

"Hey!"

She sat down with a regal air, her look pointed. "What's this about not exchanging gifts? You need to exchange gifts."

"Do you work for Macy's or something? We're not in the mood this year, and there's nothing we need." *Except our children to be home*, he thought, but he didn't say that aloud. Helena would probably organize an international kidnapping.

"Gifts for your spouse aren't about need, they're about expressing your love."

"Ah, you work for Hallmark. Got it." Evan took the coffee labeled "crankypantsmotherhumper" and then began to dig through the bag. "And Matt isn't my spouse."

The snort of derision made him look up.

"Not officially, at least," he added, calm as a cucumber, trying to remain unruffled while Helena watched him like a hawk.

No one—save him and Matt, Abe Klein, Judge Wernicky, and Miriam, who still sent them Christmas cards—knew about the trip to city hall several years ago. It was their secret; at best, everyone suspected they were engaged and would be "forever" because neither of them wanted the hassle of a wedding.

Which was entirely true, except for the part where they got married at city hall. And didn't tell anyone.

"I'm taking this delicious-looking strudel," Evan said, attempting to distract his eagle-eyed former partner. "You can have the tiny sad bran muffin."

"I already ate. They're both for you." Helena crossed her arms over her chest. "We need to get you a gift to give Matt."

"Now see, I remember talking about how we're not doing that this year." Evan took a large bite of strudel, losing himself momentarily in the obscene perfection of seventy pounds of butter, apples, and delicate dough.

"Your calendar is free around three, so we'll go out then."

Evan chewed. Matt was right—he was going to make her buy him a steak.

"HELENA SAID she's taking Evan shopping, so we can make a stop on our way back," Shane said, bopping out a festive beat on the steering wheel as they sat in traffic. Splats of icy rain hit the windshield.

"I know, I was here when you talked to her." Matt shifted again; his back was complaining about being seated for so long (not the drive, but rather all the days he'd spent being a sad lump), and that praline crap—not sitting all that well either. Maybe he really did have the flu. If he threw up in Shane's truck, maybe he'd be able to skip the mall.

"Do you have any ideas?" Shane moved the monster truck up a half an inch.

"For the gift I said I wasn't going to get Evan? No."

"Have you considered jewelry?"

Matt twisted in his seat. "Are you confusing Evan and Helena again?"

"Helena hates jewelry," Shane said, as if that was the main difference between the two. "Maybe a watch or uhhh…."

"Oh my God, what are you trying to unsubtly get at?"

Shane took a deep dramatic breath, then let it out in a slow hiss, like he'd sprung a leak. "What about a ring?"

"A…." At that moment, a jackknifing pain hit Matt in the middle. He scrambled for a moment, looking for something, and blessedly, Shane seemed to understand the blind fumbling. A small garbage bag appeared under Matt's nose right in the nick of time.

"Okay, so not a ring," Shane said a few seconds after Matt stopped throwing up.

IN HER office at Boston Celtics headquarters, Katie Cerelli Hill put the last of her belongings in a tote bag her boss had given her. Sadness over leaving the organization bubbled below the surface, but she knew this was the right decision.

She and Austin had talked—and talked and talked—about the future. Even before the big baby news (which wasn't actually big, because only three people knew), Katie felt homesick. She missed her dad and Matt. She missed New York. She hated that her stepson Josiah didn't get to appreciate the full court insanity that was her family on a regular basis. While Boston had been a wonderful experience for the past few years, it just wasn't home.

When Icahn School of Medicine at Mount Sinai came calling for Austin, Katie took it as a sign. An advanced degree in biomedical engineering made Austin a man with options, but Icahn nosed past everyone with the opportunity to move back to New York. And do his postdoc. And make Katie happy. Even Josiah climbed on board the NYC train. Win, win, win.

The double line on the pregnancy test just confirmed they were making the right move at the perfect time.

As she closed up her office, Austin was back home packing their last few possessions. A truck would be winding its way down to New York—Astoria, Queens, to be exact—where they'd rented a house, but they were driving down early to surprise her dads.

Oh man, they were going to be so damn happy. Then she was going to tell them they had to get married because as a pregnant person, she could make demands like that. Also, she was Matt's favorite.

Her phone buzzed on the now empty desktop.

Miranda.

Katie put her on speaker.

"What up, creampuff?"

"Weirdo. Listen, I wanted to run something by you. I know you're working on Christmas Eve, but maybe we can skype Dad and Matt all together?"

"Ummm…." Katie knew she was playing with fire by lying to her siblings, but they could not keep secrets at a criminal level, and no way she and Austin could pull this off if they knew. "Sure. What time?"

"Not sure yet." There was suddenly a burst of sound like an announcement over a PA system. At an airport. The sound became muffled after that.

Katie stopped putting things in the bag. "Miranda? Where are you?"

"The, uh, Underground. I have to go—my train is coming. I'll call you later bye!"

The line went dead.

Katie's Spidey sense went wild. Miranda was literally the worst liar on the planet. No wait—there was one person even worse.

She swiped down until she found her baby sister's name and pressed Elizabeth on her phone's surface. She'd get to the bottom of this in less than five minutes.

IT TOOK her ten.

TWO HOURS later, in front of her laptop in their empty apartment, Katie waited for her siblings to show up on Skype. Behind her, Austin and Josiah played basketball in the wide expanse of their living room, dodging boxes.

"If you break something…," she warned as the computer began to chime.

"There's nothing to break!" Josiah said delightedly, spinning around the center of the room.

One by one they appeared—Miranda, Elizabeth, and Danny, all looking various shades of guilty.

"You're going home and you weren't going to tell me!" she said, even as Josiah yelled, "Wait, aren't we…" in the background before his words got muffled—she assumed by Austin's hand.

"Kent's parents gave us their airline miles." Miranda sounded—and looked—defensive. "I didn't want to make you feel bad."

"I wanted to tell you," Elizabeth said primly, twisting her long brown hair around one finger, a nervous habit that narrowed Katie's gaze.

Danny shrugged, his St. John's shirt tight across his shoulders. Wait, when did her baby brother get so big?

"Well, I forgive you," she started as Austin laughed loudly in the background. "Because we're going home too."

Elizabeth shrieked, clapping as Miranda gave her a truly epic eye roll.

"Permanently," Katie added sweetly as she gestured at the empty space behind her.

Miranda sat up at that. "What?"

"We're moving back to New York! Austin's doing his postdoc at Icahn." Katie couldn't contain her delight as Elizabeth danced in her chair. Even Danny cracked a smile. "Daddy and Matt are going to flip."

"So we all show up for Christmas, you announce you're coming home, and we announce…." Miranda trailed off, a blush spotting her cheeks.

"You announce what?" Katie leaned forward, her nose practically touching the screen.

"Nothing. I'll tell you Christmas Eve," Miranda whispered as Danny snorted one window over.

"We can hear you."

Wriggling with excitement, the four siblings worked out their plans. Katie typed everyone's flight information in her phone. If the travel gods were on their side, they'd all be rolling up on Christmas Eve at about ten o'clock, with the very best present imaginable.

"Are we getting anything, you know, besides us?" Danny asked as they wrapped everything up.

"Welllll, I'd like to continue the subtle campaign to get them married," Katie said, smirking at Miranda.

She got another eye roll.

"You know I'm fine with it." The *now* was unspoken. "But they don't seem interested."

Elizabeth opened her mouth to stay something, then snapped it closed.

Danny tapped on the table. "They own a house together; they got all that paperwork and stuff. Dad hates parties, Matt hates parties that don't involve ribs...."

"All of these things are true, but there's a layer of protection that comes—legally—from being married," Katie argued. "And it's not like I'm advocating formal tuxes at the Astoria Grand Palace and a ten-tier wedding cake."

"Cake sounds good, actually," Danny mumbled.

"I just think we should let them know if they want to get married, we all support it." *Aggressively*, she added in her head. "Right?"

"Yes, we all support it. It will never happen, but we support it." Miranda raised her hands in the air. "And I think all of us showing up is a perfectly fine Christmas gift."

"We should get a card," Elizabeth added. "I'll get the card."

"Great. Card. International travel. Interstate travel. Go Cerellis and Cerellis by marriage!" Katie clapped enthusiastically. "If you're going to be late, text me. I don't want to stand out in the cold waiting for anyone."

Danny gave her a salute.

BUNDLED UP against the cold, Evan walked beside Helena, who continued to espouse potential gifts for Matt.

"No. No. No."

"We could go to Bloomingdale's—"

"And get what? I'd have to steal a roll of toilet paper from the bathroom to find anything Matt would want at Bloomingdale's."

"Can you get him something nice like a power tool? Would that make it better?" Helena's perk was starting to wane.

"We don't need anything. We don't want anything besides...." Evan sighed. "Besides the kids being home. Which they're not. No gift is going to change us being assholes this holiday." He stopped, pulling Helena closer to the building, out of the way of the rush of lunchgoers and tourists.

Her face made him sad.

"Life sucks sometimes. We both know that. We'll get over it."

Pouting, Helena wrapped her arms around his shoulders. "You shouldn't have to."

"Don't punch me in the stomach for this, but—are you seeing your folks for the holidays?"

Helena pulled back, and he felt suddenly glad she no longer carried a firearm. "We just bought the new place, and we're renovating, and I mean, after the holidays we have plans...," she rambled.

Evan held up his hand. "And I'm sure Serena and Vic understand. They aren't happy, but they understand. Your kids grow up, they make their own lives. You can't keep them little forever. It sucks, but it's life."

"Ugh. I feel so guilty now." Helena whacked her head against Evan's chest.

"Sorry," he said, though he really wasn't. If he wouldn't use parental guilt on his own kids, he was actually okay to use it on behalf of his former captain and Helena's mom.

"I swear to God. All I wanted to do was get you and Matt married. Now I want to call my mom."

Evan froze.

Helena must've registered the tension and stepped back, biting her lip. "Sorry."

"We're fine."

"I know."

"We're happy with the way things are." Not a lie. He was very happy with the way things were—married to Matt and no one knowing.

"I know."

He made a wide-armed gesture. "Then why?"

Helena stamped her foot. "I don't know. When we talk about it—"

"You talk about it? With who?" The image of a backroom conspiracy club with a secret knock began forming in his brain.

"Me, Shane. Daisy and Bennett. Jim and Griffin. Veronica, the waitress at the coffee shop near our house. The kids...."

Yeah. Definitely a secret knock.

"The kids?" Evan's growing panic took a weird left turn. He knew Katie wanted them to get married and suspected Elizabeth would be delighted. Danny existed in neutral territory at all times, and, well, they'd come a long, long way with Miranda.

But they were talking about it?

At some point they realized it would come out, but he thought they'd be old and gray and about to be parked in a retirement community. He hadn't a clue discussions were occurring.

"Yeah." Helena gave him a sheepish smile. "Sorry, this is really not going like the notes from our last meeting."

"I really don't want to see them."

Helena's ringtone began to sound. "Oh great, exactly what I need right now—some sort of crisis," Helena groused as she pulled out the phone. "No, it's Shane."

She put the phone up against her ear and said, "Hey, baby." Then her face dropped into a frown.

When she reached out to grip his arm, Evan started to internally freak out.

"APPENDICITIS," THE doctor at New York-Presbyterian Queens told Evan and Helena when they arrived in the emergency room.

"Surgery," Dr. Umrani said, sympathetic but smiling. "We'll do laparoscopic—he won't even have to stay the night if recovery goes well."

The simmering fear shaking Evan's very core started to subside. Shane's call had left him almost unable to move from their sheltered spot on the sidewalk; thank God Helena was the one with him, understanding exactly why Evan's legs were not moving.

Helena squeezed Evan's hand tightly.

"Can I see him before surgery?" Evan croaked out.

"Absolutely. I just need you to speak to our admissions person, get the paperwork filled out."

"You have a civil partnership, right? Do you need some sort of proof? I can go to the house…." Helena started babbling nervously, but Evan just shook his head.

"We're married. He's on my insurance." Evan reached into his pocket for his wallet.

Dr. Umrani just nodded, nonplussed. "Well, let's get you in to say hello, and then we'll deal with formalities."

"WHAT?" HELENA whispered as they followed the white coat down the corridor toward a small room, past hurrying staff and large pieces of equipment. "Excuse me?"

"We got married a few years ago, we didn't tell anyone, you can yell at me later," Evan said, ducking around a patient in a wheelchair being pushed down the hall. He just wanted to see Matt, hear him bitch about the pain and the noises and the smells. Emergency rooms held too many terrible memories, and he didn't want to be here unless he could be with Matt.

"We had meetings!"

In through a plain beige curtain, and Matt lay on the hospital bed, looking pale and put out. Beside him, Shane held his hand like they were floating in the middle of the Atlantic as the *Titanic* sank behind them.

Dr. Umrani—wisely—shooed Shane into Helena's arms as Evan stood at the foot of the bed, gaze riveted to Matt's face. "Mr. Haight, we'll be sending you to the operating room shortly," he said as he checked Matt's vitals. "But I'll give you a few moments with your husband."

Matt looked a little panicked, but Evan shook his head, patting Matt's stockinged foot. "It's fine," he said gently as Matt relaxed. When Dr. Umrani vacated the space at his side, Evan scooted into it.

"Hi," he said, leaning down to kiss Matt on the cheek.

"I threw up in the monster truck and Shane panicked," Matt murmured, leaning into Evan. "We came to the ER because Shane is dramatic."

"And, in this case, right." Evan took Matt's hand in his.

"Shhh, don't tell him that."

Evan wanted to be jokey and lighthearted, but all he knew was that Matt needed surgery and he hated hospitals with a violent passion. This wasn't Sherri, this wasn't the worst day of his life, but just the implication....

Matt seemed to read his mind. "I'm fine. Except for the appendix. And they're doing something fancy so I can go home later, although you'll still need to wait on me hand and foot."

"Make sure they write a prescription for that." Evan dropped another kiss, this time on Matt's temple.

A burst of hurried whispers from the corner of the room caught Evan's attention. He caught the name Miranda in the conversation and frowned.

"Hey, don't call the kids."

Helena looked up, phone in hand, guilt on her face. "But...."

"They'll freak out and try to get home—it'll cost a fortune," Matt said weakly. "I don't want them panicking."

"They'd want to be here," Shane offered.

"We'll tell them tonight, after the surgery." Outside the curtain, voices and rattling equipment; then the curtain moved.

A pink-smocked nurse smiled brightly. "Mr. Haight? You ready to go?"

"Ugh." Matt made a terrible face.

"I love you," Evan whispered in his ear. "I'll see you when you get out."

"I love you too. Don't call the kids."

"I won't."

"Tell them I love them."

"They know. And you'll tell them tonight."

"Just in case."

Evan's throat closed up, but he shook his head. "Sorry, none of that bullshit talk. I'll see you soon, you'll talk to the kids, and then Shane will never let you forget he saved your life."

Matt's eyes got moist as Evan struggled to smile.

"He'll be unbearable," Matt said in a stage whisper.

"So will you."

Evan kissed Matt then, deep and gentle as he could be, as his heart pounded in his chest.

When they pulled apart, Evan swallowed and nodded; words weren't going to come unless he wanted to get overly emotional—which would weird everyone out.

So, stoic as could be, he watched Shane and Helena give Matt a kiss, and then the pink nurse wheeled him down the hallway.

"Come on," Helena said softly, wrapping her arm around his waist. "Let's go to admissions; then we'll wait upstairs."

Evan sat in a hard plastic chair outside the surgery department, clutching an oversize coffee. Helena and Shane were taking turns being at his side, rubbing his back and patting his shoulder. A laparoscopic appendectomy took only about forty minutes, with another few hours for recovery. They were into hour two of the whole deal.

Every few minutes Helena and Shane would have a whispered conversation in the corner of the room, which Evan was determined to ignore. Questions about them being married were coming; he knew this would get back to the kids and all holy hell would break loose.

He'd deal later. Right now all he could think about was Matt.

They'd been through a lot over the past ten years. Grief, too much drinking, work and kids and in-laws and their own personal demons. Stubborn personalities coupled with bad coping habits.

Fear.

But they always found a way to make it through.

"So… I didn't call the kids," Helena said suddenly, dropping into the seat next to him. "But I called Jim and Griffin, and they are on their way."

A note in her tone made Evan look up.

"And?"

"And I cannot be responsible for what Griffin does."

Austin versus the start of rush-hour traffic from Boston to New York City the day before Christmas Eve—a battle he was determined to win.

In the passenger seat of the Dodge Caravan, Katie cried between texting her siblings as Josiah sat silently in the back seat, kicking his feet nervously. Their day-after-tomorrow plans had turned into "right now this second." A neighbor offered to let the moving people in, bags were hastily tossed in the back, and they were off—right into the middle of preholiday madness.

"Honey, you need to relax. You need to remember your health." A quick look back showed Josiah listening intently. "You need to remember what Griffin said. Matt's okay. His appendix didn't even burst."

That just made her cry harder.

"We can't change the tickets," Miranda said frantically as the cab raced toward Heathrow through traffic. "We can't afford—"

"Bennett paid for our tickets. Danny and Elizabeth are picking theirs up," Kent said, holding on to Miranda and the seat in front of him as their cabbie took every terrifying turn available to him. Thank God the twins had already arrived in London earlier in the day so they could fly home together. He was still a little dazed at knowing actual rich people who could pull something like that so close to Christmas. "We'll be there before midnight."

White-faced, Miranda clutched at his arm. "Okay, okay. Matt's gotta be okay. Dad couldn't handle anything…." Her face scrunched up like she was going to cry, but she didn't. He knew her relationship with Matt was rocky and difficult; they'd made their peace and were even friendly, but it was complicated.

"We'll be there before midnight," he repeated.

Four hours after Matt disappeared with the nurse, Evan got to see him again. Loopy as hell, he demanded a kiss and some ribs, then fell back to sleep.

"He seems fine," Evan said to a bemused orderly. Despite his smile, a weight remained in Evan's middle; it would stay there until he got Matt home and into their bed. Well and awake.

He called the precinct, then headquarters, letting them know the situation. Helena had already left the hospital to get back; there were briefings and a holiday message to disseminate, as if crime would take a holiday over the next few days. They knew better.

His phone had no messages from his kids, which meant only one thing: no one could control Griffin.

Evan sighed as he settled into the padded chair in the corner, watching as Matt continued to sleep. Well, this wasn't how he wanted to spend the holidays, times eleven. Outside the doors and down in the lobby, he knew his friends were waiting with expectations and questions. The kids would arrive, frantic.

For so long, all these tense moments had featured Matt as his partner, his backup. His rock. But now it was up to him to handle everyone's fears. To reassure and comfort. To make sure their extended family unit stayed strong.

He could do it—so long as Matt was okay.

FIVE HOURS postsurgery, Matt was awake and, though groggy, ready to get the hell out of bed. For someone who just had an inflamed appendix removed, he felt less pain than expected. (God bless Percocet.) His mouth felt gross and he wanted a shower, but otherwise it was as if he drank too much and fell down. He had experience in this, so he knew he'd be fine.

Evan's tightly drawn expression and hooded eyes were also urging him out of bed. Matt hated hospitals on his own, but Evan's experience with them pushed his legs over the side of the bed and made him smile through the ache. "I'm feeling fine. When can I get out of here?"

"Jim's bringing the car around," Evan said, helping him into his clothes with gentle hands.

"Jim? Why is he down here?" Matt groused, wobbling as Evan pulled his boots on. "They're having people over. A small city of people."

"Helena texted him; he started driving. You'd do the same."

"Griffin should have told him—"

"Griffin is waiting outside with Caroline."

A wave of dizziness swamped him, but pure grit kept him upright. Evan wound his arms around Matt's torso, avoiding his bandaged side. "Stubborn people—we only know stubborn people."

That elicited subdued laughter. "I can't imagine why."

PAPERS SIGNED, wheelchair procured, and Matt was finally rolled out into the lobby at half past seven.

"Uncle Matt!" came a wail as Caroline Shea-Drake—bundled up like she'd trekked through the Rockies to get here—ran to his side.

"Hey, Caro. I'm fine," Matt said, trying to stave off the wobbling bottom lip and full blue eyes. "I'm so glad to see you."

"Do you have a scar now? Can I see it?" she sniffled, pressing up against his arm.

"Caroline!" Griffin caught up to them, pushing his glasses up on his nose as he knelt next to his daughter. "Have some manners. We'll check out the scar when we get Uncle Matt home."

Evan snickered from behind them.

"Jim's got the car out front—I assume he's terrifying a security cop while parking in a no-loading zone, so we should go." Griffin leaned up and kissed Matt on the cheek, much to his embarrassment.

"You guys didn't have to come all the way down here."

Griffin made a "blah blah blah" face. "Whatever. Your appendix saved Jim from having to go caroling. He's so grateful right now he might cry when he sees you."

"Daddy's not going to cry when he sees Uncle Matt. He'll probably just say bad words."

Evan helped Matt up, taking most of his weight as a hospital worker collected the wheelchair and disappeared, no doubt to free another released patient. The flow of people rolled around them: a tree in the corner, lines at the desk, visitors moving in and out of the doors. They followed Griffin toward the entrance. Almost home free—until their friend turned around and gave them a look.

"So what's this I hear about you guys being married?"

THE SAD and unholidayish house in Queens was transformed.

As Jim pulled the truck into the driveway, Evan peered out the window to see every damn light was on—including the tree—and cars lined his front lawn. Beside him in the back seat, Matt snored on one side of him as Caroline motored on the other.

"Oh right, everyone is here," Griffin said, turning around in his seat. "I called the kids, I called Bennett and Daisy, and I called my family."

"Griffin, no. Your family—"

"Is having a kickass party at our house on Christmas Day. I told them we're spending tonight and Christmas Eve with our friends. They send their love." He grinned. "And it wasn't even Jim's idea!"

From the driver seat, Jim just gave a rumble. He hadn't said much since they met him at the car; he gave Matt a hug, Evan a nod, then shepherded them into the truck. Evan knew Jim enough to understand that silence was his response to tense times—and a friend having surgery fit on that list.

"Holiday decisions were made in your absence," Griffin added before quickly exiting the truck.

Evan gently shook at Matt's arm as Griffin opened the passenger door to get Caroline out of her seat. Matt mumbled and twitched before coming awake, blinking weakly in the overhead light.

"Wha?"

"We're home. And everyone we know is here," Evan said, unhooking his seat belt.

The door opened and Jim stood there, looking stern. "And everyone knows you're secretly married."

Matt rolled his head back over to Evan. "Can we go back to the hospital?"

EVAN HEARD the music before he opened the front door.

Jim was practically carrying Matt—who bitched the entire time—up behind him as Caroline and Griffin brought up the rear. Holiday tunes, the waft of food cooking. He stepped into the house and saw a fire lit and about ten strings of previously unstrung lights around his living room.

"What the hell?" Matt said as he came through the door. "Evan, call the police. Elves have invaded our home."

Caroline—now awake—shrieked with delight. Across the room, her best friend Sadie—Bennett and Daisy's exuberantly dramatic offspring and currently dressed as an elf—bounced excitedly.

"Uncle Matt! You're alive!"

It took some work, but coats and boots came off and Matt got settled on the sofa, which had been made up with blankets and sheets and every pillow in their house. Evan found himself with a beer and a shoulder rub from Helena, while Matt got gently smothered with love from Sadie and Caroline, who waited on him adoringly.

Did he need cocoa? Did he need cookies? Did he want to watch them drink cocoa and eat cookies?

In the kitchen, a crew of people (in matching T-shirts) Evan didn't know scurried about cooking dinner. Matt's richest client smiled sheepishly when Evan pinned him with a look.

"Did you throw money at my kitchen?"

"It was either that or have one of us cook, and Matt didn't need to have food poisoning on top of his appendix," Bennett said, patting Evan on the shoulder. "They'll be back tomorrow with brunch and then dinner. I've left a menu on the table so you can make your selections."

"Of course," Evan said, still dazed after all these years by Bennett's ease of spending. Like "order Chinese" never entered his mind.

The doorbell rang.

Evan waded through the chaos—six adults, two children, the tip of the iceberg. He looked through the peephole to discover a tearstained Katie with Austin and Josiah hovering behind.

The door was barely open before Katie flew in, tackling Evan in a desperate hug. "Daddy," she managed before bursting into tears.

"Shhhhh," Evan comforted her, rubbing her back and rocking her like when she was a little girl. "Come on, he's fine. Everything's fine."

Behind them, Austin and Josiah made it in and then were quickly swallowed by the hospitality committee of Daisy and Shane. And the girls, who claimed Josiah to join them on the couch with Matt while they tried to convince him to show them his scar.

"He's fine," Evan whispered to Katie. "And he's going to freak out if you're freaking out, so take a deep breath."

Nodding, Katie pulled away. She wiped her nose on her jacket sleeve, looking so young it made Evan blink.

"Let's take your coat, throw some water on your face. Then you can go see him. Although you have to fight off his fan club."

"I'm his favorite. I get priority," she sniffed.

WHEN MATT got an armful of Katie, he cried and didn't care who saw it.

Well, he cared a little.

"Are you really all right? Promise?" Katie asked, her arms tight around his neck.

"Promise," he whispered back, kissing her cheek. "You didn't need to miss work to—"

"Shut up, please." Katie pulled back. "It was supposed to be a surprise."

Matt squinted. "What? You were going to come for Christmas?"

"Yeah." She gave him a patented Katie grin. "The other kids will be here in a few hours."

Matt teared up again. "Damn, the surgery is making me have some sort of reaction…."

"Ew, feelings." Katie kissed his cheek. "I love you, Matt."

He caught Evan watching them from across the room, looking about as emotionally wrecked as he felt. They were lucky sons of bitches, and Matt hoped his expression conveyed that.

FOR THE next hour, Katie monopolized Matt's attention with chatter about her new job and their rental house, until her father arrived with a bottle of pills and a glass of water. Austin led her into the kitchen for her own water and a discreet handful of crackers and cheese, knowing she got nauseous if she didn't eat every few hours. When he got pulled into a conversation with Griffin about a book they'd both read, she wandered into the dining room, where an enormous spread of food covered every possible surface. Josiah, Caroline, and Sadie crowded around the dessert table, eyes wide over the pile of petit fours and fluffy frosted cupcakes.

"No secret licks," she teased, leaning down to kiss Josiah on the top of his head. She thought about next Christmas, when she and Austin would have their baby here with their crazy chaotic family. The image of Josiah and the new baby celebrating with everyone made her heart swell.

Sadie looked up at her with a calculated expression of mischief, but Caroline's earnestness assured her they'd behave.

"Are we going to get to eat soon?" Josiah asked, clearly weighing the no licks thing against the time constraints of not eating. Hors d'oeuvres didn't hold much interest for little kids.

"Let me go check, but I think we can arrange something." She gave Josiah another kiss.

She made it about three feet away before Caroline's little voice piped up. "Uncle Matt and Uncle Evan got married, but they didn't have any cake. Maybe we can give them that big cupcake!"

Katie skidded to a halt, nearly braining herself on the wall as she turned around. "What did you say?"

She almost made it into the living room, her brain pinging with information gleaned from an adorable child who had no idea the bombshell she dropped. So close to getting in there and yelling at her father and… oh my God! Her actual official stepfather! She was going to kill them.

But first, she felt the unmistakable gurgle at the top of her stomach and imagined herself turning an actual shade of green.

"Come on, baby, this is not the time," Katie muttered, ducking into the half bath off the kitchen. Before she shut the door, her eyes met Daisy's, who was standing at the end of the hall with a knowing expression on her face.

Crap.

THEY COULDN'T wait for the rest of the family to get there; dinner was served, much to Matt's relief.

"Starving," he reported as everyone disappeared into the dining room in a stampede formation. "What's on the menu?"

"Buttered noodles and some bread," Griffin said gently, as if breaking bad news.

"I smell better things."

"Oh God yes. Make your own nachos, braised beef and root vegetables, baked mac and cheese."

Matt frowned, placing his hand over his heart. "Why are you torturing me like this?"

"Why didn't you tell us you got married?" He sniffled dramatically. "We are your best friends. I have the key to your house. You've seen my husband naked. How could you?"

Grabbing the nearest throw pillow, Matt smacked him in the hip. "Nice mouth. My grandson is in the other room, along with your child and goddaughter."

"At some point we will discuss this."

"Can I have real food first?" Matt made his best pleading eyes, even if in his heart, he knew it was a lost cause.

"No. Buttered noodles and bread," Griffin said sternly. "Easier on the stomach. If you're good you can have a cupcake."

Matt sank back into the pillows, sighing sadly. He could smell so many delicious things. Stupid surgery. "You're a real taskmaster, Griffin."

"You have no idea." Griffin got a weird look on his face, then patted Matt on the head. "Tomorrow you can have what you want. Everyone here loves you, but we don't want you vomiting all over the place because you ate braised beef a few hours after surgery."

"Fine. But I want double your idea of a serving of bread," he said petulantly, folding his arms over his chest and ignoring the tug against his side. "And some more water. With a lemon."

"A whole lemon or just a decorative wedge?"

"Wedge."

Griffin leaned over to kiss Matt on the forehead. "Idiot. Married idiot."

"Like looking in a mirror." Matt flushed, which earned him another kiss.

As Griffin walked away, Evan came into his line of vision. "Should I be worried about you and Griffin?"

"No, you should be worried about what happens when the rest of the kids show up and someone lets it slip that we're... you know." Matt waggled his eyebrows.

"Having sex?"

"Are you drunk?"

Evan shrugged as he sat down on the edge of the couch. "Exhausted. Some guy scared the crap out of me today."

"Michael Moore?"

"That's the documentary guy. You mean Michael Myers."

Matt pointed to his side. "I think I'm still impaired." He reached up to take Evan's hand in his, twining their fingers together. "Sorry about that. It wasn't for attention or to get the kids home. I swear."

Evan made a face. "Unfunny."

"I know you hate hospitals," he said gently. "But through the magic of medical technology and lasers, I am here now and fine. Completely fine."

"Let's not do this again." Evan pulled their joined hands to his lips and pressed a kiss against Matt's wrist. "Please."

"Deal. I'm being deprived of good catered food. It's torture."

"Wait 'til the kids get here."

MATT ATE under Evan's supervision; he tried to flutter his eyelashes for a beer, but no one gave in.

The doorbell rang again.

Griffin beat Evan to the door, leaping over the ottoman with dramatic flair.

"Stand back, it's about to get crowded in here!" he shouted.

The living room was packed. Evan hugged and reassured all three of his other kids, shook Kent's hand. The rest of their friends came in to share another round of hugs and handshakes until he became distracted, wondering if their floor could hold this much weight.

"Go back and eat, please," he said, trying to sound hospitable.

Danny and Elizabeth got first dibs on Matt, affectionate and sweet at his side until Miranda stood by the coffee table and cleared her throat repeatedly.

"Hey, Miranda, happy pre-Christmas," Matt said sweetly, offering her a cheek to kiss as the twins moved out of her way.

"Hmph. You ruined our dramatic surprise." She sat on the edge of the chair closest to him, still in her coat. "Now I suppose I have to buy you a real gift."

"I'm a large in sweaters and I like the color red."

Miranda hid her smile behind her hand. "I have an extra package of tube socks with your name on it."

"Just what I always wanted." He indicated the kitchen. "There's a ton of delicious food in there if you want something."

She made a face, shaking her head. "We ate on the plane," she offered, folding her hands in her lap. "I'm good."

It was finally quiet, at least in the living room. The children had finally torn themselves away from Matt's side to descend on the buffet. Daisy handed Evan a plate of chicken nachos, which set off his hunger for the first time all day. His stomach growled dramatically as he eyed the pile of shredded meat and cheese and salsa. He dug his fork in, lifted a pile of goodness to his mouth, and nearly dropped it in his lap as Katie called a dramatic "*Dad!*" from across the room.

"Oh shit," Matt muttered from beside him. "I wonder who spilled the beans. Ten bucks says it was Griffin on a sugar high."

"How should we handle this?" Evan asked, sadly putting the plate of nachos down on the coffee table.

"Back room? A heavy dose of sympathy? A dramatic exit through the bathroom window?"

"You might need to pinch your side until you cry."

Jim appeared holding his own plate of nachos—half the size of Evan's abandoned one—and, oddly, celery. "You just had surgery, so there are two options—you sit here and we herd all the non-Cerellis into the other room, or you sit here and we herd all the non-Cerellis into the other room."

"I'm surprised you haven't yelled at us yet," Matt said.

Shrugging, Jim picked off a jalapeño, then popped it into his mouth. "Saving it. Might need it later," he said after swallowing. "Also, your kids are gonna ream both your asses better than even I could."

He walked away, chuckling.

"I miss him," Evan muttered as his four children ringed the couch, each with an expression of irritation.

"Okay, this is what happened." Evan took a deep breath. "Right before Jim and Griffin got married—"

"Ha! I knew it!" Griffin yelled from the kitchen.

"I asked Matt to marry me."

"In a parking lot."

Evan sighed. "He said yes. And we went to city hall…."

Elizabeth gasped dramatically as Katie crossed her arms angrily across her chest.

"And that was it."

The silence was deafening. Each of his children appeared betrayed; he looked at Miranda, wondering if her expression was about him being married to someone other than her mother.

She was the first person to speak. "That was kind of selfish," she said finally, her mouth tight. "You know that at the very least, we would all want to be there."

Evan could have been knocked over with a feather.

"Miranda, it's my fault. I wanted a quiet—" Matt tried to interject, but Miranda was having zero part of that.

"No—if anyone made the decision, it was Dad." She turned her laser-sharp expression on him.

"We didn't want to make a big deal about it."

"But it's a big deal! To us! How would you have felt if Austin and I eloped!" Katie stood up, then sat down again. "I mean… jeez. And then you didn't even tell us!"

"Ow?" Matt offered, giving Katie a hangdog expression. "My side hurts."

"Oh my God." Danny's strident voice—a voice no one was used to—made Evan jump. "So what? It's over with. They're married. And for a bunch of people with their own secrets, you're all very self-righteous."

Evan narrowed his gaze. "Who has secrets?"

Danny pointed at Katie, then Miranda, then Elizabeth.

Then himself.

Matt awkwardly raised his arms over his head. "Off the hook!"

IN THE kitchen, the crowd migrated their chairs close to the doorway to hear. Only the kids were immune to the drama as they sat on the floor, shoveling food in their faces in happy anticipation of dessert.

Helena didn't bother to sit; she leaned on the doorway, eavesdropping as she sipped her beer.

"Shh, shh. First secret," she translated to the rest of the group. "Danny has a girlfriend!"

Griffin shrugged as he stole a taco off Jim's plate. "He's old enough."

"She's thirty-five and a teacher at St. John's."

The adults exchanged looks.

"Where's Evan's gun?" Jim asked.

"Shhhhh! Second secret." Helena strained to hear Elizabeth. "Ohhh, she's considering the police academy!"

Helena and Jim high-fived.

"Why do I think those are the easy ones?" Daisy asked, leaning over to wipe the faces of all three of the children, who dodged her efforts.

"Miranda and Katie are going at the same time."

Austin and Kent exchanged looks, an unspoken discussion of raised eyebrows and then grins.

"Uh, that's our cue," Austin said with a chuckle, giving Kent a thump on the back.

Daisy watched them go, then broke into a huge smile. "Get ready for the explosion."

WHEN AUSTIN and Kent joined the family, Matt had a very strong feeling of what the next words were going to be. He looked at Evan's slightly stormy expression—they would discuss Danny's Mrs. Robinson and Elizabeth's career choices soon enough—and felt a peaceful wave wash over him.

He took Evan's hand, watched the two couples do the same, and held his breath.

"So weirdly enough, we just discovered that we are both…," Katie started.

"Pregnant!" Miranda finished.

Evan's jaw dropped. "What?"

Katie laughed, pointing at her sister. "She's pregnant." She pointed at herself. "I'm pregnant." She pointed at Evan and Matt. "You're gonna be grandpas."

"Holy crap!" Shane yelled from the kitchen.

"Holy crap," Evan whispered before lurching forward to hug both his daughters. "Holy… oh my God."

"Ugh, if he cries, I'm going to cry," muttered Danny as his twin burst into tears next to him. "Oh crap." Like the trouper he was, he put his arms around his sister.

Matt felt like his heart was going to burst—surely there was an appendix metaphor, but he couldn't think of it. All he could do was imagine Miranda and Katie as moms and little babies in the house and, oh Lord, he was going to spoil those kids worse than he did with Sadie and Caroline, and now with Josiah living close by—he might have to get a second job—

"Come here," Miranda said, catching him in midramble. She stood over him, red-faced and teary-eyed, arms open. "Grandpa."

In the end, he blamed the surgery for how much he cried on Miranda's shoulder.

THE BABY announcements saved them from the kids' irritation, but the kitchen full of adults giving Evan the side-eye couldn't be missed. He made another plate of food under the glares before an idea formed. Evan turned to face his friends, then pulled his Get Out of the Doghouse Free card from thin air.

"Before anyone yells at me, there's video and you are all welcome to see it."

"You're a genius," Matt whispered in his ear as they all settled into the living room to watch their wedding. Bennett and Danny fiddled with Matt's laptop as Daisy attempted to settle the kids down. "We're sending the judge a case of good whiskey and Miriam a basket of perfume and soap. Without this recording, we'd be dead."

"Is there popcorn?" Griffin asked loudly. "What's the rating on this thing?"

Helena thumped the pillow behind her, then relaxed with a loud sigh. "The only thing I want is tears. Big honking sentimental tears to lord over you both."

"Can I play Matt in the TV movie?" Daisy asked.

Bennett turned around as the television came to life. "The bar is now closed."

"Someone's cologne is making me want to hurl," Miranda muttered.

Shane scooted over to move farther away from her.

"Everyone try not to fall in love with me even more than right now. I look spectacular in my suit. And out of it—"

Evan put his hand over Matt's mouth, knowing full well there would be licking.

"Shhhh!" Elizabeth hissed from her seat on the floor.

All the laughing and chatter died as Judge Wernicky's chambers came into view.

"WE'LL BE back tomorrow," Griffin said, hoisting a sleeping, cupcake-smeared Caroline onto his shoulder. "For a Christmas Eve slash belated wedding reception slash celebration of pregnant ladies."

"The caterer said ribs and a three-tiered cake wouldn't be a problem," assured Bennett.

"We're bringing all our liquor over," Helena promised.

"You were very sappy in that video. I'm going to remember that next time you call me sentimental," Jim pointed out.

"I'm so glad I saved your life," Shane sighed. "It's like our souls are connected now on a special—"

"Okay, time to go!" Daisy called, herding everyone out the door. "You'll see each other again in ten hours! And we will be watching that video again—I like it when Matt cries."

Evan kissed everyone twice, thanking them three and four times for putting all their plans on hold to come and take care of them. Not spending the holiday together—all together, family and extended—had never felt right. A house of chaos and noise and drama—that was how it was meant to be.

The kids were all dispersed upstairs to sleep.

The house, put to rights by everyone, was finally dark except for the little tree, which didn't seem so sad anymore.

He found Matt tucked in on the couch, scooted over so there was room for him.

"We should probably go to sleep because they'll all be back soon enough." Matt didn't sound like he minded. The dopey smile on his face—half joy, half Tylenol—made Evan happy.

"Remember when we thought it was going to be a quiet Christmas?" Evan skimmed off his pants and shirt before climbing in beside Matt.

"Remember when we thought we weren't going to tell anyone we were married?"

"We're not very bright, apparently."

Evan twisted his body around until they fit, Matt sprawled on Evan's chest, his bandaged side cushioned by a pillow. He spread the blanket over them with a sigh.

"Brings back memories," Matt said, muffled against him.

"There will be no sexual exploits this evening."

"But I was so good this year!"

"Shut up."

They lay quietly, Evan listening to Matt's breathing, feeling him warm and safe and fine next to him.

It was all good.

"Our kids are having kids," Matt murmured.

Evan's heart squeezed. He remembered his girls being born so clearly, and now... in seven months, he'd be welcoming their children into the world. He couldn't quite wrap his brain around it. But whatever the future held, he had Matt by his side—and that meant everything would work out just fine.

"You should be Grampy."

"Matt…."

"Pappy? Poppy? Paw-Paw?"

Evan shut him up with a kiss.

4
HERE'S TO YOU, MRS. ROBINSON

IN THE joyful aftermath of the girls' announcement of their pregnancies, the announcement about Danny's (much) older girlfriend felt like a blip on the radar for Evan.

With the flicker of shame, Evan's first reaction—in his mind, at least—was "Cool. Congrats." He'd been in enough locker rooms in his life to call upon a retrospective of backslapping and high-fiving, all at the prospect of catching an experienced woman.

He didn't say that at the time, however. He delivered a private and stern "we will talk about this later" to his son, then promptly forgot.

A few weeks later Katie and Miranda arrived at the house on a chilly Saturday to go through some bins of baby things he kept in storage in the attic.

The numerous plastic bins were stacked in the Florida room, dusted off meticulously and waiting for a trip down memory lane. He girded his loins against the wave of nostalgia, the bittersweetness of handling little baby socks and blankets without Sherri.

God, she would have been so proud of their kids. And so excited to be a grandma. Sometimes he tried to picture her right now, the same age as he was, but she stayed frozen in youthful memories.

It was in this melancholy mood he directed Miranda and Katie to the back of the house after a bunch of tight hugs in the entryway.

"So how are you going to divide everything up if you don't know what you're having?" Evan asked as he opened the first bin. A group text called Stork Alerts kept him updated of every detail; he liked knowing what was going on with the girls' pregnancies. The discussion of whether or not to find out the gender of the babies had gone on for almost two weeks.

Under the lid, everything was neatly folded; a waft of aged fabric softener made him sniffle.

"We're going to find out at the next scan in a few weeks," Miranda said, poking through the piles. "Kent and I want to have plenty of time to put together the nursery."

"Any gut feelings?"

"I don't know." Miranda pulled a stack of receiving blankets into her lap, a rainbow of soft lavenders, yellows, and greens Evan had a vague recollection of wrapping babies in over the years. "Sometimes I'm certain it's a girl. Like—so strong. I almost bought the sweetest pink paint the other day! Then I start thinking that maybe I want a girl, so that's why I'm thinking about it." She frowned. "But I'm not going to be disappointed if it's a boy. That's not what I mean. But like—I just know girl stuff better."

"You know Kent is a guy, right? He knows guy stuff."

"Katie, last week we had a fight over a floral pattern on some throw pillows because—and I quote—the filaments were inaccurate and confusing, according to my husband." Miranda sighed. "What if we have a sporty child? They'll feel like an alien."

Katie dissolved into giggles, muffling them against her sleeve.

"You have me and Matt and Danny. And Jim! And Katie, if it's basketball. Sporty people with sports, uh, thoughts." Evan gestured at her with the bin lid. "It'll be fine."

"Did you and Mom find out before we were born?" Over her fit of laughter, Katie had opened another bin and now had both hands full of tiny onesies.

"Not on purpose. It was just a part of the ultrasound. Don't know if they even asked—they were just like, 'Hey, it's a girl, congrats and save your money for those weddings.'" Evan opened a third, finding it full of shoes—from soft and itty-bitty to Danny's first cleats. Sherri saved everything. "The twins—well, we wanted to know with them." He chuckled, absently picking up a baby-sized basketball shoe he clearly recalled purchasing when he knew he was getting a son. "Mom knew she had girl clothes, but…."

"At least we have a selection." Katie squealed as she found an "I Love My Daddy" onesie, navy blue with white lettering. "Austin will love this."

"You think you're having a boy." Miranda sorted the blankets out, placing a few in her lap—all of them traditional girl colors, Evan noticed.

Katie shrugged. "Don't feel one way or the other. Don't care. We're not going to find out. We want it to be a total surprise."

Miranda gave Evan a look. "Dare I ask your nursery color scheme?"

"We're cosleeping, so it's not really an issue."

"What if you roll over and squish the baby!"

"There's a thing you buy and attach to the bed, Miranda. The baby sleeps there. Totally safe."

"I'm going to buy you a hemp baby carrier."

"Is that supposed to be sarcastic? Because I totally want one. Oh, I have a picture on my phone."

"You have a corporate job! Why do you act like a hippie?"

The gentle bickering felt familiar. Evan suppressed a smile as he rummaged through the bin.

THINGS WERE going along nicely after a break for lunch. They ate Chinese food at the kitchen table, sharing memories that flooded back as each bin revealed another stage in the Cerelli children's lives. Baptism gowns and Communion dresses, soccer uniforms, baseball jerseys, two full containers of dance costumes and tap shoes. Lunch led to dragging out picture albums; at some point Evan looked up and realized it was nearly dinnertime.

"I should cook something," he said, unenthused as he flipped another page of the album. He didn't want to cook anything. "You two staying?"

Miranda checked her phone. "Kent's still in Chicago, so you're stuck with me!"

"Can I call Austin and tell him to bring Josiah over?"

"Of course." Evan stood up and stretched. "Matt should be back soon. I haven't heard from Danny, so I'm not sure if he'll be dropping in."

Miranda made a face that Katie echoed. Then they looked at each other and Evan's Spidey sense tingled.

"What?"

"It's Saturday night, Dad. He's out with...." Katie trailed off, exchanging raised eyebrows with her sister.

"With?" Evan's spine snapped to attention, and he crossed his arms over his chest. The rush of "cool, bro" flared back up, as did the fact that he hadn't followed up with his son.

"Leah."

Leah was thirty-five, a teacher who supervised the St. John's Spanish students when they went to Spain to study. She and Danny met in the St. John's parking lot, then again when he was studying abroad. Only Elizabeth had met her, and there was some dispute between the girls as to whether she approved.

Evan sat on the recliner, hands clasped between his knees, forehead furrowing in concern. "Thirty-five? And his teacher?"

Miranda pursed her lips. "In-appro-priate," she said, popping her *p*'s.

Even Katie nodded. "I mean, the age thing is like—to each their own, but I don't love the power dynamics," she pointed out. "She's in a position of authority over him. And who was supervising this whole shebang while they were off… uh… canoodling?"

"Basically you spent money to send him to Spain for an extended booty call."

"Miranda!"

"What?" Miranda shrugged. "It's true."

Evan felt a little woozy.

"MY FAMILY!" Matt called out as he walked in an hour later. He could smell—well, he couldn't smell anything, which sucked because it was seven o'clock and he was starving. "Did you eat everything already?"

Josiah and Austin were on the couch playing basketball on the Xbox—or rather Josiah was beating his father soundly as Austin just poked buttons with a confused expression. They gave Matt equally baleful looks as Josiah rubbed his stomach in a sad pantomime. Austin's head tilted toward the kitchen, accompanied by an eyebrow wiggle.

Code.

Uh-oh.

"Pizza and wings?"

"God, yes," Austin mouthed, while Josiah fist-pumped next to him.

Matt gave him the thumbs-up, calling up the Seamless app on his phone as he trudged toward the kitchen.

Evan, Miranda, and Katie sat at the table, an empty pitcher in the center, massive piles of clothing on every chair that wasn't already occupied, all of them sharing identical Cerelli furrowed brows.

"Hello, family," Matt said, swiping and pressing buttons until he secured a large amount of food to be delivered ASAP. The soonest of possibles possible. "Hello, Matt! We are so very sorry your kitchen is full of clothing and not food. You look so handsome today, even in your foodless fatigued state!"

"You have ego problems. Not everything is about you," Katie said, standing to give him a kiss on the cheek. He patted her teeny tiny baby bump because he had blanket permission to do so into perpetuity. (There was a signed napkin around here somewhere.)

Matt gasped in horror. "Lies."

"We got caught up in things," Miranda said, offering her cheek as Matt made his way around the table. He did not touch her baby bump because it weirded her out if anyone did it, except for Kent. Matt kept his hands to himself.

"Why am I imagining this little powwow isn't because of impossibly small socks?" Matt reached Evan, tipped his head back, and attempted to wipe that pained expression off his face with his tongue.

"Get it!" Katie yelled.

It didn't quite work. Evan accepted the kiss, then whomped him in the chest.

Matt leaned against the counter with a cold beer as his family brought him up-to-date on the Danny/Leah situation. He kept waiting for more—she was married. Or a black widow. Wisely, he kept his mouth shut as Katie got to the part where it wasn't cool for a teacher to date a student.

"And yet the plot of many porn movies," he muttered, earning a shot in the face with a balled-up piece of paper from Miranda.

"Matt...."

"I know, I know." He put his hand up to stave off Evan's irritation. "So who is the person—not it, called it fair and legal—that takes this conversation to Danny?"

"Pulling the pregnancy card," Miranda said, holding her hand up. "And pulling it for Katie preemptively."

"Thanks."

All eyes turned to Evan.

"This hardly seems fair. Or democratic," Evan said, resigned to his fate.

The doorbell rang, and Josiah's happy shouts of "Yay! Pizza!" cut off further conversation.

EVAN MULLED over the situation for the rest of the evening, through pizza and the girls doing a fashion show of baby clothes draped over their small bumps. Matt narrated like it was a pro wrestling match while

Josiah played music on his father's phone. Laughter rang through the house, but Evan managed only a smile.

"HE'S OLD enough to make choices about who he sleeps with" was what Evan ended up with, then said out loud as Matt climbed into bed. "He's twenty."

"Uh-huh." Matt smoothed the covers over his chest, leaning back against the pillows. "That's not the discussion the Cerelli Family Council had. Did you just nod to shut everyone up?"

Evan scowled, removing his clothes in as angry a fashion as he could manage without falling over. "I'm thinking about what the girls said. And I'm thinking that no, I'm not happy about it being a teacher, but—"

"Hey, I got in trouble for the porn comment!" Matt looked positively delighted. "You did just nod to placate the girls! You have no problem with your son dating an older woman! You're just as much of a jerk man as I am!"

"Shut up."

"I mean, I'm guessing your reaction would be different if Elizabeth brought home a thirty-five-year-old teacher who she'd been booty-calling in Spain—"

"Shut. Up."

Evan stormed into the bathroom to brush his teeth, just barely resisting the urge to slam the door behind him. He avoided looking at himself in the mirror, preferring to brush in the semidarkness. It was hard to miss Matt's laughter mocking him from the other room.

He hated when Matt was right.

And if Helena found out about any of this, he was a dead man.

"WHY DON'T you meet me in the city and we'll have dinner on Friday?" was all he said to Danny a few days later as he drove home from work.

The cell phone gave a staticky silence in return. Evan waited patiently, tapping his hands on the steering wheel.

"Uh, sure. Everything okay?" his son finally asked as Evan eased the car forward in the congested rush-hour traffic.

"Yeah. It's just been a while since we did a father/son thing. How about seven? Gallagher's."

Danny wasn't fooled; his tone removed any illusion of that. "Sure. See you then. Later."

The line disconnected, and Evan resisted the urge to smack his head on the dashboard. Why had his kids decided to have growing pains at the same damn time? There were four—they really needed to have a schedule of some sort.

EVAN PRACTICED all his conversation starters, muttered under his breath or played over and over in his head in the shower, for the rest of the week. By the time he got home on Thursday, he felt pretty good about the strategy and cautiously optimistic about the discussion the next night with Danny. Assure him his life was his own, but he should consider carefully his choice of romantic partners, and then a whole thing about power dynamics he'd googled on his phone. Rational Danny, rational Evan—it would all be fine.

Then Matt met him at the door, a forced smile on his face.

"Oh hey, glad I caught you. Danny brought his girlfriend over unexpectedly and they're at the dining room table with a danish ring I found on the top of the fridge."

"What?" Evan shook his head. "They're here?"

"Yes. Danny and Leah, who seems okay, but I'm pretty sure we're both intellectually outgunned. She uses a lot of big words."

Evan looked over his shoulder. "Make a break for it?"

"Oh hell no. I've been looking forward to this cage match since the doorbell rang."

REINING IN his amusement, Matt hung up Evan's coat and left his briefcase on the coffee table. He herded Evan into the dining room, firm hands on his shoulders and a smirk in his heart.

Danny—in a button-down shirt and tie, for God's sake—sat next to Leah, whose pencil skirt and turtleneck combo made her look like a central casting librarian, complete with mod eyeglasses and a neat bun on the top of her head. She was pleasant, conversational as they sat down to wait for Evan, but no mistake, Leah the teacher looked pissed off.

"Mr. Cerelli," she said politely as Evan shook her hand. Danny studied the surface of the dining room table like he was looking for clues to a murder.

"Ms...."

"Leah is fine." She folded her hands on the table. "I'm sorry to just drop in on your home like this, but Danny and I discussed things and thought we were long overdue to speak to you."

Danny's gaze never left the table.

"Uh-huh." Evan sat down in the chair across from Leah, with Matt taking the one next to him.

"I can understand why you might have some... concerns...."

"Oh good."

The tableau, already awkward, seemed to freeze in time. Matt's desire to be amused was quickly replaced by the urge to shiver because Evan's voice was basically an iceberg smacking into the table and knocking that danish ring to the floor.

What happened to "Twenty! Make your own girl decisions!" was what Matt wanted to know.

Leah straightened up a smidge more. "Danny is a consenting adult and he has a right to make decisions. A right to privacy."

"All true," Evan said, shifting in his seat. "I was going to tell him as much tomorrow over dinner."

Clearly surprised, Leah opened her mouth to speak, but Evan cut her off.

"Also true is the fact that you are his teacher. I don't care if you are a few months apart or fifteen years, you are breaking about a thousand ethical violations right this second."

"Danny does not have any classes with me. I am a teacher, but not his. I take my professional conduct very seriously."

"So you can tell me, professional conduct seriously taken, that nothing went on when you two were in Spain together."

Leah cleared her throat but said nothing while Evan turned a shade of burgundy that didn't look healthy.

Matt imagined a pin dropping. And then exploding like the end of *Apocalypse Now*.

He wanted to say something, but nothing of worth slid onto his tongue. Sarcasm? A question? A joke to break the unbearable tension currently sucking air out of the room? Instead, Matt looked at Danny.

Tiny beads of sweat knotted into the hair on his temple, his normally tanned skin pale as milk. He looked fucking miserable—not angry, not embarrassed, not indignant.

Miserable.

Matt took a deep breath. "All right, let's take a minute here." He could feel Evan's heated gaze against the side of his face, but God help him, he ignored it. "Danny? You okay?"

"Uh." Danny's head shot up, as if he was surprised he was being included in this conversation. Laid-back and easygoing Danny looked like he was about to puke.

Yeah, Matt had been a semiprofessional drunk at enough seedy bars long enough to know that look. He pushed his chair back just as Danny jumped up and ran to the first-floor bathroom like he was on fire.

"Stay here, please, and don't kill each other," Matt commanded as he stood up, then went after Danny with long strides.

DANNY WAS, in fact, throwing his brain up in the tiny first-floor bathroom. Beer. No mistaking the smell. Matt waited in the doorway, arms crossed over his chest.

"You been drinking?"

Wiping his mouth on a wad of toilet paper, Danny sat against the wall. "Three beers. I was so freaking nervous about this… this meeting."

"Was it your idea?"

Shaking his head, Danny threw the paper in the wastebasket. "I told Leah Dad wanted to talk to me, and she got all crazy mad. Said we had to confront him directly on our schedule, not his."

"And did you say, 'No, honey, that will cause me hysterical panic so much so that I'll drink three beers and barf'?"

Danny looked at him, sweaty-faced and pale, and gave him an epic eye roll.

"You think what your dad is saying is true?"

That made Danny look away.

"You hit on her, or did she hit on you?"

"God, Matt!"

"Tell me or tell your dad. Or, well, tell me and then tell your dad."

He covered his face with both hands as Matt leaned into the bathroom to flush the toilet. "Come into the hallway before that disgusting smell gets stuck in your clothes. Believe me, I know of what I speak."

THEY SAT on the floor, side by side, leaning against the hallway wall. The kitchen lay down at one end, the Florida room at the other. The latter was their personal refuge—too many sofas, the small television, and that weird window that stuck, but it was a quiet getaway when Danny was growing up and Matt just needed space.

"I'll be honest. When this first came out, I didn't think it was a big deal," Matt started. "Even that cage match out there didn't entirely sway me. But Danny, you look freaking miserable. And correct me if I'm wrong—it's not just about your dad and Leah going head-to-head."

Danny picked at his cuticles.

"Lemme ask again—you hit on her, or did she hit on you?"

"I didn't even know that's what she was doing," Danny whispered. "She did a presentation in my class about going abroad, we saw each other in the parking lot and talked. We had coffee the next day because she said if I had any questions... and I did! Actual questions. I didn't realize what was happening until she asked me to dinner and uh...."

Matt felt a twinge begin in his stomach. "First time?"

Danny writhed in embarrassment. "Maaaaatt."

"So that's a yes."

He put his hands over his eyes, rubbing vigorously. Matt patted him gently on the knee. "At her place?"

"Yes."

"And in Spain, did you?"

Danny fell sideways, leaning against Matt's shoulder. "A few times. I was busy studying, and there were chaperones. At first it was like... cool. Sneaking around and stuff. But then I wanted to hang out with the rest of the kids. Or go on side trips. I mean, Jane and Ollie and Maia and Brandon were all there, and this was supposed to be like a big adventure. But Leah got mad if I made other plans."

Matt's twinge took an ugly flare. "Why didn't you tell us? Why did you act like everything was okay?"

"Because what is wrong with me? Like, this hot and smart woman picked me and wants to have sex with me and all I can think is—why is this so much work? Why am I stressed out all the time?" Tears threatened in Danny's voice, so Matt gripped his knee harder.

"Life isn't a movie, okay? Just because someone wants to have sex with you, doesn't mean you have to have sex with them," he said quietly. "And she used her position at the school to initiate this…" Matt was suddenly loathe to use the word relationship. "This thing between the two of you. That isn't right."

Danny just sighed.

"It's not the way things should go. Problems happen even when you're both a hundred percent committed, but this—this doesn't sound like it's good for you."

"Elizabeth hates her. We all had dinner and I thought I was going to have to break something up."

"Elizabeth hates, like… bigots and people who hurt animals. Did Leah punch a chicken or something?" Matt made a mental note to give his stepdaughter an extra fifty the next time she came to the house. Because good for her radar.

Then he was going to take ten back for not tattling.

"She told me my shirt was inappropriate for dinner. It was one about laughing at my own jokes because I'm hilarious?"

"And Elizabeth got mad because she bought it for you?"

"No, because she said we were at a freaking Applebee's and that's not exactly black-tie and maybe Leah should stop telling me how to dress."

"I once arrested someone at a Subway on the Lower East Side wearing a thong and a Viking hat," Matt said, elbowing Danny in the side. "Maybe keep that in mind as a potential date outfit."

Danny snorted out a laugh, but it petered out quickly. "I don't know if there'll be another time, to be honest. Like—I have school and work, and we're talking about doing a big kayaking trip in a few months out West. I can't be like, 'Oh hey, Leah, can I hang out with my friends? Can I leave the state? Can I go home and have dinner?'"

"She didn't want you coming home for dinner?"

Danny shrugged. "She made a face whenever I mentioned it."

"Yeah, so, there are about forty red flags going on right now. I don't like the way this started, and I sure as hell don't like her isolating you from your family and friends."

He waited for Danny to defend Leah, assure Matt that wasn't the case, but his silence—and the averted face—told him what he needed to know. Danny knew this wasn't right.

Thank God.

Matt patted his knee, then twisted and turned and hung on to the wall so he could stand up. "I'm going to go ask Leah to leave and hopefully not have to hide evidence to keep your father out of jail."

"Do you want me to…."

"No, you go wait in the back room. We'll talk about you breaking up with her after the house is clear."

Danny went back to looking miserable—less green, but still miserable—and slowly got up. Matt made a calculated move, opening his arms to offer a hug. Without hesitation, Danny wrapped his arms around him, giving him a strong squeeze.

"Why are you so tall? It's disconcerting," Matt murmured, thumping Danny on the back. "Are you standing on a box?"

"Thanks, Matt."

Matt tightened his grip. "Anytime, kid."

He gently pushed Danny in the opposite direction, then counted to one hundred before taking a step. After all this was over, a long-distance call to Liz the Shrink was going to need to happen.

WHEN DANNY disappeared down the hall with Matt in hot pursuit, Evan felt everything tilt sideways. He thought he had everything under control—rational, logical, trust your adult son. But one look at "Call Me Leah" at his table and his terrified-looking kid—because he was still a kid, and no matter what Evan's life was like at twenty, Danny wasn't him—and oh. Yeah. The sudden anger took him by surprise.

"Maybe I should—" Leah started, but Evan held his hand up.

"No." He breathed. "Please."

She settled back in her chair, her gaze direct and unflinching. She wasn't going to back down, even if she knew she should. All those interrogations proved helpful in real humdrum life.

"He desperately wants your approval," Leah said, folding her hands on the table in front of her. "About me, about school. I've tried my best to help him… separate himself from wanting a committee vote on everything he does. Particularly with regards to his sister."

"So he just needs your approval?"

She wrinkled her nose. "That isn't what I said."

"Elizabeth and Danny are close—always have been. No girlfriend is going to break that apart."

She bristled at that, shoulders going up to her ears. "While I can appreciate the twin dynamic, Danny has to be able to live his own life. Make his own decisions. I merely suggested that to him. Unless you're suggesting he live the life of a monk because his sister—"

"His sister is my daughter, so let's dial back the criticism." Evan used the same tone he did in meetings where his presence felt like window dressing and all he wanted to do was quit on the spot.

Or throw a couch out the window.

Leah's face pinched with displeasure; she sat back with a huffing sigh, all pretense of calm and collected discarded.

"This seems a lot of work to date a twenty-year-old," Matt said, walking back into the kitchen.

"That isn't your choice," Leah snapped, standing up as she slammed her hand on the table. "And I don't appreciate your implication."

Matt put his hands up in supplication. "No implication. Just saying, there have to be better choices for a relationship, unless this is about to turn into you telling us you'd like his hand in marriage."

Evan bit his tongue at the hypothetical. If she said anything of the sort, he was going to require a sedative.

"You're being ridiculous." Leah gathered her purse and coat off the chair next to her. "Blowing everything out of proportion. We were trying to be proactive—"

"We're being concerned about our son. I'm not going to apologize for that." Matt crossed his arms over this chest, a wide-legged stance Evan labeled *security professional* in his head.

"Danny is free to make his own choices, Leah. I've already said that. But this family... we're involved with each other's lives. Not apologizing for that either."

A cold silence settled over the room.

"Leah? Can we talk outside?" Danny ducked out from behind Matt, still looking pale and shaky. "I think we're done here."

Like magnets, Evan's gaze snicked with Matt's; the serious cop face wavered briefly as his husband tried not to laugh. "You okay, Danny?"

"Fine." Danny walked toward the living room, clearly expecting Leah to follow him. She did, looking none too happy about it. "I'll be back in a minute."

Leah shot them each a glare, then hustled out, nearly hip-checking Matt on her way.

"Not going to lie—I'm really glad she hates us," Matt said as they disappeared.

Evan heard the front door open and then close with a slam. "Good. As long as he doesn't, I don't give a shit." He rubbed his forehead. "That was—I don't know what that was. Is he all right?"

"Stress and panic with a beer chaser." Matt sat down at the table, pulling the danish ring box closer. "This whole thing was a lot more serious than we thought." Matt frowned as he opened the box. "She did a number on him."

Evan's stomach dropped. "I should have handled this better. I should have talked to him sooner…."

"Yeah. Not gonna lie." Matt tore off a hunk of danish, dropping bits of walnuts and sugar coating on the tablecloth. "Not our finest moment."

"I want to go stand by the front window like when Katie used to come home from dates." He walked toward the living room, then back again, digging his hands into his pockets. No, he shouldn't do that. No— he really should.

"He came out to handle it—that's something. A good sign."

Evan knew when Matt was sugarcoating something to keep Evan from losing his shit. The tone of his voice, the way he avoided eye contact.

"What should we do?" Evan hovered between the living and dining rooms.

"Give him a few minutes. If he doesn't come back, we kick open the door and you flash your damn badge." Matt wiped his face on a napkin. "But uh—after that? I'm calling Liz. And then we're contacting that goddamn school."

Evan's brain tried to process everything; his blood pressure peaked into a painful headache at the back of his head. Anger and a ton of shame rushed through him. They'd failed Danny on this one.

"How can she be wrong and right at the same time?" he mused.

Matt ripped off another hunk. "Meaning?"

"He's allowed to make his own choices. He's his own person. He's twenty! He should stand up to us." Evan sighed, picking walnuts off the ring. "All of that is true. And his sexual—" He swallowed. "—relationships are his own. I don't want to meddle in that."

"But."

"But. He's also young. Maybe younger than we realized."

"Might be. Then again, he could have stayed hidden in the back, but he chose to come out and face her." Matt shrugged. "That's something."

THEY FINISHED the danish and two beers each before the front door opened again. Evan had remained at the table, and Matt's "leave him be" speech worked well on both of them, because Matt wanted to check on things himself about a hundred times.

Matt's knee did a jig that rattled the table as Evan tightened his grip on the bottle.

Only Danny returned, looking worn-out and cold as he walked back into the dining room. "Is it stupid to want a beer right now?"

"Yes. Because you're not twenty-one yet," Evan said as he got up. "But I can get you coffee." He didn't resist the urge to wrap his arms around Danny, hugging him tightly.

When he felt Danny relax a bit, Evan let him go. "Milk and sugar?"

Danny nodded, his entire body sagging as he plopped into an open chair. "Is there anything to eat?"

"That's a good sign." Matt winked up at Evan. "I'll make coffee and dig out the Drake's Coffee Cakes I hid in the pantry. Talk to your father." He leaned over to ruffle Danny's hair. "Then take a shower, you're disgusting."

When they were alone, Evan cleared his throat. "So. Are you single again?"

Danny thunked his head down on the table. "Ugh."

"I'm sorry, Danny."

"Why? Because I'm an idiot? Probably not your fault."

"We can debate that after you have a coffee cake in your system."

"I broke up with her, but like—awkward because we are on the same campus."

Evan shifted in his seat, leaning against the table. "You have any classes with her?"

"No. Just—I see her around, you know?"

"If she gives you any trouble, you tell me."

"Daaaaaaad."

"I'm serious."

Danny sat up abruptly, his expression a view of stubbornness Evan remembered seeing in many a mirror. "I'm a man. I can handle myself."

Evan suppressed a wince. "I know," he said gently. "But she is still a teacher at the school, and I don't want her to start any trouble." The fact that Danny went to a place of protecting himself made his stomach twist. "And… if she confronts you on campus or your dorm, if she seems like she's going to put her hands on you…."

With a swallow, Danny shook his head. "Dad, she's never done anything like that."

"Okay, okay. Good." Evan put his hand on Danny's shoulder. "If that changes, you let me know."

Matt's whistling broke the tension slightly as he returned, carrying two cups and a coffee cake under each arm. "You need a restraining order?"

"Matt. Not funny."

"Security cameras?"

Danny laughed weakly. "I'm okay. Leah's not dangerous. Just… intense."

"Blow-up doll?"

"Matt, I swear to God." Evan tried not to crack, he really did. "This is serious."

"Have you considered men?"

"Matt!" He barely managed to choke back laughter—something Danny didn't bother to do.

Matt put a mug in front of Danny, then lifted his elbow so a cake fell in front of him. "Just for that, you don't get a Drake's."

"My first relationship was a doozy," Danny said finally, wiping his eyes with the sleeve of his shirt. "I think I'm going to take a break for a while."

"Good idea," Matt said, sitting down. "You should try sleeping around."

"*You're* sleeping on the couch forever."

Matt ignored Evan entirely. "There's some learning to be done here, okay? And I think maybe you should talk to someone...."

"I'm talking to you," Danny pointed out.

"Right, but there's this whole thing that goes along with talking to your father, and your incredibly cool stepfather, that might not be the most helpful solution."

Danny frowned. "You mean like a shrink?"

"I get ninety-nine percent off all services from my friend Liz, and you don't even have to lie on her couch. Just... give her a call."

Evan cleared his throat. "I know it's easy to brush this aside and pretend like it's no big deal."

"I like that idea better."

"But."

"This sucks."

Matt unwrapped a coffee cake, then nudged it in front of Danny. "Sucks hard. But you ended it, and that's great. Now, you just have to deal with your...."

Danny shoved nearly the entire cake into his mouth.

"Feelings," Evan provided as Danny covered his eyes with both hands. "Sorry."

FIVE WEEKS later Evan's phone buzzed as he walked from the car to the house, a bag of takeout in one hand and a briefcase overflowing with paperwork that represented the rest of his evening in the other. Juggling everything, he managed to pull it from his pocket.

No text, just a picture—of Danny and a young woman Evan had been acquainted with since the twins were in kindergarten. They were smiling, heads pressed together, his son looking glowingly happy.

Five weeks of conversations with Liz the Shrink, and a meeting with the dean no one wanted to have. Five weeks of Evan making an effort—with support from Matt and the rest of the kids—to keep Danny talking and finding comfort in his family. A few days' worth of gut-busting stress aside, Danny seemed to be coming out the other side with a better sense of himself and a mature attitude that settled Evan's nerves about his future.

And this text suggested Danny's future had just gotten a bit more populated.

Jane says hi, Danny texted him a second later. Then, *dinner soon?*

Absolutely, Evan sent back, a smile spreading across his face.

5
It's Always the Quiet Ones

Evan wasn't sure when it happened. One day he was bringing the twins home from the hospital, and the next Elizabeth was sitting across from him and Matt at the kitchen table with police academy brochures.

A flicker of pride, coupled with pure abject fear, tempered him as he listened to his youngest daughter—and the quietest, most sensitive of the bunch—rattle off thoughts about the orientation she'd just attended.

Her liberal arts credits weren't a waste, she insisted. No, they'd just provided her with a feeling of the world around her, and history and abstract thinking. She'd take some criminal justice in her junior year and then move to the academy when she graduated.

It was decided.

Except Evan's brain jumped and danced over a list of things, both rational and not, that kept him nodding and nodding and not much else. In moments like this, when Evan disappeared into a whirling mass of overthinking and panic, it was Matt's job to rescue everyone until Evan came back online.

Those were the rules. Except, of course, at this moment, when Evan's nodding was coupled with Matt's silence.

Stone.

Cold.

Silence.

Silent enough to signal Evan's brain. He blinked a few times, then tried to emulate WWMD (what would Matt do)—just in the nick of time.

Elizabeth finished her breathless recitation, then looked expectantly at her father and stepfather.

"How does that sound?" Her eyes were big and excited, and for a young woman who scarcely peeped louder than a whisper, she seemed to be almost shouting now. *I picked this. This is my decision.*

"Wow, you've really thought this out," Evan said, testing each word on his tongue before it slipped out. "What do you need your old dads for?" The latter was a joke that wobbled on its landing.

Elizabeth's smile deflated a watt or two. "Well—I mean, you guys have both done this, and I... I wanted to make sure you thought it sounded right. The way I want to do it."

Still nothing from Matt. Evan didn't chance a glance.

"Matt and I both went into the academy with different circumstances. At a different time." Did he sound diplomatic? He was still parsing out his own feelings on this. "You need to make your own path."

She nodded enthusiastically. "I just feel like... like maybe a different perspective will help the police force and then help the citizens of New York! Community policing, Dad—that's where the future is."

Evan felt Matt's lips purse and the tensing of his thigh where their legs touched under the table.

"We need people who want to shake things up—and that's me. I want to be that person." Elizabeth paused and took a deep breath. "Like you, Dad."

"I am so proud of you," Evan said, and that was sincere, truly. Because his sensitive little girl was a smart young woman with a true goodness inside her. He wanted her to succeed.

Even as he worried she wouldn't.

THEY SENT her back to her dorm at Stony Brook with five bags of groceries and clean laundry in the back of her Toyota. Matt slipped her fifty bucks as he hugged her goodbye tightly; he assumed Evan did the same. Elizabeth would probably stop and buy food for the homeless on her way back.

Nothing about how he handled her announcement sat well with him, but the red alarm claxon in his head was unrelenting. Jim and Helena were thrilled with Elizabeth's choice, peppering her with advice and pep talks and "insider info." So far none of the other siblings expressed concern over Elizabeth's career aspirations, or maybe—as a sympathetic Griffin pointed out—they didn't think it would come to pass, so they weren't worrying.

Having his best friend's husband play agony aunt three times a week over the phone would be embarrassing, but Matt was starting to feel crazy. Did no one but him think this was a terrible, terrible idea?

Evan hadn't made a comment about Elizabeth's choice one way or another but seemed—to Matt at least—to be going along with it. Griffin told him to just ask, for God's sake, and Matt called him a name, but he wasn't wrong.

But.

Matt was still the stepfather. He wasn't the moral authority of the family, and he wasn't comfortable contradicting Evan. He didn't want to do that. He wanted to skate along at Evan's side, cheerlead, support, and manage him when necessary. He loved the fact that the kids came to him—even Miranda texted him "just to chat" twice a week. He loved these kids, would take a bullet or a speeding car to the chest.

But.

Mulling and mumbling, Matt ambled back into the house, where Evan was already shutting down the first floor for the night.

"Danny's coming tomorrow. We need to pick up more groceries and laundry detergent," Evan commented from the kitchen, where Matt heard the clank of glasses.

"When did we become a rest stop? I'm thinking of putting a Popeyes in the backyard."

"The future is franchised chicken." Evan came out of the kitchen, two glasses of water in hand. "The weather's starting to get nice, speaking of backyards and chicken. We should get everyone together for a barbecue in a few weeks."

Matt grunted a response and then focused on punching some throw pillows on the couch.

"What?"

"What what? We'll have people over and cook meat. Sounds good."

"Matt…."

He knew that tone, that warning concern that said, *I am probably not going to drop this and the silent treatment lies ahead.*

Matt sighed, throwing himself onto the couch dramatically. At least he could get a head start if this devolved into a fight and he ended up sleeping on the couch. "Do you really support this? Elizabeth's decision to be a cop?"

Boom. There it was. Out in the open.

Evan seemed to freeze for a long moment before slowly making his way across the room to sit on the edge of the coffee table. The glasses of water ended up gingerly placed on a day-old copy of the *Daily News*. "I wondered why you were so quiet."

"I can't…," Matt started, shifting on the couch. "I can't pretend I think this is a good idea. The academy is going to eat her up and spit her out, and if by some miracle she survives that, she's going to walk into a precinct…." Matt ran out of words, feeling his heart bumping again his rib cage. "They're going to take one look at her and draw a giant target on her back."

"Women police officers—"

Matt put up his hand. "No. No. This isn't me being backwards and stupid. We both know a hell of a lot of women in the department who could break us both in half physically, mentally, and verbally. Helena, for example, who I pray to Jesus never thinks I think that."

Evan nodded. "Fair enough."

"This is about her being so fucking sweet and good and decent a human being." Matt's chest hurt just thinking about it. "She's going to always want to do the right thing."

"Maybe she's right. Maybe the force needs people like her," Evan said, his tone indicating that he was only about 40 percent convinced.

"Yes. She's right. But her? Even if she succeeds the tiniest bit, they will extinguish her enthusiasm and her heart and make her a bastard like you and me."

"Helena is still a positive person."

"Helena makes speeches and serves on task forces and makes recommendations in meetings," Matt responded bluntly. "She couldn't do it anymore. She got out before they ruined her, even if she doesn't want to admit it."

Evan's shoulders went up the tiniest bit, and Matt felt the inevitable fight whistling its presence from the next station. He opened his mouth to speak, but Matt cut him off.

"And before you dump this into my lap because of my experience with the force—stop. Please. I went in an asshole and I came out a bitter asshole. This isn't just about being positive or naive. I knew what the world was like." Matt leaned forward. "You know what the world is like. But you and me and Jim—we have shields."

Evan deflated. "And even with shields…."

"Jim's retired. I got bumped out the door. Helena's got a desk job. You have a desk job. We're all alive and whole, but there were some shaky-ass times in between."

Silence echoed loudly through the house.

After a long and awkward moment, Evan rubbed his palms over his eyes. "I want to believe in her," he said softly. "I want to support her and her enthusiasm and her dreams, but my God. I'm terrified for her."

THEY TABLED the discussion in favor of sleep—or mostly a night of shared tossing and turning until the alarm went off. Evan cycled through endless arguments in his head, from not putting his fears and prejudices on Elizabeth (would he have this reaction if it was Danny? Was this misogyny? Why didn't he believe in his own child?) to being firm in his conviction that, as a father, didn't he have the obligation to help guide her away from a seriously negative—and potentially fatal—choice?

Dawn didn't break the tie between the two voices, and neither did Matt's equally troubled expression over shared coffee and eggs over easy on toast.

They separated at the driveway, Matt heading upstate to work with Jim at his home office, and Evan into the city for another day as captain, but this time carrying a magnifying glass in his mind's eye.

All day he watched how the female officers in his command were treated. How he treated them. Did he assign the same amount of gravity to their concerns and hunches? Did he hand out cases fairly between the male and female detectives? Did he even have a fair ratio to make that decision?

The answer to that last question was no.

His own tokenism seemed to slide into the mental battle almost unnoticed. The first "out" gay captain. Trotted out when One Police Plaza had another PR nightmare to battle or when they wanted to remind everyone of their "diversity."

"If you were black, this would have been even better optics," someone had remarked once at a community luncheon, with Evan left blinking in surprise and unable to respond before the man drifted away to shake more hands.

Matt had thrown their rake across the backyard when he shared that little tidbit.

The number of female, LGBT, and nonwhite officers had grown over Evan's years on the force, but the ratio was hardly balanced. There were "optics"—oh yes, so many smiling faces on those brochures and campaigns—but too many meetings for captains and higher-ups featured far more people who looked like Evan than Helena. Or Austin.

Or Elizabeth.

His gentle-hearted, fair-minded girl. Optimists didn't last long in this job.

HE GOT home later than usual—too many hours woolgathering at his desk in between phone calls, office visits, meetings, and conferences. His precinct was small and the crime percentage low—another "optic" he wanted to smack in the face—so days of deadly mayhem were few and far between.

How many days until retirement?

Danny's car was parked in the driveway, but Matt's was missing. Evan checked his phone and discovered three texts: Matt saying he was staying for dinner at Jim and Griffin's, Danny saying he was at the house and had ordered pizza because Matt was not coming home for dinner, and another saying they were out of laundry detergent. Also from Danny.

In the middle of everything Elizabeth-related, Evan took a moment to be grateful Danny was back on track and their relationship on solid ground.

"Sorry," Evan called out as he unlocked the door and stepped through. "Can you squeeze some extra out?"

Danny sat up from where he was sprawled on the couch, his face suspicious. "I really hope you read your texts and that wasn't some weird sex thing."

Evan threw his keys at his son's head.

"My reflexes are better than that," Danny said, dangling them from two fingers. "Pizza just got here."

"Want me to run out and get more detergent?"

"Nah. Found some samples they send in the mail—more than enough for me to finish. Thanks." Danny—all legs, arms, and skinny torso—unfolded off the couch, heading toward the kitchen.

"Ingenious." Evan hung up his coat, left his briefcase by the door. Paperwork could wait; his intent was focused on his son and spending some quality time.

They sat at the kitchen table, splitting the pizza clean in half, a basketball game on the television, all the lights blazing—ideal circumstances for a moment of relaxation as far as Evan was concerned. They ate the first pieces in silence before Danny slowed down enough to breathe.

"Elizabeth called me today."

Evan swallowed and sighed. "She was here last night," Evan said, neutral as he could be.

"I know. With all her brochures and grand ideas."

Danny's tone intrigued Evan; he took a sip of soda, nodded slowly. "You uh—talk to her about her decision?"

Danny folded his crust in half, then shoved the whole thing into his mouth. The mischief in his eyes reminded Evan that his kid might have a deep voice and six-foot wingspan, but he was still... a kid. He swallowed dramatically, drank half his soda, then spent an inordinate amount of time wiping his mouth.

"Daniel!" Evan finally yelled, dissolving Danny into laughter.

"Sorry, sorry." Danny winked. "I was wondering who would crack first—you or Matt."

Evan pretended he didn't know what Danny was talking about as he reached for another slice.

"Yes, I talked to her. A lot. Before she talked to anyone else." Danny leaned back in his chair, an easy sprawl. "You know Elizabeth—she doesn't like to create drama. I'm surprised she didn't have, like, a whole PowerPoint presentation."

"She seems very, uh… committed to her decision."

"Wow. Very diplomatic, Dad."

"What?" Evan tried to look indignant but, failing that, took a defiant bite of pizza.

"You and Matt hate the idea, I know. She knows. She's all insecure now." Danny scowled. "I wish you'd just come out and say it. She can read your disapproval on your faces, and then you're all like—good luck with that."

"What about you? What's your opinion?"

"I think she's nuts."

"Did you tell her that?"

"Of course I did! She expects me to tell her the truth, like she does with me. And because I'm the only person she'll yell at when I do." Danny shrugged. "We've done like twenty rounds on this. I keep telling her if she wants to do good, there are a thousand things to do in the world other than joining the NYPD."

Evan sagged in relief. And a bit of shame, because Jesus, where was his backbone? "You know I only feel like this because of her… her gentle nature. Not because she's a girl. Woman."

Danny gave him some epic side-eye. "Don't say that again. Not until you're one hundred percent committed to it being true."

LATER, ON the couch—more basketball, more cold Cokes, half an apple pie and two forks—Danny turned to Evan with a serious expression.

"Elizabeth is, like, the nicest person I have ever met. She doesn't even curse at other drivers on the expressway. But… I think part of this is her wanting to not be a wallflower anymore."

"So she wants to be a cop? That doesn't make sense."

"She wants some control. Some—power isn't the right word. She wants some respect. She wants people to see her as more than just nice, quiet Elizabeth."

Evan thought of his handling Miranda's intense teen years and Katie's energetic aura. Their conflicts: the yelling and door-slamming. Elizabeth and Danny were like their quiet mirror. Aside from Elizabeth's need to shadow her brother (and his desire to escape), they never gave him a problem. Good grades, good behavior, good manners.

Stress saved for Evan.

Internalized struggle for Elizabeth.

"And a uniform gets people to notice her."

"Yeah. And it's gonna give her some power to do something good. None of which is bad." Danny let out a frustrated sound. "But she's just… I try to picture it and I can't. Which sucks because I'm always on her side and this time… I just can't be."

Evan poked the pie with his fork.

"We can't let her…," Evan started, but Danny smacked his arm with a throw pillow. "Sorry."

"You need to be honest with her. Maybe let her…." Danny hit himself with the pillow. "Crap. What the hell do I know? I still haven't declared a major."

MATT AND Jim spent the day in Jim's home office, mapping out security camera placement on a floor plan—not exactly glamorous, but it paid the bills. Like college and weddings and grandbabies making their arrival in a few months. Matt didn't complain as they ran into yet another too wide blind spot, sending them back to square one for the boutique hotel's lobby.

"I mean, I know my knees couldn't handle it, but it might be nice to chase someone down an alley right now," Matt quipped, swiveling his chair around a few times.

Jim smirked as he saved their work on the huge monitor they did floor plans on. "That's it, we're breaking for lunch. You're clearly light-headed."

"You don't miss it?"

Jim didn't answer for a few minutes; he tidied up his desk, shut off the monitor. Pretty sure he already knew the answer, Matt creaked his chair back and waited.

"Well?"

"Well what? You miss it, after all this time. All the shit." Jim gave him the stink eye. "But would you really go back?"

"In time? Or for a desk job?" Matt looked at his sneakers, at his well-worn jeans. Sometimes he wore a tie for meetings, but generally he dressed the way he wanted, made his own hours, and cashed bigger checks than he ever had as a detective. Benefits included not getting shot at. Ever.

"You wouldn't change a thing."

"Damn, you sound sure of yourself."

"We are cut from the same cloth, my friend. Bitch as we might about the sedate and safe lifestyle, we aren't going anywhere." There was something wistful in Jim's tone.

Matt grabbed a piece of paper off the closest desk, crumpled it, and threw it at Jim's head. "Suburban logical you is so fucking boring. We need to get you into the city."

Jim easily ducked out of the way. "Queens is not the city."

"Well, now we have to duel."

BACK IN the house, Jim made sandwiches. They bullshitted and bantered, the well-worn groove of their friendship making for a pleasant hour of leaving business behind. The previous topic didn't make its way back into rotation—there was preseason baseball, after all—but as Matt finished his last bite, he let his gaze rest on Jim.

"Whoa. That's a pretty serious expression. I just asked who you thought the Yankees' starting center fielder would be."

"Me and Evan talked to Elizabeth the other night. She's going full steam ahead with this police academy thing."

"Good."

"Good?"

"Smart people with good morals joining the police force—I'm not going to try to stop that." Jim leaned his elbows on the table. "She reminds me of my former partner, Terry."

"Didn't he leave homicide?"

"Yeah. Not everyone can do that job. He's fucking fantastic where he is now—and happy. Doesn't make him any less of a good cop because he couldn't handle death every day." There was an edge to Jim's tone that Matt knew well.

Matt put his hands up. "Not saying he's a bad cop."

"You want only adrenaline junkies on a power trip with a badge?"

"Yes. That's all I want. Asshole." Matt got up and straightened his back, the creaks and cracks echoing in the kitchen. "She's my kid. You look me in the eye and tell me if Caro came to you with the academy brochure, you would be happy."

Jim shifted in his chair. "Griffin would shit a fucking brick."

"She'd be in a convent in ten seconds."

They shared a quiet laugh.

"It's dangerous, yeah. Just the thought of all the guys I've listened to "Taps" played for…." Matt dug his hands in his pockets, walking in a circle over the neatly tiled floor. "But it's more than that. Even if she retires without a scratch on her head, it's a mindfuck. It's a goddamn trench, and you're down there with the worst of people, and people in agony…." He trailed off and then looked at Jim imploringly. "It's not just that you can be physically hurt. It's the wear and tear on your soul."

"That's poetic." Jim sighed as he stood up. "And true."

The ghosts of the Kelly family—Carmen, the victim, and her parents, Ed and Della—sat quietly in the room, heavy on Matt's mind and, he knew, Jim's.

"So what's the answer? For all the garbage, Matt, we helped people. That's the job—it's not pretty, but it's necessary. Why assume Elizabeth can't do the job? Or at least a piece of it."

"Support her now, pay for her therapy later?"

"I know it's been a while, but there are other jobs besides homicide detective in the department. Maybe this isn't about Elizabeth with a badge but Elizabeth with the… right badge."

EVAN SEPARATED his issues—there was Elizabeth, and then there was the overwhelming inequality of his station house and department—and stewed over his words after Danny collected his laundry and left. It would be easy to ride the wave of self-loathing for letting his younger kids get to their early twenties carrying baggage of his making. In fact, he let it swamp him in the shower before bed and punched the hamper afterward for good measure.

Then he was done.

The past was the past. No time machines were going to appear in the living room to take him back so he might do things differently. He needed to deal with the here and now, with Elizabeth the adult and her choices. They were hers—but that didn't mean he had to keep all his opinions to himself.

Sounded good in his head, at least.

MATT SNUCK in late. The lunchtime chat with Jim had turned into a deeper one, this time about giving Elizabeth advice and direction to the type of work within the NYPD that might suit her. There was even a list—which Griffin tore into tiny pieces when he got home from the city.

"She has to make her own mistakes. Or maybe, just maybe, she knows herself and knows this is the right choice."

"And if Caro came home—" Jim started to say.

Griffin held up his hand. "If Caroline comes home with police academy brochures, you are more than welcome to bring up this moment. But until then, you can't use hypotheticals to get yourself out of this. She's an adult. You and Evan raised her—do you doubt she's capable of making important decisions? Could you just slow down and let her live her life?"

Matt turned to Jim, waving his phone in his face. "I recorded it. You know, for future reference."

And that's when Matt found himself buying Jim, Griffin, and Caro dinner at the most expensive restaurant in town.

He was sorry to miss Danny. They exchanged a flurry of texts throughout the evening, partially about the Yankees' opening-day center fielder and a bit about school. The *talked to Dad about Elizabeth. Have fun with that* made Matt wish he could have a beer or six with dinner.

Settling for one out of the fridge, Matt sat on the couch, SportsCenter volume low.

Non-black-and-white ethical dilemmas were not Matt's forte. So far everyone presented logical counterarguments to whatever fears kicked around his gut. He might even give the same advice if it wasn't his kid.

For some reason he harkened back to Katie's wedding and all his fears and concerns, Katie's worries she wouldn't be a good stepmother when anyone with a brain knew she would be.

Except Katie.

Matt took a long swig of beer.

Undertaking (step)parenting proved to be the biggest challenge of his life. Unprepared and unsuited, Matt bumbled about, trying to forget the lessons of his childhood, which hadn't prepared him for fatherhood. Or giving and receiving love. Hell, Evan's childhood was shit too. And yet four incredible adults had come out of their home with their heads screwed on straight.

"Goddamn it," he muttered. He hated when Griffin was right.

"Matt?"

The stairs creaked as Evan walked down. He sounded too awake to have just woken up, which meant they were avoiding sleep together.

"Hey, sorry about that. Was the TV too loud?"

"No, couldn't sleep."

Matt waved the beer around. "Just sayin'."

"Nah." Evan sat next to Matt, leaning against him with a sigh. "How was dinner?"

"Expensive."

"What did you do?"

"Eh. Griffin turned out to be right about stuff, so you know, there will be no living that down."

"We'll babysit for a weekend and all will be forgiven."

They sat in silence, sharing warmth and contemplation as Matt felt himself relax.

"Danny and I talked about Elizabeth," Evan said finally. "He had some good points."

"So did Jim. And Griffin. Caro has no opinion on the matter, just for the record."

Evan chuckled. "I envy her ability to remain neutral."

"Which we can't do."

"No. I think we have to share our feelings, but in the end…."

"It's up to her."

They sighed in unison.

A MONTH later they moved her out of the dorm at Stony Brook so she could spend the summer at home. St. John's had another week, so this delightful chore would be repeated in seven steamy days for Danny.

Evan stacked another bin of linens into Matt's arms, then turned him toward the door. They were down toward the end, only a few more bins and boxes of books to load into the car. Elizabeth darted in and out, taking something to the car, then being distracted by friends who wanted to say goodbye.

The line of girls and guys who poked their head into the room stayed steady for the entire two hours they were there.

"Sorry!" Elizabeth called, over and over, before disappearing into the hallway for hugs and squeals.

Her voice carried into the room, full of excited chatter and laughter.

"See you soon!"

"Carrie's party—no, definitely!"

"Oh my God, have fun in Barbados!"

And on and on.

Matt came back, red-faced and sweating. "Is Princess Popular going to grace us with her presence?"

"I feel like this is Katie 2.0," Evan mused, unplugging the floor lamp near the desk. "Remember? I didn't think we'd get out of there without twenty kids hanging on to the back bumper."

"She had like four friends in high school," Matt said, sitting down on the edge of the narrow bed.

"Yeah."

Elizabeth bounded into the room, long hair swinging. "I'm sorry, I swear, that's it. I'll help you finish," she said, giggling as she threw herself on the bed next to Matt. "We're going to see each other in, like, a week, I don't know what the issue is."

Evan blinked and blinked, as if his vision was clearing and he could see Elizabeth for the first time.

"They're going to miss you," Matt said as Evan floundered. "We, on the other hand, will quickly grow tired of your niceness and cleanliness."

"I'm going to start leaving my laundry on the floor!"

Matt stared at her. She stared back. Then they both started to laugh. "No, you're not."

"You'd need to tranquilize me." Elizabeth knocked shoulders with Matt. "Oh hey, you know who called me the other day? Uncle Jim!"

"Oh really?" Matt asked, suspiciously casual.

"Yeah. He had some really great advice for stuff I could study next year to prepare for the academy. And he told me to email his friend Terry, who does Crisis Management, which totally sounds so interesting."

Matt and Evan shared a look.

"That's fantastic," Evan said finally, busying his hands as he picked up the lamp. "I'm really proud of all the work you're doing, you know. Figuring out what you want."

Elizabeth's smile beamed brightly. "It's a lot of information, but I figure I have you and Matt and Jim and Helena to give me good advice."

"Always." Evan started to walk the lamp out of the room but paused to drop a kiss on her forehead. "Whatever you need, you just ask. We've got your back."

"Well, I need to get all my stuff into the car so we can get home."

Matt nudged her shoulder. "Hot date?" he teased.

Then Elizabeth flushed a shade of red Evan had never seen before, and the world tilted again.

6
DECISIONS, DECISIONS

EVAN'S CELL phone rang at six thirty in the morning, as he was pouring coffee into his travel mug. Having two pregnant daughters and two kids living away at college—not to mention a traveling husband—meant that thing was never more than six inches from his hand.

But it was none of those people. The number was Helena's.

"Hey, good morning. What's up?" he asked his former partner as he screwed the top of the mug on with his other hand.

Evan had known Helena for going on fifteen years. Her uneven breathing scared the living crap out of him.

"What?"

"Vic had a stroke. I'm in a car to the airport. My mom is freaking out," she said in a rush. "I already called the office—"

"If they have any questions, they can call me," he said firmly. His stomach roiled with tension. "What do you need?" Their old captain was a special person in both their lives—but he was also her stepfather.

"I… I don't know. I'm just—I'll know more when I get down there and talk to the doctors. Mom isn't…." She sighed. "You know Mom."

He felt her burden as an only child used to being the adult, and purposely made his voice as soothing as possible. "She's scared and upset. I'm sure once you get down there—"

"I'll take over and it'll be fine," Helena cut him off, her tone weary. "Just—can you keep an eye on Shane? He wanted to come with me, but they have to get these rewrites done or the whole schedule is fucked."

"Soon as I'm off the phone with you I'll call Matt. Putting my very best man on it."

"Thanks." She laughed halfheartedly. "Just—thanks. Soon as I know something more."

"Call when you can or when you need something. If I can manage it from my phone, it'll be done."

"Thanks."

He chose his next words to be carefully gentle. Helena didn't like being handled. "And if you need me on a plane, just ask."

"Only if… you know. I'll call," she said again. The noise in the background got louder. "We're at the terminal. I'm going to go."

"Okay. Be safe."

Her thank-you was lost in the flurry of speaking to the driver and opening the door. Evan disconnected the call, a heavy weight in his stomach.

After Sherri died, Vic and Helena in particular kept him alive and afloat until he found his footing again. Until he met Matt. And after that, when he was stupid and reactionary and wrong, they stood by him. Kicked him in the ass as appropriate. Fed him. Fed his kids. Vic's compassion and his quiet acceptance of Evan and Matt as a couple were invaluable.

His gratitude felt inadequate.

Evan didn't know his father, and he'd never had a quality relationship with his late mother. His in-laws were both dead, and his interactions with them after Sherri died had been contentious at best. Vic was at once friend and father figure, a guiding hand offering wisdom and advice, correcting him when Evan's stubbornness bred more panic.

How many nights had he sat in Vic's office, distraught and sure his life was over? A decade later, he couldn't have predicted how his life would reinvent itself again.

Evan finished his morning tasks, heading out the door a few minutes later than usual. He sent a message ahead to his second-in-command, then dictated an email about Helena's family emergency to the chief's office.

As he eased into the bridge traffic, he ordered his phone to call Matt, hoping he was awake.

"Live from New Orleans" were Matt's first words, gravelly and grumpy as he was first thing in the morning. "Is this about babies?"

"No. Helena called me this morning—Vic had a stroke."

Evan heard the change in Matt's demeanor through the line. "Shit. Shit."

"She's on her way to Florida. Soon as she gets there we'll have an update."

"Shit."

"Yeah."

"Goddammit."

Evan let Matt process it. Last year his former partner and their sweet best man, Abe Klein, passed from cancer, and Matt took it very badly. With Katie and Miranda being pregnant and the younger two away at school, it upped his protectiveness off the charts.

"She wants us to keep an eye on Shane."

"He didn't go—oh right. I don't even fucking know what rewrites are, but I am completely aware of their schedule at this point."

"Can you let Jim know?"

"Yeah. We've got breakfast with the clients at eight thirty. He's at the gym now because he's insane," Matt grumbled. "You want me to call Shane?"

A smile played on Evan's lips. He was glad Matt couldn't see him. "Would you mind?"

"No problem. And I'll text Griffin a heads-up so he knows what he's walking into." Evan heard the covers and pillows scattering off the bed. Matt was a tornado in the morning. "Probably should let Daisy and Bennett know…. I'll do that too."

"Thanks. Don't want to bug you while you're out on business, but you're better at this stuff."

"Sending texts? Oh wow, I'm blushing." A pillow hit the wall.

"Tip the maid extra," Evan said as he moved forward another inch in the traffic. He knew what that room looked like, and it wasn't pretty.

"I always do." Matt yawned loudly. "Unless you want to take this call into the john and ruin all sexy illusions."

"Too late. Bye."

MATT WAS only five minutes late to the meeting, which meant he was fifteen minutes early. Jim's military clock—set permanently at uptight—kept them on schedule and made everyone else apologize when they arrived, which made them spend more on security.

Something psychological at work, clearly.

"Griffin's leaving early so he can pick Shane up on the way to the office" was how Jim greeted him at their table in the hotel restaurant. Somewhere out there in New Orleans there existed delicious wonderfulness, but here they were, doing the hotel breakfast buffet for twenty-five bucks.

"Thanks for taking care of that. Shane sounded like shit when I talked to him."

"Doubt they'll get any work done today—he should have just gone." Jim unfolded the white napkin and dropped it into his lap.

Sometimes his rich-boy fancy-pants manners came out, making Matt feel like a slobbering caveman. Not that he did anything to change it.

"Then he would feel guilty because of the rewrites." Matt air quoted the last word as he sat down. The latest project for Griffin and Shane, for Bennett's production company, was hush-hush, not that Matt pushed too hard for details. It was a play he'd be forced to see and probably not understand, just like all the others.

A server dropped by with coffee for Matt and a large ice water for Jim; his name tag said Trevor, and he had a smooth demeanor that Matt felt guaranteed that unobtrusive refills throughout the meeting would be swift.

Matt poured two sugars into his coffee, because Evan wasn't here, and risked a glare from Jim…

Who wasn't paying attention as he emptied five pills, in various sizes, out of a tiny pill holder into his palm.

"Vitamins?" Matt asked casually, even as he knew that wasn't what they were.

"No." Jim tossed the pills into his mouth, then drank half the glass of water.

"You going to tell me what they're for?" Matt's chest tightened.

"No." Jim's steel-blue gaze pinned him into place. A wordless moment passed over them, two stubborn men facing off until Jim's gaze fell away. "Later, okay?"

Before Matt could protest, Trevor the server was bringing their clients to the table, and business took over.

EVAN KEPT his phone muted but in his line of vision for the entire day.

He considering calling Helena during lunch but refrained, even as his finger hovered over her number. She was probably still traveling, in a car speeding toward the hospital somewhere in Orlando. Maybe traffic, maybe delays. Evan's chest felt tight, his hands twitching every second they didn't hold a pen or cup of coffee. Even after all this time, the memory of rushing to Sherri's side came back in vivid color.

The twin distractions—potentially losing Vic and, oh God, the guilt for not visiting, and worrying about Helena—kept him off-balance all day. He fielded a dozen calls from One Police Plaza about a fundraising event they wanted to trot him out for, but he kept putting them off with a growing sense of annoyance.

Yes, he was the first out police captain in the city, but he was no longer the only one. His old friend Chris had taken over a precinct on the Upper West Side, and Norman Bell—black and gay, "PR Bingo," he would say dryly—was downtown. They'd moved past this, right? Taken pictures of him and Chris and Norman at a "summit" with the chief and the mayor, discussing both sides of the aisle. LGBT officers. LGBT community policing. Things that mattered.

And with every snap of a camera, every comment or line in an article, Evan felt a cringe of guilt.

The road Chris and Norman took to get their captainships was infinitely more difficult than Evan's. They fought being out and gay on the force, discrimination at every turn, fellow officers and perps alike throwing hate in their direction. They'd earned these positions.

Evan had just fit a scripted package they needed as a placeholder.

His office phone buzzed, pulling him out of his inner monologue.

"Captain Callas for Captain Cerelli." Chris's thick Queens accent came through the line, as if he'd summoned her.

"Weird. I was just dodging the mayor's office. Are you calling to make me go to this stupid reception?"

"God, no. Montgomery has a chest cold, so I gave him ten bucks to breathe on me. Maybe I can get pneumonia and they'll give me a pass." She cracked up at her own joke. "Those grandkids born yet?"

"No, we're a few weeks out."

"If at least one of them can time it to around the shindig, you might be able to skip it."

"Your mouth, God's in-box." Evan switched ears, fiddling with a pencil to divert some of his pent-up anxiety. "What can I do for you, Chris?"

"The grapevine got ahold of the news about Vic. Just wanted to check and see if you had updates."

"No, no word yet." He checked his phone just to make sure. "Helena'll call me when she can."

Chris gave a heavy sigh. "I hope he pulls through. Good guy."

"The best."

"When you talk to H, give her my love. She needs anything, you give me a call."

"I will, Chris. Thank you."

They chatted a bit more about the reception they both wanted to skip, the new crime stats, and a neighborhood initiative with some good ideas and about half the funding it needed.

"I swear, Evan, sometimes retirement can't come soon enough," Chris said before they said their goodbyes and hung up.

The comment hovered in the back of his mind for the rest of the morning.

HELENA DIDN'T call until almost five, but the lining of Evan's stomach remained mostly intact thanks to a text from Shane.

Vic's stable. They were waiting on test results. Serena was medicated thanks to Helena's persuasive personality. She'll call when they get back to the town house.

When his phone went off, Evan was just wrapping up a meeting with the second shift, discussing open cases and the potential problems a local hotel strike might cause. Picketers, tourists, and theatergoers were a bad combination when it came to shared sidewalks. Seeing it was Helena, he finished his thought, then waved them out of the office.

"Close the door," he said to his assistant, pressing the green dot on his phone to connect the call. He'd deal with everyone thinking he was an abrupt asshole later.

"Hey, how are you holding up?" he asked gently.

"Thank God for Xanax," Helena muttered. He heard a rustle of clothing. "Vic is sleeping. So far so good. They'll evaluate him again in the morning."

Evan felt light-headed in relief. "That's great to hear." He quickly put the phone on speaker so he could text Matt. "Your mom?"

Helena grunted. More rustling of clothes, and then a door slammed. "She's, uh, had a little white pill, and that is why we are both alive."

"Sounds like you might need something."

"I have a tumbler of scotch, thank you for knowing me." She heaved a dramatic sigh. "I love my mother like crazy, but holy Christ, she does not handle stress very well."

Matt texted back his relief on the hopeful prognosis for Vic and sent his love to Helena, which Evan passed along.

"Are you going to be able to handle her?" Because Helena did not want to be coddled right now, that much he knew.

"For a little while. I told Shane fuck the schedule—if he wanted me home sane and whole, he needed to be down here." Helena's voice wavered. "Because I can't...."

Evan let her breathe through the line, get herself under control. In fifteen years of knowing her, this part of Helena's life had flared every year or so, when her mother's demons spilled up and over into her relationship with her daughter.

"Concentrate on Vic, talking to the doctors. When Shane gets down there, he can take some of the load." Evan said a silent apology to his friend; when this was all over, he would buy his friend a giant steak and all the scotch he wanted. "Matt and Jim are in New Orleans. Do you want me to reroute them?"

"Oh God." Helena started laughing, real and hearty. "I... wait. Is that a real possibility? Seriously, don't tease me."

He should really check his joking tone.

"Let me text. Matt might be available—Jim has a kid to get home to."

"Matt has you."

"Eh, I kind of enjoy having control of the remote."

Evan could hear Helena's mood plunge suddenly. Shallow breathing, a little hiccup. Her trying to keep control of herself and of the situation. It wasn't difficult for him to imagine himself in her position; they were truly two peas in a pod.

He texted Shane quickly: *Call your wife, right now, and tell her when you are flying down there.*

Shit. Okay came the response.

"Listen. I want you to take a deep breath and just try to—"

"What's going to happen? If Vic lives, or if...." Her voice trailed off. "They can't live down here without anyone to help out. She can't be down here if he dies." Her tone grew more frantic.

"Okay, okay. Helena? You can't make that decision based on the current situation. You have to get through this part, and then you talk to them. You talk to your mother and convince her to move back here."

Helena moaned. "Fuck."

"Too much for right now."

"No shit."

Evan heard the buzzing through the speaker and felt no small measure of relief when Helena said, "That's Shane."

"Call me later."

"Okay," she said, distracted, and disconnected the call.

Evan got up in search of more coffee. Today was the ideal day to perfect his growing ulcer.

AFTER A day of wining, dining, and contract negotiation, Matt and Jim returned to Matt's room with a six-pack and containers heaped with red beans and rice, and shrimp po'boys. Well, a po'boy for Matt and steamed shrimp for Jim.

"I was afraid that family in the elevator was going to jump us for our food," Jim said, tossing his jacket on the second bed. "They were drooling."

"I'm glad they were able to maintain their composure. I don't make a habit of punching grandmothers." Matt kicked off his shoes, grateful to be free from their prison until their next business meeting. "You having a beer?" he asked, laying out the food on the room's small table before divesting himself of his jacket and tie.

"Subtle." Jim was already rolling up his shirtsleeves. "And no."

"Start talking, James. I want to know what's going on."

Matt leaned against the desk, arms folded over his chest. The entire day was an exercise in self-control: he wanted to fly to Florida for Vic and Helena; he wanted to shake his best friend and business partner until the truth fell out. Instead he talked security with hotel owners, joked and laughed and tried not to let the ugly oily rumble of his stomach be noticeable.

Jim sat on the edge of the bed, clasping his hands between his knees. "So a few months ago…."

Matt made a sound of frustration. Months?

"A few months ago," Jim repeated, his gaze unwavering, "I had a physical because my husband is secretly paranoid about me being so much older than he is, and because I like his brain unscrambled by stress, I went."

"They found something?"

"They found… an inherited thing. Basically a dangerous spike in my cholesterol, which increases the chances of a heart attack. Familial hypercholesterolemia, if you're going to google."

"You're the healthiest person I know," Matt said, shifting his weight. He didn't quite know where to put his worry and concern. Clearly they'd caught it in time. Jim was taking drugs; he seemed okay.

He'd just never thought too much about the age differences between the people in their circle. Yeah, Griffin and Daisy were babies; Bennett,

Shane, and Helena were a few years younger. Evan had a few years on them—and Matt a few more years than that. But Jim—Jim was older than them all. No one noticed because he could also fight a moose and win.

"Weird, right? I work my ass off to stay healthy and find out my father's genetics put a time bomb in my body." He laughed. "There's a metaphor in there, I think."

"How the hell is Griffin functioning after that news? I mean, Jesus, I'm about to make you lie down with a cold rag over your eyes. He let you leave his sight?" A thought popped into Matt's head, and he squinted at his best friend, his frown deepening. "Wait—you told him, right?"

That got a rise out of Jim. He sat up straighter, a snarl of anger on his upper lip. "You think I'd keep something like this from him?"

"I think you're taking little pills and dealing with something fucking scary, and yet you are also sitting in a hotel room a few thousand miles away from home. If I had a fucking head cold, Evan wouldn't let me leave the house." Matt's voice kept rising.

"Griffin is not the kind of person—"

"Oh my God! No, don't even. Don't try to bullshit me." He threw his hands in the air. "Griffin is exactly the kind of person to threaten to cut off your balls over something like this."

All the fight seemed to whoosh out of Jim, his shoulders sagging as his head dropped.

"He knows," Jim said quietly when he finally spoke. Matt struggled to hear him over the buzz of the air conditioner. "We, uh, have a deal. I do everything the doctors say, I get tested every few weeks. The tiniest change and I'm grounded."

"No more traveling," Matt said, though he knew in his gut it was more than that.

"No more work." Jim took a deep breath and leaned back on his hands. He still didn't meet Matt's gaze. "I retire to the couch and let Griffin run my life."

"Jim."

"He's scared. And mad. Come to think of it, so am I."

Matt couldn't think of anything to say.

EVAN STAYED late at the office. He'd texted Matt a few times but got no response. A call went to voicemail. It didn't worry him—he knew they were working. He knew that Matt and Jim on a business trip involved a healthy amount of beers, steaks, and cigars.

Once upon a time, the green-eyed monster would be sitting on his shoulder, whispering innuendo and worries.

He clearly remembered the anger he'd felt toward Jim, the jealousy sitting deep in his stomach every time his name was mentioned. But it had been a long time—a long time for him and Matt to be together and steady and good. Years of Jim and Griffin being more family than friends. For Evan, a man without siblings, Caroline was the closest thing to a niece he could imagine.

So no, nothing worried him about the silence.

Unfortunately it left him with an empty house.

And worries about Vic. Concern for Helena.

Weirdly, though, the main course in his dinner—besides take-out meatloaf, mashed potatoes, and string beans—was Chris's comment about retirement.

He had the time in to get his full pension.

He hated sitting behind the desk.

Evan dipped a forkful of potatoes in a puddle of gravy.

If money wasn't an issue, his next concern fell to mental health, because he'd been working full-time with very little time off since the age of eighteen. What would fill his hours after he let the police force go?

Two sonograms sat tacked on the front of the fridge, in plain view. The new babies, Josiah living so close—did Evan have the fortitude to spend his time spoiling grandchildren?

"Seen the Visa bill?" Evan muttered to himself, stabbing some green beans. Maybe he could convince Matt to take only local clients. Or he could join the security firm; him, Matt, and Jim traipsing all over the country, making money and being charming and—no.

God no. Retirement meant burning his suits.

Evan sent another text to Matt before getting into the shower. *Good night. I love you. Don't smoke too many cigars.*

MATT LAY in the hotel bed, wide-awake and feeling waves of guilt.

He'd texted back only an *I love you* to Evan, not wanting to engage his husband at this moment, when he felt so unbelievably raw. It was only when he got under the covers, tossing and turning, that he realized he hadn't asked about Vic.

Goddammit.

They'd sat and eaten in silence, he and Jim, then watched ESPN until Jim got up to go to his room. Words sat in Matt's throat—some angry, some emotional—but all he managed was *good night*.

Two more days in New Orleans, three meetings, a dinner, and a tour of the facility they were bidding on. Professionalism and charm got Matt far in life; he depended on those two things to work him out of situations dramatic and dangerous. Working while sad was an entirely different prospect.

There was a luxury in having his husband behind a desk and his best friend pushing paper. All the years of friendships being tainted with the undercurrent of "I hope you don't get killed" had faded into the mist. No one carried except Evan. Once in a while, he and Jim went to the range for some good old-fashioned dick measuring. Life and death seemed to be held in reserve for that third drink, when reminiscing felt called for.

All the danger was behind them, or so Matt had thought.

Love came to Matt later in life, and it brought along with it friendship at a level he hadn't known possible. The thought of not having his best friend in his life was fucking terrifying.

He should have called Evan and told him, instead of lying there with his throat clogged and his heart beating way too fast.

EVAN WOKE to a phone full of texts, both mundane—joint baby shower planning—and profound. As in his husband loved him and Vic seemed on the road to recovery.

He leaned against a stack of pillows, answering each message with a sense of odd contentment. At first he attributed it to the roll call of "everyone's okay" that settled any panicky vestiges of not having eyes on his loved ones. But then it crept into Evan's brain that he'd made a decision, somewhere between his shower and falling asleep to MSNBC.

Retirement.

He took a deep breath, let the certainty fill his lungs. There would be resistance from the commissioner. Evan could expect a call from the mayor's office. Chris might give him shit for getting out before she did.

He'd want to have some input on his replacement; his precinct deserved the best. Or at least someone slightly less grumpy.

Tossing the phone onto the covers, Evan kept one eye on the clock as he let himself sink into the mattress. Such a confluence of events to make this decision for him, without his usual forty days and forty nights of self-flagellating inner turmoil.

Maybe he was growing as a person or something.

BREAKFAST WAS just the two of them, Jim and Matt, sitting silently at the hotel restaurant, poking at their biscuits and gravy. Or rather Matt poked at a plate of cholesterol while Jim had a bowl of oatmeal and a plate of melon.

"We just paid twenty-five bucks for oatmeal," he groused as Jim continued to eat.

"You've had about forty dollars' worth of coffee, so I think we're coming out on top," Jim said, wiping his mouth with his napkin. "You're going to be vibrating all day. Don't want the clients to think you're a coke freak or anything."

"I'll tell them I'm stress drinking." Matt glared as he flagged down their waitperson.

"Matt, I'm not doing this for the rest of the trip. I'm fine for now. It's under control." Jim managed not to raise his voice, but Matt had no problem imagining that heavy white mug at his fingertips smacking him in the side of the head. "Trust me, okay? I wouldn't be here if things were critical. I'm not in any hurry to be dead," he snapped.

The only thing Matt could manage after that was, "Can we get the check, please?"

"THEY'RE MOVING back to the city," Helena told Evan as he stood in line at the deli, waiting for his breakfast sandwich and coffee.

"That didn't take long."

"Shane is very persuasive." She sounded exhausted, raspy like she got when days went on too long and sleep eluded her because of work. "I told him since he's her favorite, he can handle the moving details and figuring out where they're living."

"I'm surprised he didn't invite them to come live with you," Evan said lightly.

Helena coughed out a laugh. "My husband knows the chances of him ever seeing me naked again would drop to negative a million if those words came out of his mouth. I'd move in with you and he could live with my mother all by himself."

"Sounds like a play he'd write." Evan gave a nod to the counter guy as he took his bag and coffee, the phone balanced between his shoulder and chin.

"Let's not mention that idea to him." She sighed. "The issue now is the transition. Vic's going to be in the hospital for at least two weeks; then he'll go to rehab for a month or two. After that, we'll have to get them up here."

"Doesn't give you a lot of time to find a place." Evan held the door open for a few customers, then ducked onto the sidewalk. "Or sell their house."

Helena groaned. "And pack them up. And a billion other things. How the hell am I supposed to work and take care of all of this? From hundreds of miles away!"

He winced in advance of her reaction to his next words. "I think you might want to consider a leave of absence."

"If you were next to me, I'd punch you in the freaking face."

"Helena—"

"I already called my boss," she cut him off. "Three months in Florida as I try not to lose my mind, while my husband has to go back to New York tomorrow morning because goddamn rewrites." Helena's voice caught on her words. "I literally hate everything right now."

Evan dodged commuters and tourists who were trying to get a head start on the day. He wanted to help Helena, be there for her—hell, just give her some good advice—but nothing good seemed to be making itself known. Just random pops of "you need some help" but nothing concrete to add beyond the obvious.

"Hey, it's Florida—we'll all want to come visit you!" was the best he could come up with.

"You should start booking plane fares now," she said darkly. "I'm not even joking."

"Soon as Matt gets home. We want to see Vic, and we can run a little interference." He reached the precinct, nodding to several detectives as they hurried past him. The decision about retiring came back in a rush as suddenly a countdown timer appeared in his mind as he stepped through the front doors. "I'll make it happen, I promise."

EVAN NO sooner hung up with Helena than his phone buzzed again.

Matt.

"Hey, everything okay? I missed you last night. Just talked to Helena—looks like Vic is going to be okay." Evan got in the elevator with two people with visitor's passes, each holding a stack of manila folders. He prayed they weren't headed for his office.

The long pause pricked Evan's radar.

"That's great to hear about Vic," Matt said finally.

Evan felt his grip on the bag tighten, palms sweaty. "You all right?" The elevator jolted to a stop; then the doors slid open. "Are you two okay?"

Matt took a deep breath and let it out slowly through the line. "I'm fine," he said finally, the emphasis on *I'm* very clear. "I'll… I'll call you tonight. At nine your time. We can talk then."

"I think I can work you into my very busy ESPN schedule," Evan said lightly as he walked to his office, nodding at every person whose gaze met his. Clearly the mental line outside his office had been forming since dawn.

"Nine o'clock," Matt repeated.

A heavy pause gave Evan a moment to take a deep breath. "Impress the hell out of them today," he murmured, purposely adding a tender lilt to his voice. He stepped into his office, a sanctuary at the moment. "Love you."

"Love you too."

Evan let Matt breathe through the line for a moment, then heard the call disconnect.

The phone felt heavy in his hand.

7
THE SHOWERING

THE WAIT for the grandbabies felt endless and far-off, until suddenly Evan was attending a joint baby shower at a Queens party space, where a hundred people ate baked ziti and a cake shaped like a giant carriage under a ceiling strung with paper flowers.

"Dazed" didn't even cover it.

Matt, on the other hand, won diaper bag bingo and finished Evan's cake when he wasn't paying attention.

Simmering in melancholy, Evan blinked at the girls—his little girls; how were they old enough to have children?—who sat at the head table, morphing between toddlers and grown women. They sat with their husbands, happy, bright, and loving couples; he couldn't have chosen better partners for them. Now living so close again and sharing parallel major life experiences, the once bickering sisters had mellowed into friends. The couples spent time together—dinners and weekend excursions, sporting events. And Miranda, working from home, became Josiah's regular after-school pickup.

They weren't starting out in crisis like he and Sherri did. They were adults with jobs—careers. Nice homes. Support systems. He chose to believe he was a good father, good father-in-law; they knew he was there for them, whatever they might need. They had Matt as well, and quite frankly, in case of a fight, break the glass and activate *him*.

Around the room were scattered their extended family. Josiah, Sadie, and Caroline darted between tables, playing with Austin's little cousins. Jim and Griffin were at their table, sitting across from Matt, enjoying coffee.

Everything was perfect—or as perfect as Evan might allow himself to consider—and yet the tide of tears threatened to drown him. He didn't even remember feeling this emotional when the announcement of babies happened at Christmas.

During his scan of the room, he spotted Cornelia by the gift table, shifting presents and straightening corners over and over again. If anyone understood his feelings of melancholy and joy, it was she.

"I'll be right back," he told Matt, who nodded as he read over the card for the next game (something about advice for the new parents with a hangman theme). "Anyone need anything?"

"A dolly to roll me out of here," Griffin moaned, patting his stomach. "Or another piece of cake. Whatever you come across first."

Smiling, Evan made his way over to Cornelia and the gift table. He recognized people as he passed: Miranda's former roommates, Katie's coworkers, mutual friends from their old neighborhood, cousins of Sherri's. Sherri's sister Ellie sat with Helena and her mother, Serena—they waved as he walked by. Danny's girlfriend, Jane, helped Elizabeth set up the crepe paper–decorated chairs the girls would sit in to open gifts. He'd been warned that this was the longest part of the day.

"Hey," he said as he made it to Cornelia's side. She was wearing a pale pink sweater in honor of her soon-to-be-born granddaughter, and a long skirt, hair tucked behind her ears. Behind her glasses, Evan spotted unshed tears in her eyes. "How's it going?"

She smiled and shrugged. "Everything turned out so nicely. Elizabeth was such a great help."

"She and Jane made about six thousand paper flowers at my dining room table," he said, remembering the chaos of his house the past few weeks. "They absolutely loved doing it. And you know I appreciate you and Beverly handling the planning and execution. I had no clue where to start."

"We appreciated your check," Cornelia said wryly as she winked. "I enjoyed every second of it. Plus Beverly and I are a team now—the christening will be a breeze."

In a bright yellow-and-green floral dress, Beverly, Austin's mom, sat on the other side of the room with a table of relatives who'd driven down from Boston in a caravan. She spotted Evan and Cornelia together and began waving.

"I love her. It stinks she and Fred are three hours away from us," she added, a touch of sadness in her tone.

The unlikely friendship between Miranda's in-laws and Katie's began with a Skype meeting set up between all the in-laws to plan the joint shower. Evan and Matt were of little help, while Blake and Fred, the respective fathers-in-law, looked just as confused. Cornelia and Beverly ran away with the conversation. In the end, Matt said, "I'll get the checkbook," and they were done with it.

The planning led to dinners and then weekends of hanging out. Blake and Fred shared an epic love of discussing lawn care, which came in handy while Cornelia and Beverly ditched them for hours to lunch and shop and discuss new grandbabies to spoil.

Evan wanted to feel left out, but frankly he hated talking about his lawn.

"I don't know, I kinda want to go outlet shopping now," Matt said one night after hearing a report from Miranda and Kent about how his mother never seemed to answer the phone these days.

"Is the hotel all right? I wish we had the room to host everyone. Matt offered to buy an RV for the driveway, but I felt that was a little excessive." His husband, Evan noticed, had left their table and joined Beverly's, and was currently trying to read her game card, which she clutched to her chest in mock horror.

"The hotel's lovely." Cornelia shook her head, watching Matt's antics. "We closed down the bar last night, which I haven't done in about twenty years."

"You'll be back down here in a few weeks when the babies are born—try to pace yourself."

They spent a quiet moment looking out over the crowd of joyful attendees. Elizabeth darted by wielding paper plates and tape while Jane perched on a chair with paper and pen in hand.

"Opening presents next," Cornelia said briskly. "I went completely overboard, just to warn you. Beverly and I did a weekend at the outlets, and let's just say these babies won't need a lick of clothing until college."

"I just bought two sets of nursery furniture—believe me, no judgment."

"I saw Matt carrying in some large bags."

"He said we couldn't show up with pictures of the furniture, so he went shopping." Evan trailed off. "I don't have a clue what he bought."

Cornelia started to laugh. "Sporting equipment?"

"Could be. He wouldn't tell me." Evan had brought two gifts of his own, framed pictures of Sherri with each of the girls when they were born, for the nurseries. He debated sharing it at the shower, but Elizabeth took the decision out of hands.

Crying is okay at a shower, Dad. People want to have a reason— and this is a good one.

He sincerely hoped crying was okay, because his throat had been clogged for hours.

"I hope it's something entertaining," Cornelia said beside him, twisting her hands. "Because I'm pretty sure I'm going to start bawling when Miranda opens the quilt."

The quilt was Cornelia's special gift for Miranda and Kent. It had been in their family for three generations, and each mother added a border of baby clothes to the piece before handing it down to the firstborn. A lovely tradition that made Evan wish he had something like that to pass down—hence the photos.

"I've been collecting pockets full of napkins since we got here," Evan said, light as he could manage. "Stick by me. We'll get through this."

Cornelia fixed him with a curious stare. Then her expression softened. "I dug out my old journal from when I was pregnant with Kent. Every time I see him these days, I imagine he's…."

"A little kid? I feel like my brain has a glitch." Evan watched Miranda getting up from her chair, Kent at her side to steady her. Her dress was pink like Cornelia's, the confirmation they were having a girl the perfect bow to the top of her pregnancy.

"I swear I had sympathy labor pains last night."

He wrinkled his nose. "That might have been the binge-drinking."

They laughed, watching as Kent helped Miranda navigate the chairs and tables, directing her toward the restrooms in the back corner. He was so serious and careful with her, hovering at a respectable distance. Kent's attentiveness to Miranda, the way he listened to her, balanced her out, reminded Evan of Sherri. That Miranda would find someone patient and strong like her mother made perfect sense.

Back at the table, Katie and Austin were making terrible origami hats out of their napkins, laughing loudly at their own hilarity. An absentminded professor with a dry sense of humor felt like the ideal match for independent Katie, and if no one else saw the character resemblances between Austin and Matt, Evan wasn't going to point them out.

"You get the name out of them yet?" Cornelia asked, breaking the quiet. "Or even the gender?"

"No to both. When Matt tried and failed, I realized we would find out when they tell us. Or in the delivery room."

Austin and Katie kept the baby's gender between them and kept wraps on their name choices like these were state secrets. At Miranda's gender reveal party, Katie remained in a state of polite eye roll (though she shed a tear when they announced the baby's name would be Shelia—a combination of Sherri and Cornelia) and was tight-lipped as a spy under the hot lights.

"I realize this might be against your ethics, but what about bribing Josiah?" she teased.

Evan sighed dramatically.

The weekend after the gender reveal party, Josiah had arrived to spend the night with his grandfathers. They had big plans—pizza and wings, an Xbox marathon, and staying up late.

Austin and Katie were dressed up for a work event at the Knicks, with Katie already bitching about her shoes as they walked in.

Josiah dropped his backpack and jacket on the ottoman, bouncing around the house so much that Evan suspected presugaring.

"LeBron!" he yelled as Katie gave Austin a smirk.

"Now see, I know who that is," Austin called as Josiah cracked up, jumping next to Matt on the sofa.

"Do I want to know?" Matt asked as he grabbed Josiah for a wrestling match.

"My son has decided the baby should be named after an NBA player."

"Shaq!" Josiah squeaked as he wriggled out from under Matt and onto his back. "Kobe!"

"Hey, what did I tell you about that name?" Katie warned, wagging her finger. "Come give me a kiss and don't break Matt."

"So does that mean it's a boy?" Evan asked, fake casual.

"I will neither confirm nor deny the baby's gender." Katie gave her father a saucy look. "Nice try, though."

"Dominique!" Josiah darted away from Matt's grab, running to give Katie a hug.

"How much sugar did you give this child?" Matt grumbled, rolling off the sofa.

"A spoon and the bag of Dominos. Was that wrong?" Austin asked, innocent as a babe, picking Josiah up for a tight hug. "Be good for your granddads. Brush your teeth."

Josiah kissed his father on the cheek. "Isaiah? Charles Barkley?"

After dinner and surprise cupcakes, thanks to Matt, they settled down on the sofa to play basketball on the Xbox.

"Why do you think the baby should be named after a basketball player?" Evan asked, settling into the side chair and putting his feet up.

"Because they're all rich and have their own sneakers," Josiah said, biting his lip as he concentrated on his controller.

"Baby's not going to need a shoe deal for a while," Matt pointed out.

Josiah focused on the game, the only sounds the clicks and clacks of their controllers. Evan dozed a bit, happy to be an observer and not have to figure out how the damn thing worked.

"Why is Aunt Miranda naming her baby Shelia?" he asked finally.

Evan and Matt shared a glance.

"Well, you know Aunt Miranda and Katie's mom died when they were teenagers…," Evan began.

"Like my mom, only I was a baby," Josiah said, his brown eyes wide.

"Right. Her name was Sherri. So they took the *Sh* from her name and the last few letters of Kent's mom's name—which is Cornelia—and that spells Shelia. It's a nice way to honor their moms." Evan smiled at the thought. He loved the name, loved the sentiment behind it.

"Oh." Josiah went quiet again, gaze locked on the television screen. Matt gave him a wink—which Evan easily translated into "good job."

Matt and Josiah continued their play until Josiah suddenly hit Pause.

"Bathroom break?" Matt asked as Josiah got up abruptly and then ran into the hallway, toward the kitchen, not the first-floor guest bath.

"Josiah?" Evan called, getting up to follow the boy, with Matt close on his heels.

They found him in the kitchen, marker in hand at the white board on the fridge, scribbling.

He wrote a few letters, then wiped them off with his sleeve. Did it again and again. His little body blocked Evan's gaze, so he couldn't see his calculations.

Josiah muttered to himself, stepped back, then tilted his head.

"That works," he said before stepping to one side.

In big letters, he'd written *Mavan*.

"Two letters from Matt," Josiah explained, gesturing to his work. "And the end of Evan. Mavan! Mavan Frederick, after all the grandpas! That's what we should name the baby!"

Now, Cornelia giggled behind her hand.

"He refers to the baby as Mavan," Evan sighed. "Austin and Katie thought it was cute for the first few days, then they thought it was a joke, and now they're worried he really thinks that's what they're naming the baby."

She cleared her throat, dabbing at her eyes with her fingers. "I mean, it's kind of a cool name. Unique!"

"Maybe he thinks they'll reconsider LeBron if he keeps saying Mavan enough."

"Works for a boy or a girl." Cornelia began to giggle again.

Evan felt himself succumbing to her amusement; he covered his eyes with his hand.

"You know Matt's rooting for it."

He moaned in response. "Oh God, what if he got the baby something with Mavan embroidered on it!"

Cornelia lost it completely.

OPENING THE gifts? The longest part of the day.

Jim covertly watched a baseball game on his phone as Griffin and Matt played dirty word hangman on a series of napkins. Sadie, Caroline, and Josiah gathered all the bows and ribbon for Elizabeth to make hats as Jane dutifully wrote down each gift and who gave it.

Danny showed up halfway through with his friend Ollie in their gym clothes; they raided the kitchen where the food had been moved to, and emerged with two huge plates of food, bread tucked under both their arms.

"Well, now I'm hungry again," Matt muttered.

"Hurry up if you're going for what? Thirds? They're getting to your gift soon." Evan gave him the side-eye. "I assume you want to see them open it."

Matt said nothing but laughed evilly as he walked away.

"Bring us ziti," Griffin stage-whispered.

"And bread," Jim added, though he wilted at Griffin's side-eye. "I mean salad."

"What did you two get them?" Evan asked, convinced the pile was not going down but rather reproducing bags and boxes for each one opened.

"State-of-the-art Diaper Genies," Griffin said. "Like they're practically sentient."

"And money." Jim looked up from his phone. "Because kids are expensive."

Evan put up four fingers, then pointed to himself.

"Thank God we need a woman to get pregnant." Griffin drained his cup of punch. "There's no such thing as an accidental artificial insemination."

"Eating," Danny mumbled.

"Wasn't there a TV show," Ollie piped up before Danny elbowed him.

"Don't encourage them."

Katie opened a baby tub, and then Miranda got a bottle warmer, and the assembled guests cooed. Evan saw Matt's bags getting closer to the assembly line of Cornelia and Beverly, and then looked back toward the kitchen to see if Matt had emerged. There was a fifty-fifty chance on whether the gifts would be sentimental or ridiculous; if it was possible for them to be both, Matt would have figured that out.

He came back to the table right as Cornelia and Beverly wrestled the Santa's sack–sized bags toward where the girls were sitting.

The tray he'd commandeered, packed high with food, dropped in the center of the table.

"Perfect timing," Danny said, grabbing another hunk of bread.

"Excuse me, I'm moving up closer for the big reveal," Matt said, rubbing his hands together with childlike glee.

"Do I go with him or hide?" Evan asked no one in particular.

MATT KNEW it was mean to tease Evan, convince him his gift was outlandish or bizarre. He cultivated a sense of "what did you do, Matt?" in everything he did, and this wasn't an occasion to let pass by. He "excuse me'd" his way to the front, pulling an empty chair so he was front and center to the girls.

"Let me guess, this is from you?" Miranda asked, shifting her weight on the chair.

He fluttered his eyelashes in response.

"Did we decide," Katie asked loudly, "on Grampy or Poppy?"

"We should take a poll," he started, moving to stand up. "By applause?"

"Sit down, Groppy." Miranda looked at the giant sack in front of her. "What did you do?" God, she sounded just like Evan.

"Should we open them at the same time?" Katie asked, hands hovering over the top of the bag. "You are dying to do a countdown. I can see it on your face."

"Oh how well you know me. Five… four… three… two… one!"

Like toddlers on Christmas morning, Miranda and Katie tore into the bags.

"What in the world?" asked Miranda, coming up for air with handfuls of clothing. But not clothing clothing. Oh no.

"So people apparently dress their babies in costumes while they're sleeping and take pictures, then put them on the internet," Matt jumped in. "Passes the time, I guess."

Katie shrieked with laughter as she pulled out a mermaid tail in shiny aquamarine and a tiny Viking helmet.

"It's a hot dog costume!" Austin and Kent crowded over their wives' shoulders as Miranda flapped the bitty wiener over her head.

The doctor coat and stethoscope in Katie's bag reduced Austin to clapping like a madman.

Laughter rang through the catering hall as more and more costumes made appearances. Dogs, cats, firemen, ballerinas, construction workers. "It's like baby Village People," cooed Katie.

"There better not be baby chaps in here, Matt, seriously," Miranda whispered.

Eventually they got to the bottoms of the bags and Matt smirked. Did they think it was over? Surely they knew better.

"Box," Katie said as Austin leaned over to grab it out. Kent did the same.

"On three." Matt raised his hands like a conductor. "One, two, three!"

Inside the navy blue box sat tiny pairs of mouse ears.

"Disney?" Katie asked, holding the sweet little ears over her head. "Infants in Disney?"

"Noooo. You can take them whenever you want. There's a condo in Orlando with your names on the deed," Matt said smugly. "Sorry, you have to share."

Josiah, who'd been hovering around the piles of costumes with a delighted grin, looked up with his eyes wide. "Disney? We're taking baby Mavan to Disney?"

Miranda's face read shell-shocked. "You got us a vacation condo?"

"Got a good deal." Actually Bennett sold it to him for a song; it probably cost the same as the robot Diaper Genies. "I figured this takes part of the worry out of figuring where you go on vacation."

Kent shook himself out of his shock. "It's really too generous—"

"Hey, you still have to buy the plane tickets and stuff," Matt said, holding his hands up. "This is just a little something to help you out." They hadn't opened up Daisy and Bennett's gift yet, and he knew plane tickets and Disney passes weren't going to be a problem either.

"Help us out!" Katie put the mouse ears on her head and then pushed off the chair to give him a clumsy hug. "You're nuts! You bought us nursery furniture!"

Matt pulled her close, pressing a kiss to her forehead. "That's from Dad and me. It's practical," he whispered. "This is fun grandpa stuff."

When he let her go, Miranda was standing there, hands on hips.

"You're crazy," she said. "Literally." She opened her arms and he went with a grin on his face; they were never going to be best friends, but every step closer felt special to Matt. Part of it was Evan's peace of mind.

And part of it was ego. All would love Matt, all hail Matt.

He murmured that in her ear until she pulled back, punching him in the arm.

"Ow. I gave you a hot dog–shaped baby costume and real estate."

"Wait, do we have to pay taxes on this property?" Kent was asking Austin.

"Disney," Josiah said dreamily from the floor.

"WE NEED to buy those kids rocket ships for their first birthdays," Griffin said to Jim as they watched the chaos. "Because we have been so upstaged."

"I didn't realize this was a competition."

Griffin gave his husband a shocked face. "Matt and Evan gave Caroline a pink plane for her birthday."

"Not a real plane." Jim brushed crumbs off the nearly wrecked tablecloth. He smothered a cough; this cold was taking forever to go away. "I mean, if he'd gotten her a real plane...."

Caroline rushed up, breathing heavily. She ducked between her fathers, hair flying in every direction.

"Can I go to Disney with Josiah and Sadie and baby Shelia and baby Mavan and Uncle Matt?" she asked, sucking wind as she collapsed against Jim's side. "Josiah said we could go with them, but you have to say yes."

Griffin pulled her up into his lap. The shower was making him nostalgic, more than he'd thought it would. Did he miss diapers and 3:00 a.m. feedings? Were they worth it when you got bright-eyed little girls with perpetually messy hair and endearing personalities?

"Can we come with you?" Jim asked, making a halfhearted attempt to gather Caroline's hair into a ponytail.

Caroline considered that for a moment. "I'll have to ask Josiah and Uncle Matt." She leaned around her father, spying Danny and Ollie. "You want me to ask if you can come too?"

"Maybe you shouldn't be inviting half of Queens on this vacation." Griffin kissed her cheek, sticky with sugar. "We'll talk to Uncle Matt, okay?"

Jim got her hair into a lopsided bun on the top of her head about a second before she slid out of Griffin's arms and onto the floor. Like a cartoon character with a plume of dust behind her, she took off to rejoin Josiah and Sadie and their vacation plotting.

"She can fly her pink plane down there," Jim said wryly.

"Don't say that in front of Bennett. He'll probably buy her one."

EVAN STOOD in the center of the catering hall as Matt's gift brought down the house. Fortunately Cornelia and Beverly had saved it for last, knowing full well nothing normal would be popping out. He felt a mixture of love and exasperation, as the costumes were delightful and *so* Matt, and the condo was…

Crazy.

Expensive and crazy. He wanted to be practical, ask to see the paperwork because what was he paying? They were paying—shouldn't this be a discussion between them?

"Oh my God, your face," Matt said, kissing him on the cheek. Evan startled.

"What?"

"Stop doing math. Please. You know I am impulsive and ridiculous, but you also know I am a responsible adult."

Evan squinted. "Responsible."

"Shut up. Bennett sold it to me for next to nothing. It's a good investment because now we have a place to go on vacation, a place to take the grandkids, of which we now have three, not to mention Sadie and Caroline and the other grandchildren that will pop up once Danny and Elizabeth are allowed to procreate. Also it was a surprise I didn't want to be talked out of." Matt gave his most innocent face—and Evan tried not to kiss him on the mouth. He couldn't resist that face.

"How many bedrooms?"

"Five."

Evan blinked. "How big is this thing?"

Matt waggled his eyebrows dramatically. "Down, boy. We're in public."

IN THE end ("That's what he said!" Matt was on a roll) Evan got numbers—real numbers, numbers that didn't make him twitch—and moved on from Matt's clutches. Calm now, Evan set him off on the rest of the room, reminding him to be nice and not dirty.

"I make no promises, I've had a lot of sugar," Matt said with a salute and then went to charm Beverly's cousins.

In the gift corner, Danny and Ollie had been recruited to bag up the gifts under the direct supervision of Elizabeth, Jane, Cornelia, and Beverly. Evan skirted past the taskmasters, ducking to where Miranda and Katie sat, admiring their bow hats.

"I don't understand the bow hat tradition or why I couldn't use a knife to cut anything," Katie said as Evan pulled a chair up to sit with them. "Also your husband is nuts."

Evan kissed her cheek. "No comment."

"Dad, you can be honest. Can you guys afford this? And the furniture?" Miranda fussed with a few of the streamers attached to the back of the hat. "It's a lot if there was one of us, and there are two!"

"We will be totally fine if you need to drop one of the gifts, seriously."

"You know me, I'm being honest when I say it's fine." He reached out to take Miranda's hand. "Matt got a deal, and he's right, it's a great idea for us to have a place to stay that can accommodate this huge pile of people."

Miranda and Katie exchanged looks.

"How did he convince you to do something this crazy?" Katie asked.

Evan ducked his head. "Uhhhh…."

"Oh my God!" Miranda snorted out a laugh. "This was a surprise? I wish I'd known—I'd have had the guys take video of your face."

Katie gave him an expression of pure awe. "Who are you and what have you done with our uptight father?"

"I got old and chilled out, apparently." Evan tilted his head to one side. "Chilled out—do people still say that?"

"So old," Katie mouthed to her sister.

"Okay, one more present," Evan said, looking over to the gift table.

"No, absolutely not." Miranda stomped her foot. "You've done too much already."

"Stop. This didn't cost me a thing." Evan got up and went to the now empty table. The pictures were in a small bag he'd left underneath. He took a deep breath as he returned to sit with the girls again.

People like to cry at showers.

"So, not real estate, but, uh, I thought you'd like these for the nursery." Evan took out the wrapped squares, a rosy pink for Miranda and a shiny green for Katie.

He waited quietly as they opened the paper slowly. No mistaking them for anything other than pictures; Katie gasped a little as she turned hers over first.

"Oh man." Her eyes began watering instantly. "Look how young Mom is," she whispered as she trailed her fingers over the photo. Evan had it memorized; Sherri's triumphantly tired smile, the yellow cardigan over her hospital gown because she was cold, blonde hair falling over her eyes. "I look terrible," she'd laughed as Evan wielded their camera. They were exhausted, giddy, and too happy to be terrified. Young parents with a toddler and an infant. Evan walking a beat, Sherri cutting coupons so they could eat dinner.

"Beautiful and strong, like her amazing daughters," Evan said softly. Next to Katie, Miranda stared at the back of her photo, not turning it over yet. "Miranda?"

"Give me a sec," she muttered. "I'm trying not to embarrass myself."

"Come on, join me," Katie cried, half laughing as she leaned against her sister's side. "Turn it over—Dad's close and about to lose it."

Miranda sucked in a breath, then turned the photo over. Tears began flowing, twin tracks down each cheek and staining the front of her dress as she trembled.

Evan dropped to his knees, taking Miranda's hand in his. "Blame Elizabeth. She said people liked to cry at showers," he choked out, suddenly fearful he'd miscalculated his gift.

Eighteen-year-old Sherri, newly married, vaguely terrified and clutching Miranda close to her chest. No poses or laughter, just quiet awe and unspoken panic until a moment when Sherri pressed her forehead to Miranda's cheek and seemed to just... relax. "Hey, baby girl, I'm your mommy," she'd whispered, and Evan snapped a picture as it dawned on him that he was that little girl's daddy and they were a real family.

"It's so beautiful. Thank you." Miranda's voice cracked as she wrapped her free arm around Evan's shoulders. "I wish she was here," she whispered in his ear.

"Me too," he whispered back as his own tears fell.

MATT DISTRACTED anyone who spared a look into the corner where Evan and the girls huddled. He whipped the little ones into a Disney frenzy, leading them in a rousing—full of wrong words—rendition of "It's a Small World" to the delight of the guests.

He knew about the pictures. Elizabeth couldn't keep a secret to save her life.

Sherri's ghost and Matt shared an uneasy relationship. Sometimes he felt like he knew her and her life with particular intimacy. Other times he feared her memory left him only a tiny part of the Cerelli family to make his own. Those days were mostly gone; even right now, as he watched Evan pull napkins out of his pockets to dry the girls' faces, Matt didn't feel left out. This was a moment that didn't belong to him.

It didn't need to.

WHEN THE party space manager poked his head in the room, taking a dramatic look at his watch, Matt enlisted Jim and Griffin's help in clearing the place out. They began to go table to table, herding folks toward a line forming near the exit. Tears wiped, the guests of honor kissed everyone goodbye, with thanks and promises to let them know when the babies made their appearance.

Kent, Austin, Ollie, and Danny lugged bag after bag of gifts into the waiting cars out back.

"Don't forget the leftovers," Danny said to Matt, as he walked past with a portable crib on his shoulder. "The caterers wrapped everything up in boxes. Don't leave them behind."

"He really needs to learn to get by with less food. I just bought a condo," Matt said to Evan. "You okay?" he asked under his breath.

Evan smiled wanly. "Yeah. We were invited to cocktails with the other grandparents, by the way."

"Great. I googled some fun facts about Kentucky bluegrass."

Matt caught Ellie in a tight group hug with all four of the Cerelli kids near the door; his throat clogged a little as he watched them break apart, wiping their eyes in near synchronization.

"Let's see if Ellie wants to come," he said, clearing his throat. "And Walt. And the rest of the gang."

"That's a lot of people in the hotel bar, and what are we doing with the kids?"

Matt sniffled, then gave his husband a smirk. "Send everyone to the house."

"Maybe," Evan said, hoisting up one of the robot Diaper Genies in his arms, "you should have bought a bigger house *here* rather than Florida."

"Well...."

"Matt!"

8
DON'T ANSWER THE PHONE

FOUR DAYS after the shower, Matt was still eating leftovers for late breakfast/early lunch—not that he minded. Pasta tasted better after a few days in the fridge—he knew this from his bachelor decades. It also meant he didn't have to order in or, God forbid, cook. And maybe Evan was giving him side-eye across the dinner table when they ate the same thing again, but hey. Work-at-home-husband privilege. Also, it was delicious.

He licked his fork as he read over a series of emails; the security business was good at the moment. People feeling financially secure? They want to protect their assets. People feeling financially insecure? They want to protect their assets. Recommendations fleshed out their roster of clients; money came in on the regular—Matt couldn't ask for more from this little business, particularly with grandchildren due in a few weeks and the twins having two more years of school.

And now with Evan moving forward with retirement, for real this time, it looked like Matt's income would be their primary support.

Not a problem. He planned to use it to leverage more sex.

Between the office and the kitchen, plate in hand, Matt heard his cell phone ringing back at his desk. He hesitated, thinking *voicemail* since it was his general ring, but something made him pivot.

When he saw Griffin's name on his phone, he didn't panic.

When he heard the voice of Georgia, the housekeeper, speaking breathlessly about Jim, he dropped the plate and grabbed his keys.

IT TOOK him almost two hours to get to the house, due to an abnormally busy Taconic Parkway, pushing the speed limit and generally driving like a cop chasing a suspect. In the back of his mind, he knew he needed to let Evan know what was going on, but his hands gripped the wheel a bit too tightly to grab his phone.

When he reached Jim and Griffin's house, he found the driveway and front of the house full: their cars, Daisy's Volvo, and a dark sedan he didn't know but suspected belonged to the housekeeper. The lack of an ambulance settled his heart rate a bit.

From the car to the walkway, Matt texted Evan, giving as much information as he had now.

Jim's not well, Griffin freaking. At the house.

Evan texted back immediately. *Let me know if you want me to drive up after work.*

Matt sent a heart in response, then finished the trek to the front door. Two knocks later he heard Daisy yell, "Come in, Matt!"

He walked into subdued chaos. Daisy and Shane sat in the living room, each with a tumbler of far-too-early-in-the-day brown liquor while raised voices drifted from upstairs.

Throwing his keys onto their foyer table, Matt chose the living room.

"Hello, Matthew, welcome to the Thunderdome," Daisy said drily, saluting him with her glass.

By her side, Shane vibrated like a nervous purse dog.

"The housekeeper said Jim was sick." Matt settled into Jim's chair, a giant leather monstrosity that he coveted. "His lungs sound okay."

"Griffin dropped the girls off at school, picked Shane up from the train station, and they came back here to work." She indicated Shane should continue.

Eyes wide, he leaned forward, clutching the glass in both hands. "We were writing at the dining room table, and he was like—where's Jim? And went upstairs, and then all I heard was freaking out. Jim was sick, so Griffin went, you know."

"Ballistic," Daisy added. "Which led to me being called, which led to Georgia being told to call you."

"But not an ambulance."

Daisy squinted at him. "You've met Jim. He refused to go to the hospital despite having trouble breathing and feeling light-headed. Griffin told Georgia to get you up here, indicating you are the big guns." She air quoted the last two words with one hand.

"We've been sitting here for two hours listening to World War III," Shane added.

Matt relaxed only slightly. "So I have to walk into the middle of the battle? Into the middle of my best friends' marriage? I did not wear a cup."

Daisy indicated her drink. "You want one?"

"After." Matt took a deep breath and forced himself out of the truly comfortable chair. "Only come up if you hear a series of thumps and crashes."

"We love you, Matt," Shane said gravely. "Godspeed."

Matt gave him the finger.

AT THE top of the stairs, Matt followed the sound of Griffin calling Jim a "fucking stubborn son of a bitch" and knocked on their bedroom door like he was serving a warrant.

The fighting paused.

Matt clearly heard Jim say, "You called Matt!" and turned the knob.

Inside, Matt discovered pillows on the floor, Jim on the bed in a bathrobe, and a wild-eyed Griffin pacing around in circles.

"Hey," Matt said, clearing his throat as he shut the door behind him. He gave Jim a critical look, returned the withering stare he got, and then crossed his arms over his chest. "You look like absolute shit. Why aren't you at the hospital?"

Jim's pallor could only be described as gray. His hands, folded in his lap, shook slightly, and Matt could see him holding back a cough.

"I don't need—" he started, but Griffin cut him off.

"You are going to the fucking hospital if Matt and I have to carry you," he snapped, kicking the corner of the bed. "Do you want to die here? Are you going to let your daughter come home to a coroner's truck?"

Eyes narrowing, Jim struggled to get up. "Don't."

When he got to his feet, he went still and stark white. Matt reacted so quickly he barely felt himself move. He and Griffin met in the middle, catching Jim before he fell.

The ambulance took only eight minutes

"I AM at the hospital. Jim has pneumonia," Matt said wearily, sitting on a bench outside the emergency room three hours later. On the other end, Evan made a frustrated noise.

"Jesus. Every time the phone rings lately, someone's in the hospital."

"Good point. I'm not answering my phone ever again."

"It's not related to that thing he has, is it?"

"No. Just him being a stubborn son of a bitch, to quote his husband." He rubbed his hand over his eyes. There'd been some terrible coffee at some point, and at least two Diet Pepsis from the vending machine, making him both tired and twitchy.

After an endless wait, Jim got wheeled out for tests, leaving the three of them climbing the walls, texting Daisy nonupdates as she waited home to watch the girls. With Jim, Griffin, and the doctor back in the tiny emergency room pod, Matt and Shane headed out to place phone calls to their respective spouses.

"Are they keeping him overnight?"

"At least. Maybe the rest of the week. Might be for his own safety, because Griffin is fucking pisssssed." He drew the word out, wrinkling his nose as the smoker's circle of hazy smoke reached him from a few feet away. "I'm going to wait until he's settled into a room, drive Griffin home, lock him in a closet, and then head back."

"If you need to stay, it's fine," Evan said gently. "I have a meeting at One Police Plaza after work, so I won't be home until eight."

Matt kicked a piece of gravel from under the bench. "What's up?"

The long pause caused momentary concern.

"Chief wants to talk about my retirement," he said finally. "The term used was 'unofficial,' so I assume it's a move to convince me to stay on."

"And what do we say when they make fancy promises they won't keep?" Matt coached.

"Name, rank, and serial number, repeat November 1 retirement date, and don't drink anything they offer me." Evan laughed as he repeated Matt's "advice."

"Fantastic. I hope you wore a severe tie today."

"Every day."

Shane's purple Converse appeared in Matt's line of vision; he looked up to find his friend with pursed lips, showing his phone screen and a text from Griffin.

"Okay, gotta go put Griffin in a headlock. Love you."

"Love you too. Give everyone my best."

"I'll call you if I end up staying." Matt hung up, stretching and standing off the bench with a creaky stretch. "How's Helena?"

"She offered to come up and kick Jim's ass." Shane's wan coloring and tight-lipped frown worried Matt. Shane spent more than his fair share of time at hospitals lately.

"That's our girl." Matt put his arm around Shane's shoulders as they walked back through, noting the tension in his muscles. "Why don't I drop you at the train station when I take Griffin home? Or I can ask Daisy to send Georgia."

Shane withered a bit under Matt's arm as they entered the raucous emergency room. "I hate to abandon you guys."

"Stop. I got this. I'll deal with Griffin. Daisy has the kids. Honestly I'll probably head home after all this," he said, lighthearted as he could manage. When they reached the front desk, he winked at the receptionist, with whom he'd put in some solid flirting time earlier.

"Wendy, can we go back? They're taking him upstairs."

Wendy—dimples and pink hair; Matt wished he had a brother to fix her up with—smiled and nodded as she picked up the ringing phone.

"You're scarily good at that," Shane muttered as Wendy pressed the button and the automatic doors swung open.

"Glad you noticed. You want me to flirt with you until you do my bidding?"

In actuality, Matt didn't want Shane to leave. He wanted to keep up the banter and joking and distraction so he didn't have to examine the wave of pure terror currently bouncing against his organs like a hurricane.

He focused on Shane, tucked against him, as he wove his way through doctors and nurses and techs, frantic family members, and weary people being discharged. They reached the pod where Jim rested on a bed, a white-faced Griffin at his side. The oxygen—and Jim's exhausted expression—brought the seriousness of the situation home.

Matt plastered on a smile. "I heard you're getting an upgrade. You hold out for a room with a view?"

"Balcony too," Jim said tiredly. He turned his head to look at Griffin— who was looking at the side of the bed. "You're driving Griffin home?"

"I'm staying," Griffin snapped. "I'm so mad right now I could punch the wall, but... not leaving you."

Jim opened his mouth, but Griffin's expression kept whatever he was going to say unspoken.

Matt bit the inside of his lip, feeling Shane uncomfortable at his side. "So, I'm going to drive Shane to the train station, then run home, get some of Griffin's stuff, and be back before bedtime." Jim's mouth moved again, but Matt raised his hand. "I will remind you of the time you gave up Christmas caroling to pick me up after my appendix operation. I owe you."

Jim sank back into the pillow, nodding. That he didn't argue felt most upsetting to Matt; in all the time he'd known Jim, he'd never seen him look so defeated.

Or... his age.

Shane slipped around him to give Jim a gentle patting hug, and then squeezed Griffin until Matt heard his ribs creak. The writing partners whispered for a few seconds before separating.

"Your turn," Shane said, fake cheerful.

I should have been an actor, Matt thought as he pulled Griffin into a tight embrace. "I'll be back in like an hour, maybe an hour and a half. What do you need from the house?"

Griffin clung for a second, then cleared his throat and stepped back. "A sweatshirt. Top drawer of the bureau by the window, any one will do. My shaving kit is on the top shelf in the bathroom."

"Check and check. Real food?"

"No."

"Turkey on rye, three Diet Cokes. Got it."

"Matt...."

"Daisy took the girls to her house for the night," he said briskly. "I'll stop by and deliver some hugs before I head back here."

Tears began to form in Griffin's eyes, so Matt ruffled his hair affectionately, trying to stave off a total meltdown at the mention of Caroline. He got a nod, which let him feel okay about turning to Jim.

Jim, his best friend and onetime lover, business partner—Matt wasn't quite sure how to manage the next thirty seconds of his life. Seeing him so pale and helpless triggered something in Matt's middle.

"You need anything, young man?" he asked, his jovial tone cracking a bit as Jim looked up at him.

The pale blue eyes, so wide and afraid, did him in.

"Just... kiss Caroline for me," Jim murmured. "Tell her I'll be fine."

"That's exactly what I was going to say." Matt heaved a deep breath and then leaned down to kiss Jim on the cheek. "Behave yourself. Do what the doctors tell you."

Jim nodded, drifting off a bit as Matt straightened up.

"I'll be back as soon as I can." With one more look at Griffin, Matt turned and walked out of the pod, Shane at his heels.

DURING THE silent drive to the train station, Matt's heart raced. He imagined his blood pressure numbers in big red print, throbbing in time to the pulse in his temples.

"Maybe we shouldn't have left Griffin alone," Shane muttered. "He's going to worry himself into a stain on the floor."

"There is literally nothing outside an Army extraction that would have gotten him out of that hospital," Matt replied, because he'd been there, done that, and Evan wasn't even his husband at the time. Hell, they were so new the tags were still on them, but seeing his lover in that hospital bed? No. Just no.

"I can't imagine what he's going through. It's like with Serena and Vic." Shane trailed off as he looked out the passenger window. "Watching them struggle while he's been in the rehab place has been god-awful."

Matt's hands tightened on the steering wheel. The GPS gave cheerful commands from the dashboard, which Matt wanted to punch. Hard.

"Not easy," Matt said, for lack of anything reassuring coming to mind. The twilight made it hard to see the road; all he kept hearing was Jim's admonishment to be on the lookout for deer every time he drove back from the house.

"Crap!" Shane let out an annoyed sound. "I left my bag at the house," he said apologetically.

Matt shook himself back to paying attention to things and began looking for a place to make a U-turn. The clock on the dash had him calculating his time limit to get everything done and still make it back before visiting hours were over.

"Would Helena mind if you stayed at the house tonight? I might be running out of time." Truth was, Matt didn't imagine himself going home after all this. Between the long drive and his own anxiety, it'd be easier to sleep over.

Shane gave a heavy sigh. "No. But I need to get back tomorrow morning. Helena and Serena alone in the apartment for long periods of time is a bad scene. I have to play mediator at least until they head back to Florida."

"Forgot about that." Matt spotted the U-turn sign and moved into the right lane. "Okay, we go back to the house, get your stuff, you drive my car back to the city, and I'll take the train when I'm ready to go home."

"You have to go to the hospital."

"Don't they have car services up here?"

"It's the wilderness, Matt, I have no idea."

BACK AT Griffin and Jim's, Helena—who told Shane to stay put—made the decision.

"I can not kill her for one night," she assured, as Matt listened in on speakerphone.

"Well, that sounds promising," Matt said after Shane hung up.

Matt put everything Griffin asked for in a cloth shopping bag he found in the pantry, adding a cute picture of Caroline in her dance costume from the mantel. "Has Serena found a place up here yet?"

"Soon as she wins the lottery." Shane kicked off his sneakers as he lay down on the couch. "Senior housing in the city is a nightmare. We can manage Vic's rehab because of his insurance, but Serena doesn't have a pension, just Social Security. Even between them, it's going to be next to impossible to find an affordable place he can get around in."

"Bennett Moneybags can't help?"

Shane gave him a dirty look. "I know it's a joke that he pays for everything, but the new play is costing him a lot of money. It'll be a while before he sees some returns on the investment."

Matt put his hands up. "Mostly kidding."

"If this play bombs, we are all going to end up living in your basement," he muttered, rolling over onto his side.

"Good to know," Matt said, checking his watch. "I've delivered hugs and kisses to a small child. You can feed and water yourself. I have everything on the list. Going to pick up Griffin's food, then head back to the hospital."

"Do you want me to go?"

"No. Because you're keeping the home fires burning and going to sleep because you look like crap."

"I am tired of hospitals, Matt." Shane gave him a sad look. "Helena flies back to Florida in two days to sit with her mom in the rehab place. I'll go down next weekend...." His voice drifted off. "We're both just... tired."

Feeling guilty for Shane staying the night, Matt picked up the bag, fiddling with his keys in his free hand.

"Fly back with them. Griffin's not going to be working for the next week at least. You don't lose any time with your wife," he said gently. "Bring your expensive fancy computer, work while you're there."

Shane perked up. "I could get all our notes transcribed so Griffin doesn't have to worry about it."

"See? Brilliant—I'm full of brilliance." He winked in Shane's direction. "Go to sleep—we've got this."

"Thanks, Matt."

"I live to serve."

"YOU CAN'T retire," the NYPD chief of police said outright twenty minutes after Evan sat down in his office. They'd talked about the weather, the last crime stats the mayor's office released, how much of an idiot the mayor was, then… boom.

Name, rank, and serial number, Evan thought.

"Chief, I have my years in. More than enough years, actually. I think I've served my city well. Now…." He spread his hands out as if he could encapsulate how much waited for him outside the badge. "It's time to move on."

The chief scowled, more artful Botox and smooth white hair than the central casting jowls and liver spots of the typical chief of police. "You've been a pain in the ass for years, you know that."

Evan smiled, crossing his legs, ankle against his knee. "All the more reason for you to be anxious to see me go."

"We gave you an incredible opportunity—"

"While using me as a poster child for inclusion and trotting me out like the Stanley Cup for photo ops," Evan finished. "Sir, I am grateful for my time as captain. But it's time."

A shrewd look, and Evan resisted the urge to sigh out loud.

"Are you planning to run for office?"

"God no!" Evan coughed into his hand. He should probably play things cooler than this.

"So you're really just quitting, moving into the private sector?" The chief squinted as if trying to read Evan's mind.

"I'm retiring." Evan emphasized the word. "Moving into the grandchild sector."

The chief's eyes all but disappeared into his unnaturally smooth face. "Bullshit. The Democrats want you to run for mayor." Suspicion oozed through every syllable. "They're grooming you."

"No. Sir. I don't know the Democrats and I don't think they know me, particularly not enough to uh… groom." Evan uncrossed his legs, leaning forward to emphasize his point. "Sir, I've been a cop since I was barely out of my teens. I have a scar on my chest from being shot, bad knees, and no stomach lining left. I owe the department so much—but I also owe my family a few decades of spoiling to make up for everything I've missed over the years. I want to take care of my grandkids and spend time with my husband."

He dropped the last word, watching the chief's reaction carefully.

The nose wrinkle was barely evident. But Evan could see it—he'd been seeing it for years.

"Fine. You set on November?" The chief flung himself back in his chair, rocking slightly from the recoil.

"I have about ten years' unused vacation time," Evan said drily. "Might as well use it up."

"I'll get PR on it. I want coverage—I expect you to make yourself available for interviews. And a ceremony."

Evan cringed inwardly. "Of course."

"No statements until we prepare something." The chief tapped his fingers on the arm of the chair. "Lucy Childress will coordinate."

"Nothing's been said publicly. I haven't even talked to my squad."

"Give me a few days to get something together." He looked put out. "Lucy'll call you."

It felt like a dismissal. Evan hovered for a second, then made to stand up. "Thank you, sir. I appreciate your time."

The chief waved his hand, making a noise that sounded like "hmph."

"Good night, sir," Evan said sweetly, before gathering his things and heading for the door.

MATT RELIEVED Griffin when he got back to the hospital.

"Wash your face, take a walk," Matt insisted in a hushed voice as Jim slept on, breathing shallowly. "You're going to be here all night."

Griffin's glasses were dirty, his face drawn. He fumbled with his shaving kit, then nodded. "Text me if he wakes up."

"Promise. Scout's honor."

"I mean it."

"Griffin, go take a piss. Take care of yourself. I refuse to have Jim give me shit because you drove yourself into a nervous breakdown."

Eyes closing, Griffin swayed for a second. "He's sick and he won't stop working. He's got this… fucking ticking time bomb in his body, and he won't stop. I've yelled and I've begged and I've fought dirty and it just…."

Matt swallowed a throat full of barbed wire, then put his arms around Griffin. "I'm sorry."

"He's not allowed to die. I will fucking kill him," Griffin muttered. "I swear to God."

Matt rubbed Griffin's back until he could answer. "I'll help."

"He has to stop working, Matt. Please, you have to help me convince him."

The narrow bar between Matt's feet got smaller—a tightrope walk between his best friend and the shaking man in his arms. Griffin wouldn't be happy until Jim retired, and Jim would never be happy if he retired…

but he'd be miserable if Griffin was miserable. A terrible mess, and one that Matt could cast himself in without a struggle.

"Let's wait until he's home and then, uh, we'll talk. We'll sit down and talk about the business." On the tip of his tongue came promises of making Jim take it easy or giving up the travel, but Matt wasn't a liar and Griffin wasn't dumb.

Griffin heaved a sigh, pulling back. His expression said it all. "Okay, thanks," he said, all the anger knocked out of him. "I'll uh, be back in a few minutes."

"At least twenty. I'm blocking the door."

Nodding, Griffin walked to Jim's bedside and bent down to kiss him gently on the cheek. He didn't say anything else when he left the room.

MATT SAT down at Jim's bedside in the world's most uncomfortable leatherette chair. It creaked as he settled back, his gaze locked on Jim's still form.

Guilt marinated his guts. He should have insisted Jim quit as soon as he heard about his condition. Put his foot down—right up until Jim ripped it off and shoved it up his ass.

Yeah, that wouldn't have worked.

But truth be told, Matt's real reason for not saying more was pure selfishness, bathed in deep-down understanding of his friend's plight. If someone told Matt to stop working, go sit on a couch—not because he wanted to but because he had to....

He'd go ballistic.

So Jim would be mad and bitter and hate it—but fuck that, he'd be alive.

"You're fired," Matt whispered sadly as he watched his friend sleep.

EVAN DROVE home, enjoying a post–rush-hour commute. He turned on the radio, whistled along with the oldies station, and imagined himself putting a big red circle around November 1 on the calendar when he got home. It was real. Official. Retired captain Evan Cerelli, husband, father, and grandfather, settling in to civilian life in a matter of months.

Maybe he'd call Fred and Blake, start discussing the care and proper feeding of a lawn. Maybe he'd grow a beard. It would offset all the hair he was losing on top.

"Text Matt," he said as his phone lit up from its holder on the dash. "Meeting over. November 1 is a go. Call as late as you want. Let me know how Jim is doing."

The polite voice asked him if he wanted to send.

"Send."

Evan went back to whistling.

He pulled into the driveway, turned off the lights. The engine. Hand on the door, ready to open it. Thinking about leftovers, because yes, Matt was right. That ziti from the shower....

His phone lit up with his son-in-law Kent's face, and Evan's entire evening took a left turn.

"CONTRACTIONS ARE three minutes apart," Kent babbled as Evan met him in the hallway outside Obstetrics. The young man's hair was askew, his gym clothes ill fitting, like he'd grabbed someone else's when he heard Miranda was in labor. "I called Mom and Dad and Katie. And you." He took a breath. "It's early."

"Only two weeks," Evan said, laying a soothing hand on Kent's arm. "What did the doctor say?"

"First babies don't usually come this fast, but Miranda is impatient, so he wasn't really surprised," Kent quoted. He twitched a smile. "She didn't like that too much."

"I'm sure she didn't. Get back inside; I'll wait for everyone here, okay?" What he actually wanted to do was run down the hall, find his daughter's room, and make sure she was okay. But that was her husband's job. "Give her a big kiss from me."

Kent nodded. He still looked frazzled, so Evan made a calculated decision, pulling him into a backslapping hug. "You can do this, Kent. Just stay calm and… and enjoy the moment. Your little girl is going to be here soon."

MATT FIDDLED with his phone, checking sports scores, the weather. Anything to keep his mind occupied. He stole one of Griffin's Diet Cokes and ten of his fries, his stomach suddenly reminding him he hadn't eaten since lunch.

The phone vibrated in his hand with a text.

Red Alert! Miranda's in labor!

9
RED ALERT

JIM BOBBED, nodding in between sleep and wakefulness, catching snippets of conversations. A scatter of words, a burst of emotionally pitched voices. The quiet movement of nurses who changed his IV. He always knew when Griffin was at his side, the touch of his fingers twined, thumb rubbing back and forth quickly against the inside of Jim's wrist.

Matt was restless, crossing and uncrossing his legs. Shifting in his seat. Muttering while he texted on his phone.

He never did remember to silence it, and Jim heard the clicking as he drifted off again.

The fever gave him terrible dreams, loud and red and frightening retellings of memories. Chasing a suspect through dark alleyways, listening to a fellow officer's death rattle during a domestic violence call gone bad. That day in court with Tripp Ingersoll, when grief killed Della Kelly.

Those were bad, but nothing touched the dreams where Tripp Ingersoll escaped from prison and came after Griffin and Caroline. Jim searching the house frantically for his family but finding only Tripp, smiling maniacally and covered with blood.

Jim forced himself awake, swimming up to consciousness with a start. He gasped out loud, triggering a coughing fit that shook the bed. His eyes stayed closed—because opening them felt like too much effort—so when someone touched his arm, he tried to get away.

"No, no, it's me, relax," Griffin murmured, stroking Jim's arm and shoulder until he caught his breath. "I'll get the nurse."

Jim's eyelids fluttered. He reached for Griffin and shook his head.

"I don't have to leave, just…." There was a moment of fumbling in the bedclothes; then Griffin went back to comforting Jim.

The cough finally slowed, every breath a painful rattle.

The door creaked open.

"See, the nurse is here," Griffin whispered, brushing a kiss against Jim's temple. "She's going to give you a breathing treatment."

He opened his mouth to protest and was cut off by a mask being lowered over his face.

WHEN JIM woke up again—really woke up, rooted in reality—the sun shone through the blinds of his hospital room. IV, check. Oxygen, check. Breathing? Not bad.

Relief coursed through Jim's entire body.

No one sat in the chair next to his bed, so he allowed himself to be emotional, at least for a moment. Not being able to breathe now sat atop his very private list of Shit That Scares James Shea. Tears filled his eyes as every moment of the past… twenty-four hours?—he was guessing—came back to him. Feeling like he was going to die. Fainting in the bedroom at Matt's feet. Griffin's fury. Griffin's *fear*. Their ridiculous fight, part stubbornness and just… due. He'd been honestly waiting for his husband to lose his shit since the diagnosis, because Griffin didn't do emotion halfway.

Too calm. Too accepting of Jim's continued work schedule.

The first time Jim went away for business, he expected to come home to an empty house.

A tear rolled down Jim's face.

Someone knocked at the door. Jim raised the arm not attached to the IV and quickly wiped his eyes. "Come in," he croaked.

A smiling Daisy ducked her head in, followed by the rest of her body. She wore a Yankees baseball cap, yoga pants, nylon jacket, and a tank that proclaimed her a member of the Goddess Squad, her typical running errands/trying not be recognized outfit.

"Hey! You look a lot better. That's a human skin color." She let the door close gently behind her. "How are you feeling?"

"Better." He attempted a smile and wink, but Daisy rolled her eyes as she threw herself into his bedside chair.

"You better work on that before Griffin gets back."

Jim worked his head back and forth, trying to crack the tension in his neck. "I feel like a tank ran over me."

"Better," she said, smirking.

"Where is he?" They'd mellowed into a friendship over the years, bound together by a mutual love of Griffin and now the bond between their girls. "Is he all right?"

"I made him go home to shower and spend some time with Caroline."

Jim squinted, suddenly concerned about how much time he'd lost. He looked around the room, trying to find a clock.

"It's Friday. She had a half day," Daisy said gently. "Last day of school is next Wednesday. You didn't miss anything."

"Oh. Thanks." Jim settled back against the covers. "Is she upset?"

Daisy pursed her lips. "We told her you were sick and you didn't want her to catch it. She's drawn you about three hundred pictures."

Jim's lungs tightened with grief. He hated letting his little girl down. "They won't let her come here, will they?"

"We tried. But honestly I agree—seeing you hooked up to machines will mess her up." Daisy had opinions about children, mostly about protecting them from real life for as long as possible. As a pragmatist, Jim usually disagreed, but maybe not this time. "You go home, lie in bed and let her snuggle you, and all will be well."

Nodding, Jim nervously twisted the blanket between his fingers. "You didn't answer the question about Griffin...."

"He's mad and scared, in equal parts." He appreciated her matters-of-factness. "He wants to throttle you, so I would consider playing up the feeling shitty angle a while longer."

Jim sighed as he stared up at the ceiling. "I should have just gone to the hospital when he wanted me to."

Daisy gasped dramatically. "Holy crap. Can you say that again? I wasn't recording."

"Be nice to me, I'm sick."

"You're stubborn. It's not the same thing." Daisy tapped her feet against the bed. "You know you have to retire, right?"

Even at this moment, Jim couldn't resist the urge to protest. "Technically this has nothing to do with the familial hypercholesterolemia."

She moaned, covering her face with both hands. "I'm going to have to testify when he murders you."

"Drama queen," he said under his breath.

Daisy peeked out, a knowing smile on her face. "You're going to retire and let him spoil you. Or else you're going to be buried in the backyard under an ornamental well."

"You're getting violent in your old age." He scowled at her.

"Watch it." She twisted on the chair, reaching into her pocket to pull out her phone. "Text from your husband. He is on his way back and wants to know if you need anything."

"Can I eat real food?"

"You want something hot?"

"He's just going to bring me something healthy and low-fat. And no salt."

Daisy made mmmmm noises. "He's bringing you soup. Probably something disgusting like lentil."

She texted back, fingers flying for at least a paragraph of words.

"What?"

"What what? I told him to bring me a salad and an iced tea."

Jim tried to calculate how long it would be before Griffin arrived and how much groveling he'd have to do to smooth this over. Retirement was the least of it.

"I feel like an idiot," he murmured, staring at the bathroom door.

"You are an idiot, but Griffin loves you more than anything," Daisy said briskly. "And I get it—you are not a couch person. You're not going to go gently into that good night either." She paused. "We will absolutely have to find you a hobby."

Jim made a strangled sound.

"Bowling. Woodworking? How are you with a saw?"

"*Your* hobby is tormenting me." He turned to face her. "I will be spending time with Griffin and Caroline."

"Griffin has a career that takes up long hours, and Caroline goes from school to camp to soccer to dance." Her serious expression caught Jim's attention—Daisy was the consummate professional with a perky "public" face. The real Daisy Mae didn't show up very often.

She was here now.

"I'm serious, James. You have a health issue that means cutting back on stress. But you are not any less yourself. Your drive is still going to be there. You're still going to wake up ridiculously early, you're still going to insist on exercising like a psycho. You're still going to resist sitting around all damn day. You have to figure out a way to occupy your mind and your time," Daisy said passionately, leaning forward in emphasis. "Believe me when I say this, Jim. I love my life more than I can articulate to you. I love my kid and my husband. My workshops. The odd acting job. It's all good. But."

She stopped abruptly. Jim couldn't look away from her. It hadn't occurred to him, all these years, the things they had in common.

"But," he said softly. "You miss who you used to be."

Her lips went tight, a straight line of denial, but she nodded.

"My life ten years ago doesn't even vaguely resemble this one. It was terrible! Toxic. And yet sometimes I think—I used to live in a mansion. An assistant followed me around, doing my bidding. The money, the clothes, the pampering. I was a movie star, Jim. A fucking movie star." She took a deep breath. "On the other hand, today I had a moment of sadness because school drop-off was almost done for the year and I'll miss seeing some of the moms in the line every morning."

"Weirdo," Jim said, feeling his nose and throat clog up. Stupid pneumonia. Stupid medicine.

Daisy reached over to grasp Jim's hand. "I. Love. My. Life. But sometimes the old Daisy gets sad and frustrated. It's why I teach. It's why I do at least one acting job a year. It's why I am telling you to be prepared for when you miss your old life, even if it was killing you."

GRIFFIN DID not expect to walk into Jim's hospital room, hands full of bags from Molly's Kitchen, to find his husband and his best friend holding hands, exchanging looks that could only be described as… meaningful.

"Is there something you kids want to tell me?"

Both snapped their gazes to him, pulling their hands back like he'd caught them doing something naughty.

"Yes, I'm running away with Jim. We're going to move somewhere secluded and annoy each other into insanity," Daisy said primly, wiping her eyes discreetly.

"That sounds about right." Griffin put the bags down on the bedside table.

"Hey," Jim said almost casually, avoiding Griffin's eyes.

"Hey." Griffin leaned down to kiss him on the cheek, happy to find the skin under his lips cooler than a few hours ago. "Looks like the medication is working pretty fast. You look a thousand times better."

Jim nodded. When he finally tipped his head enough so Griffin could see his eyes, his expression was one of incredible guilt. Griffin kissed him again, this time on the lips.

"I love you," he said quietly.

"Griffin…."

"We'll talk after you eat some soup." Griffin straightened up, ducking around Daisy, who was already elbow-deep in the bags, searching for her salad.

"Where are the girls?" Jim asked.

"Georgia took them to the pool." Daisy gathered her food and iced tea and then bussed a kiss to Griffin's cheek. "I'm heading out."

She did the same to Jim, the look of understanding that passed between them piquing Griffin's interest. He set up a container of lentil soup on Jim's tray, letting the moment happen without his interference.

By the time the door closed behind her, Griffin had settled down in the vacated chair, waiting for a story.

Jim poked the soup with a spoon, a look of distaste on his face.

"Enjoy," Griffin said perkily, faking it as he opened his tenth Diet Coke of the day.

A tiny dab on the end of the spoon finally reached Jim's tongue.

"So, what's going on with you and Daisy Mae?"

Jim shoveled a far larger portion into his mouth instead of answering.

"I have plenty of time," he said lightly after taking a sip of his soda. "We can cover you and my best friend having feelings. We can talk about you getting out of here. And then…."

Swallowing, Jim dropped the spoon on the table, then settled back against the pillows. "I know it's hard to believe, but she had some good advice." He shrugged. "When can I leave?"

Griffin watched his husband throwing his walls into place, the same thing he did every time Griffin challenged him. And Griffin usually responded by deflecting and charming and teasing Jim into a compromise.

And maybe that meant part of this was his fault. For keeping calm and not laying down the law when it came to Jim retiring—which meant it was time to rectify that.

Griffin wouldn't be deflecting this time.

"They want to run a few tests, and you'll probably get another breathing treatment. Maybe a few hours and they'll spring you," Griffin said, shaking the bottle to make more bubbles appear. "And we can do this at home or here, doesn't matter. But this conversation is happening."

The tension in the room notched up. Jim shifted under the covers and then picked up the spoon to play with his soup again.

"You need to let Matt know you're not going to be able to keep working with him." Griffin dropped it casually, even as his heart banged against his ribs. He wanted the words out of his mouth. For a long quiet moment, everything felt fragile, precarious.

Jim swallowed, his gaze locked on the take-out bowl of soup in front of him. Griffin waited for the shouting, the anger. The resistance. But seconds stretched out to minutes without the expected explosion.

Finally Jim raised his eyes to meet Griffin's.

"I can't just sit on a couch," Jim murmured. "I can't just… stop. I'll go crazy, Griffin." His tone and expression implored Griffin to understand.

"I'll stop traveling, I'll stop going to meetings in the city, I'll eat every boring piece of cardboard health food you put in front of me, but I can't...."

Griffin nodded, fingers tightening on the bottle. "Okay. But if you keep working with Matt, it's only a matter of time before you get the itch again, and I refuse. *Refuse*." He stressed the word with a hitch in his voice. "To fight you again about this."

"So, I don't work with Matt." His shoulders slumped in defeat, and it took every bit of Griffin's strength not to break down, give in. Denying Jim was torture. "There has to be something else I can do."

Griffin didn't trust his voice, so he took another drink, blinking rapidly to keep his emotions at bay. He hadn't slept in almost two days, running back and forth between the house and the hospital, soothing Caroline, who just wanted to know when Daddy was coming home.

"We'll figure it out," he said finally. Faintly. "We love each other."

"You called me a lot of names recently." Sad yet sweet Jim was like fucking Kryptonite; Griffin girded his loins.

Griffin put his soda down on the side table, then leaned his elbows on Jim's bed. "Your stubbornness has been setting records, so I'm pretty sure you deserved at least forty percent of them."

Jim's expression softened as he reached out to stroke his fingers against Griffin's cheek. "I'm sorry about that. I can't help myself sometimes."

"I'd apologize, but frankly if it took another hundred swear words to convince you to keep living, I'd do it." Griffin's glasses caught the few tears that escaped.

"I'm not going anywhere. Promise." Jim tugged Griffin's wrist until he got out of the chair, and then pulled him closer. Griffin rested their foreheads together, breathing in the moment. "Promise."

"Let's not tempt fate, okay? This decision is not entirely in your hands," Griffin whispered, brushing their lips together. "Please."

"Promise," Jim repeated, tipping his head just enough to kiss Griffin tenderly.

Griffin didn't realize he could cry and kiss at the same time. It wasn't a skill he wanted to use on the regular. He had the urge to deepen the moment, to let the familiar rhythm take over, but his tongue remained dutifully in his mouth.

The oxygen nodules were digging into his face, reminding Griffin where they were and why they were here.

He pulled away, dredging up a smile as best he could. "Easy. If a nurse walks in on us, I might be permanently psychologically damaged."

"Too late," Jim said, clutching Griffin's hand so he couldn't move too far away.

"Sweet talker." Griffin sat down again but kept his upper body close to Jim. "You should eat your soup."

"It got cold while you were pawing me."

Griffin rested his head against their joined hands. "You're not going to wriggle out of this after you're home, are you?"

The quiet made him peek up.

"I have never, nor will I ever, wriggle," Jim said sternly.

"Is that a challenge? Because you're going to be in bed for a while, and I work from home…." Griffin felt his anxiety dissipating, melting a bit more with every twitch of Jim's lips. They would be fine. Everything would be fine.

Jim's serious façade broke as he chuckled weakly. "Pretty sure that won't be in the discharge orders."

They sat quietly for a moment—a comfortable silence that Griffin had been missing desperately.

"I should probably call Matt, talk to him privately," Jim mused, prompting Griffin to remember the thing he forgot to tell his husband.

"Matt is currently occupied, waiting to become a grandfather."

"*What?*" Jim's eyes went wide as he sat up. "Which one?"

"Miranda went into labor. That's why he isn't glued to your side." Griffin kissed Jim's knuckles. "I'm sorry I forgot to tell you."

"Did you send flowers?"

"Not yet. She's still laboring. Soon as Shelia is born, the order is ready to go." While he wasn't sleeping last night, Griffin had searched every flower delivery website in existence, looking for the most over-the-top pink bouquet he could find. The one he settled on would require Teamsters to get it through the door and included a four-foot pink floral-pattern stuffed giraffe. He loved it. "Matt's going nuts."

"God, when it's Katie's turn…."

They exchanged amused looks.

"What's wrong with them? We were so calm when Caroline was born," Griffin deadpanned. The memories of them Keystone-copping it all over the maternity ward made him feel warm all over. And oddly sleepy.

"Your father threatened to hit me with a chair if I didn't calm down," Jim said fondly.

Griffin settled his forehead against Jim's shoulder, still holding his hand tightly. "Remember when the nurse got mad because there were thirty-six people in Farrah's room?"

"Thankfully she didn't pop in when there were forty-eight."

Jim rested his head atop Griffin's, pushing him a little deeper into sleepiness. He'd wreck his back leaning this way, probably wake up with cramps—but for now, Griffin tolerated the discomfort to soak in the warmth of Jim's body, the comfort of his breath against Griffin's hair. His eyes fluttered closed as he drifted off.

DAISY DROVE to the community pool and parked the Volvo under a tree to steal some shade. Beyond the bushes and Japanese cherry trees, a wrought iron fence separated the lot from the patio and, farther on, the pool. They also belonged to the local country club, but Sadie preferred the public pool, so they joined. Once a week, she played tennis among the Dutchess County elite—had a drink, ate a salad, and then escaped here, to watch Sadie and Caroline race each other from one end to the other, showing off their swimming skills.

She sat for a moment, watching the comings and goings of the pool. Mothers and their damp children, faces pouty to have to leave so early (and it was always early, even five minutes before closing). A few nannies stewarding their charges to the concrete snack bar, waiting in long lines for churros and pizza and ice cream.

If this were a movie set, Daisy would declare it wholesome and family-friendly.

Her talk with Jim left Daisy distracted. She wanted to drive back to the hospital and clarify her own position. She loved her life. So much. She wouldn't trade Sadie or Bennett or her freaking Volvo for anything. Hollywood could show up on her doorstep and she wouldn't answer.

"Gut check, Daisy Mae," she whispered to her dashboard. "If Hollywood knocked, you wouldn't at least listen?"

The good parts—money and attention and people fussing over your every whim—whispered to her sometimes. The stage had never called to her like the lights of Los Angeles; she never expected to live in New York, doing a stage play a year. Teach little kids who wanted to pretend to be popcorn in the pot or animals in a zoo on the moon.

In her lowest moments, she wondered about a comeback.

They could all move to California. Bennett would do it—Bennett would do anything for her. Sadie was young enough; she might even think of it as an adventure.

Daisy blinked as the pool took shape in front of her once again. And what if that adventure turned her back into the woman she once was? The drugs, the petty, ugly behavior. Treating other people like they were disposable.

Griffin forgave her years ago. She would never forgive herself.

"If it knocked, I would turn up the music and pretend I wasn't home," Daisy said out loud, feeling a little foolish. She probably needed a nap or a hug from her precious little girl.

She got out of the car, bag and keys in hand. A few of the moms from the pickup line waved from across the lot as Daisy walked toward the entrance. Sadie's soccer coach yelled hello as she showed her badge to the teenager at the gate.

No one asked for her autograph.

"Mommy!" Sadie shrieked. Daisy scanned the pool, spotting her daughter waving frantically from the deep end, Caroline bobbing behind her.

"Hey, sweetheart!" Daisy located Georgia in her favorite chair, tucked under a large maple that leaned over the back fence. Her wide-brimmed hat and lightweight long-sleeve cover-up protected her pale skin from the sun. A magazine was spread across her lap, but Daisy could see her monitoring the girls.

"Georgia, I am here to relieve you," she said, reaching the housekeeper's side.

"How's Jim doing?" Georgia smiled up at Daisy.

"Grumpy, so he's clearly feeling better." Daisy settled down onto the lounge chair next to Georgia. The girls' pool bags were piled up between the chairs, along with a soft-sided cooler. "Thanks for watching them this afternoon. They really appreciate it, and so do I."

Georgia began to gather her belongings, slipping her magazine into her straw bag. "Not to be crass, but you all pay me enough—more than enough—to take two sweet little girls to the pool."

Daisy laughed. "I appreciate the honesty."

"Taking my nieces on a Disney cruise for Christmas," Georgia confided as she swung her legs over and stood up. "You need anything this weekend, I'll be around."

"We should be okay, thanks."

Georgia patted Daisy's shoulder and then hefted her bag up. "Fridge is full. They have plenty to get them until Monday."

"You're a saint." Daisy smiled up at her.

"Eh, I'm a stress cooker. There, uh… might also be some stuff in your fridge," she said sheepishly.

"This is my mac and cheese pleading face."

Georgia gave her a wink. "Tell the boys to take it easy and I'll see them Monday."

"Thanks, Georgia."

Daisy watched her leave, saw her pause at the water's edge to say goodbye to the girls. They'd never gotten nannies, always preferring to share the load of taking care of Sadie and Caroline between them, but Georgia filled in more and more each year. Daisy and Bennett chipped in for her salary—and clearly it was time for a raise.

She checked her phone: a series of reminders for various appointments, a list of dance camp supplies Sadie needed, emojis from Bennett intimating he'd be late but wanted to have sex with her. And then one message from Griffin: *V is for victory.*

Relief washed over her. She hoped Jim could create a life post–everything else that filled him with as much joy as she had.

"Mommyyyyyy!" Sadie said, sprinkling Daisy with water as she ran up.

"No running, miss." Daisy opened her arms, accepting a soaking-wet Sadie into her hug. "Did you have fun today?"

"Yes." She smacked a damp kiss to Daisy's cheek. "Georgia made us lunch and we've been here for *hours.*"

"Did you leave Caro in the deep end?"

"Nope, I'm here." Ever the quieter of the two, Caroline dutifully walked up, her hair tangled every which way.

Sadie shifted without being asked; Daisy pulled Caroline into their pile, letting her clothes get wet.

"How's Daddy?" she whispered against Daisy's ear.

"Ooo, so much better! He was eating soup when I left." She gave Caroline her biggest, brightest smile. "He might be home later today or tomorrow morning."

Caroline's face broke into a happy grin. She wiggled closer to Daisy, letting her cuddle her a little tighter.

"You guys want to swim some more? Or maybe we should go home, have some showers, and watch a movie." Daisy inhaled their sweet suntan lotion and chlorine scent, comforted by their arms around her and each other.

"Home," Caroline said immediately, even as Sadie chimed in, "Let's stay!"

"Compromise? Another half hour, then we go home." Daisy let the girls sit up, assessing their feelings about that. Sometimes Sadie got her way by default of being older and more aggressive, while Caroline tended to just agree.

Sadie watched Caroline, while Daisy attempted to get the hair out of her eyes.

"Actually," she said, feigning a yawn—badly, in Daisy's opinion—"I am a little tired. We should go home."

"Only if you want to." Caroline shivered.

In full caring mode, Sadie got out their towels, handing the first to Caroline before draping her sparkling unicorn one around her shoulders.

"Oh, I do. I think it might even rain," she said, peering up at the cloudless sky.

Her daughter, Daisy concluded, was a truly terrible actress.

CAROLINE FELL asleep during *The Little Mermaid*, not even twitching as Daisy and Sadie sang along to every song. In the nest of blankets and pillows on the family room floor, Daisy let her daughter's weight ground her, contentment spreading over her like warm honey. Caroline curled up in a question mark, her head on Daisy's hip. Sadie drifted off as the credits ran, allowing Daisy the chance to change the channel.

Griffin texted her that Jim would be released in the morning sometime around ten. She happily spammed him with emojis while HGTV rumbled in the background—hearts mostly, and then a squirrel for no real reason. It made her smile.

At nine she heard the key in the lock, the beeps and pops of the security system.

"Quietly," Daisy stage-whispered preemptively. "Sleeping children."

Bennett, still dashing in his suit after a full day at the office, appeared in the archway, a fond smile on his face. "Room for one more? I have some apricot brandy and a lascivious mind." He held up a small brown bag.

"Ooo, that sounds delightful. If you can help me get them upstairs, I might be able to fit you in." She didn't mean it dirty, but the second it left her mouth, she heard it. And the expression on Bennett's face told her he heard it too.

They broke into undignified laughter at the same time, with Bennett doing something stupid with his eyebrows that made her laugh harder.

"Shhh," she giggled, feeling both girls stir.

Restraining himself, Bennett picked Sadie up; she sleepily wound her arms around his neck as he murmured to her. Daisy watched her husband and daughter, her heart full. *Second chance at life, second chance at love,* she thought. How fortunate they were to survive Bennett's indiscretion.

Caroline snored quietly as she was hefted into her godmother's arms. Not everyone got to live next door to their best friend, but both she and Sadie got that pleasure.

She followed Bennett up the stairs to Sadie's room, whispering to Caroline. "Daddy's coming home tomorrow. It's all going to be fine."

10
WELCOME, SHELIA. AND MAVAN.

EVAN MASKED every emotion—mostly fear—coursing through his veins as he sat in the waiting room, keeping his face neutral. Or so he hoped. They'd pretty much taken over the small space: Cornelia and Blake, Elizabeth, Danny, and Katie, who was updating Austin back at home. They cycled through everyone being loud and then shushing each other as they excitedly waited for Miranda to give birth.

He held a cup of Starbucks Danny'd brought him almost forty-five minutes ago, presumably cold and disgusting at this point, but Evan held on to it like a lifeline.

Matt was on the road, speeding back from Jim's bedside. Evan's phone buzzed repeatedly, as Helena wanted to know if there was any change to the situation as she packed to return to Florida with her mother. Evan just sat and held his coffee, hoping his smile conveyed polite anticipation.

"You look like you're going to explode like a piñata," Cornelia whispered as she sat down next to him. She clasped his free hand in hers. "You okay?"

"I, uh, hate hospitals," he murmured. "Also, the control freak in me feels way, way too far from my kid right now."

She tightened her grip. "Miranda's doing great. Kent said it shouldn't be long now." Cornelia sounded like a flight attendant giving crash directions, but her expression was basically the visual of Evan's internal freak-out voice. "Shelia's almost here, and you'll have a better memory for a hospital from now on."

Evan started at that, the coffee cup wobbling in his hand. Oh.

He offered Cornelia a smile, grateful his daughter had married into such a lovely family. "Thank you. That's a really nice way of looking at it."

They sat quietly as the rest of the family took group selfies "for the baby." A few minutes later the door to the waiting room flew open and Matt bounced into the room, trailed by a half-dozen balloons celebrating a new baby girl coming into the world.

MATT BLEW through a hundred dollars at the hospital gift shop, purchasing all the giant pink balloons they had, a bag of assorted chocolate bars, and two sodas. That—along with the adrenaline coursing through his body—would get him through to little Shelia's birth.

Given the past twenty-four hours, Matt did not imagine ending his day in the maternity ward waiting room, kissing his husband on the mouth, and waiting for his granddaughter to be born.

"Did you save any balloons for other children?" Evan asked as they sat down on the creaky chairs, upholstered in nubby red fabric circa 1989.

"Nope. Only Shelia deserves them." He offered Evan one of his sodas. "How's Miranda?"

"Do you want dilation numbers or just general information?"

Matt's face did a grossed-out thing. "General information regarding the well-being of Miranda and our grandchild. Everything else I'll take a pass on. I'd like to be able to look her in the eye."

"She's getting close to pushing." Evan smiled weakly. "Kent said he'd let us know when."

"And Miranda's okay? No problems?" Matt asked.

"Miranda is doing great."

Nodding, Matt settled back, opening his soda.

"Jim?"

He shrugged as he took a sip. "Better. He's getting out of the hospital tomorrow. Griffin is making him retire, and I am now down a business partner." He tried to make it sound like a joke, but it fell flat. "You need a job?"

"I'm retiring so I can spoil grandchildren." Evan rubbed Matt's arm gently. "Maybe you can join me?"

Matt considered this potential solution for about four seconds, but he was already shaking his head in response when he answered. "We need the money. Kids in college, still paying off the house. Plus—and I can't stress this enough—retirement will make me loco."

"If I can manage it…."

"Which you haven't yet. So I'll keep that job open just in case," Matt deadpanned. He'd believe "relaxed, retired Evan" when he saw it in person for at least six consecutive weeks. "I can do it by myself, but it kind of sucks. I've gotten used to having someone to bounce ideas off of. Someone to do all the things I don't want to."

"You need an intern," Evan said absently, leaning forward as the door opened again. Kent, red-faced and sweaty, stuck his head in.

"Pushing, we're pushing. She's pushing." He took a breath as Cornelia and Blake rushed to give him a hug. "Shouldn't be long now."

The room erupted in cheers.

EVAN GAVE up the pretense of calmness, pacing in large looping circles around the waiting room. He dodged the balloons, Cornelia and Blake, his children, and Matt, who was reading a *Woman's Day* from last June in between texting Griffin.

"How long has it been?" he asked.

Danny looked up from his phone. "Fifteen minutes."

Mumbling to himself, Evan did another loop around the waiting room. Were the walls closing in? He was starting to think the room had gotten smaller. Fifteen minutes—was that enough time to push out a baby? He racked his brain to remember each of Sherri's labors.

When he recalled Katie taking almost three hours of pushing, he felt a little faint.

God, waiting—not his strong suit.

"At least you're not Kent," Matt commented as he did another pass through the room. "I imagine he's a lot more stressed out right now."

"That doesn't actually help." Evan kicked at Matt's sneakers. "I'm worried about him too."

Matt patted the seat next to him. "Please sit down. Please." He pulled a chocolate bar from the bag next to him and then waved it enticingly. "Have some candy?"

"Your sex games are really disturbing." Katie, or rather Katie's belly, squeezed between them. She plucked the candy from Matt's fingers.

Evan gave her a sideways hug. "How do you feel?"

"Hungry. And impatient. I want to meet my niece." She lowered herself back into a seat, rubbing her side. "Just think, everyone, you get to do this all over again three weeks from now!"

ANOTHER HOUR ticked by. Matt fed Evan chocolate and parsed out the rest of his treats to the group as if they were crashed into the side of a snow-covered mountain. A rousing game of paper football broke out, boys versus girls, but that got curtailed when another family of seemingly normal people came to wait. Their bacchanalia was over.

"I hate having to behave," Matt muttered. He texted everyone in their friend circle who was not in this room, sharing his tale of woe.

Evan tapped his feet until even Elizabeth began to glare.

"Oh, this is driving me crazy," Cornelia said loudly, startling everyone in the room. "Sorry, sorry." Blake drew her back down, wrapping his arm around her.

Katie shifted in her seat, then struggled to stand up. Danny gave her a hand, steadying her as she tried to gain her balance.

"Elizabeth, walk me to the little girls' room." She held out her hand for her sister. "Given the law of averages, as soon as I sit down to pee, that baby will be born."

"Damn, why didn't I think of that?" Matt watched them go, contemplating a trip to the vending machines for more caffeine. He'd drifted into a sugar/soda walking coma, both incredibly awake and sleepy at the same time. Maybe the other family wouldn't mind if he lay down on the floor and took a little nap—

The door flew open, setting the whole room into an uproar.

Matt had never seen Kent show that much emotion. Still in sweat-stained scrubs, he burst in, grinning from ear to ear, vibrating with joy.

"Shelia's here, she's here." His voice broke as Cornelia enveloped him into a hug.

EVAN STOOD up as soon as Kent entered the room. For a second he couldn't react—everything just seized up inside him. Then he opened his mouth to speak… and nothing came out.

"Congratulations, Grandpa," Matt whispered, wrapping an arm around his shoulders. "Breathe."

A quick intake of air; then Evan cleared his throat. "Miranda…," he managed.

"Oh." Kent pulled away from his parents for a second. "Oh, she's amazing. Just amazing. I have to get back to her. God. But she's fine. She did great." Kent collected himself and then kissed his mother one more time before ducking back out.

Evan nodded, letting himself be folded into a tight embrace from Matt. He held on, struggling to keep himself in check. His firstborn was a mother. Little Shelia was here, and God, he couldn't wait to hold her.

SECRETLY, MATT imagined being emotional when Katie gave birth, given their relationship. He and Miranda were good now, but it wasn't the same as with the other kids, so he'd be happy but not… dramatic when she had her baby. At least he didn't think so until he started tearing up as Evan hugged him back.

"Oh crap" was all he managed as Evan chuckled weakly against his shoulder. "Wow."

A tap on the shoulder made him lift his head. Danny stood there, smiling with his arms outstretched. "Someone hug me, I'm an uncle!"

"I told you!" Katie's voice broke up the group as the door slammed open. "I went to the bathroom and Shelia was born!" Then she burst into tears.

"Don't go into labor, please," Matt muttered as he and Evan hurried over to help Katie back into a chair.

Evan left Matt to soothe her as he did the rounds of hugging Elizabeth, Cornelia, and Blake. From the other side of the room, the second family watched them with polite but concerned smiles.

They would be so happy when this crowd cleared out, Matt thought.

"Hey, kiddo. These happy tears or giving birth tears?"

"Ha-happy." Katie dug into her pockets for tissues. "Oh my God, Miranda had a baby!"

Matt wrapped his arm around her shoulders. "True story."

"I'm having a baby!" She blew her nose loudly. "Oh my God!"

One-handed, Matt texted Austin the good news, then recommended he find a way to get here. Soon.

Neighbor's watching Josiah. There ASAP.

"I mean I knew it was happening, but oh my God…."

Evan returned, settling down on Katie's other side. "Hey, Katie? You okay?"

She nodded, wiping at her eyes. "Miranda's a mom. We're going to be moms together. I never thought this would be such a great thing, after all the years I just wanted to drive her as crazy as possible."

WITHIN TWENTY minutes a cleaned-up Kent returned. "Who wants to meet Shelia?" he asked the crowded room. Two more families had arrived, and things were starting to get a little tense in terms of allocation of chairs and noise level. Evan began to get concerned they didn't have enough air.

"How many can you take in?" he asked eagerly. Part of him wanted to argue grandparents first, but Katie needed to get home before she fell asleep.

"We can do everyone so long as we're quiet." Kent waved them out the door.

He didn't have to ask twice. They followed him down the hallway, Evan speed-walking to the front of the pack. Every inch of him vibrated with nervous energy; he wanted to cry and celebrate and then cry some more.

When Kent reached the door, giving them one more *shhhh* before opening it, Evan felt Matt's hand in his. From the doorway, he could see Miranda in the bed, a pink-blanketed shape against her chest.

"Come meet Shelia," Kent whispered as Evan pushed his feet to move.

At Miranda's bedside, Evan let himself drink in her smile, her tired eyes, her rosy complexion and damp hair. He could see Sherri in her so clearly as he reached out to brush his fingers across her cheek.

"Congratulations, sweetheart," he whispered, leaning down to kiss her forehead. "I love you so much."

"Daddy." Miranda's voice wavered. She moved her arms slowly, gingerly, revealing the tiny face of his granddaughter. Little wisps of blond hair sat on the top of her head, her apple cheeks moving as she breathed in and out. "This is Shelia Cerelli Moran," she said, breathless and proud as she gazed adoringly at her daughter.

"She's perfect." Evan stroked the baby's chin, seeing both Kent and Miranda in her features. "Absolutely perfect."

MATT LET go of Evan's hand, letting him bond with the baby. The moment his husband got that little nugget into his arms, it was like a light was switched on from inside. He beamed with the joy of it, making Matt's heart flip a few beats.

He watched Cornelia and Blake meet their granddaughter, sniffling a little as a beaming Cornelia held her for the first time. Elizabeth and Danny were both rapt in their attention, marveling over her tiny hands and her tiny dimples. Then Katie sat on the bed next to Miranda, introducing

Shelia to her bump—"This is your cousin, and you're going to be the best of friends"—and there wasn't a dry eye in the house.

"YOU'RE NOT getting off the hook. Come meet your granddaughter," Miranda said when she'd gotten a handful of tissues to clean up her face as Kent cuddled his daughter.

Rubbing his hands together, Matt presented himself bedside. "I have all the balloons to give you, but I forgot them in the waiting room."

"She doesn't care, and I'm happy you're here." Miranda's eyes filled up again, and Matt crossed his arms over his chest.

"Stop that."

"Say hello to her," Miranda ordered, starting to cry again.

"You're doing this on purpose." Matt put his arms out, trying to remember when he did this with Caroline and Sadie. Support the head, hold the butt.

Kent deposited little Shelia into his arms, and Matt fell in love.

"POPPY."

"No."

"Grandpappy?"

Evan leaned back against the headrest. Having adult children meant getting driven home from the hospital, so Elizabeth was at the wheel of his car while Danny followed behind in Matt's car.

Matt sat in the back seat, throwing out honorariums.

"We need to come up with something."

"There's time!" Elizabeth laughed as she turned down their street. "She can't talk yet."

"Miranda and Kent are very smart. You don't know how quickly Shelia is going to pick things up."

Evan and Elizabeth shared a quick smile as she pulled into the driveway.

"I think we have a few weeks, at the least," Evan said, unhooking his seat belt.

"Until Mavan is born, and then we'll be out of time! We have to pick something before Fred and Blake get the good ones," Matt insisted as he got out of the car.

Elizabeth laughed as she walked around to the other side of the car. "Dad, you can't sleep in the car." She offered her hands. "Come on, Gramps!"

"See, Gramps, I like that."

Evan let Elizabeth pull him out of the seat. "I will be Grandpa Evan. That's what Josiah calls me. That's what Shelia and… Mavan… will call me. I don't see why we have to get fancy."

Danny joined them on the walkway. "That's you, Dad. We're talking Matt here. Grandpa seems so… pedestrian."

It was hard for Evan to miss Matt's triumphant expression, and impossible to miss the fist pump over his head.

MATT SLEPT ten solid hours, missing Evan's departure for work and both the kids leaving for the day for their summer break activities. When he rolled out of bed, he found a ton of texts and missed calls, mostly from Griffin.

"What's wrong?" he asked, halfway into his pants when Griffin picked up.

"Nothing. Sorry, do I call too much? I was trying to find out about the baby," Griffin rambled, not taking a breath. "We're home, Jim's home. In bed, where he's staying until I tell him he can leave."

"He just got out of the hospital—curb your crazy sex games." Matt dropped his pants, then got back into bed. "I'll be up there in a few hours."

"No, don't. You have family stuff to do."

"Tell him to stay home!" Matt heard Jim's voice in the background.

"I'm offended by how you think I can't do two things at once in two different places."

"Um, you can't?"

"Put your husband on the phone, please." Matt rolled himself in the sheets, settling into his comfortable groove in the mattress.

"Hey."

"You okay?"

"I'm fine."

"I was coming up so we could talk about… stuff."

Jim sighed, a noisy exhale that ended with a slight cough. "We can do this now." He cleared his throat. "I'm retired, but I don't want my investment money back. That's yours, to run the company."

"James."

"Matthew."

"I'm not taking your money. We'll dissolve the partnership, you'll get your—" Matt didn't get very far.

"Matt!"

He blew a raspberry into the phone. "Fine. You can be a silent partner and my sugar daddy. But you can't work."

"Fine."

"I'm going to come up and get all the files and the desktop, and I will be changing the email password so you can't get in."

"Fine," Jim said, but Matt could feel his grimace as clear as if they were in the same room.

"Okay." Matt pulled the sheet over his head. "You mad?"

"If I had the strength, I'd get up and throw this couch through the picture window." Jim sounded like himself again, and for that Matt was grateful, even if this sucked. "Daisy said I had to get a hobby."

"You don't know how to do anything."

"Therein lies the problem."

EVENTUALLY MATT got dressed. He answered approximately a thousand texts, sharing Shelia's adorable pictures with everyone whether they asked or not, all while finishing the last of the shower food, which felt fitting on Shelia's first official day on earth. He checked in on Katie—then checked in with Austin to get the straight talk on Katie.

"She's fine but very emotional still. Also she's making Josiah help her clean out the linen closet, so uh, I'm sticking close to home today," Austin said with a nervous laugh. "I suspect we have entered the nesting stage."

"I'll be home all day. Holler if you need anything. Grampy is here."

Austin coughed.

"Yeah, I know. I'm still working on it."

When he finally sat down at his desk, Matt's emotional high took a direct hit. With Jim sick and Matt being at way too many hospitals in seventy-two hours, his work emails were backed up, and several proposals sat unfinished on his desktop. Jim's expertise and ability to handle all the stuff Matt hated left a huge void, even beyond the "I won't be hanging with my best friend all the damn time" loss.

"What the hell am I going to do?" he muttered before tackling his work.

Two hours passed in irritated work mode before he heard the front door.

"Matt!"

"In here." He printed out another proposal, his eyes dry from staring at the screen without blinking.

Elizabeth plopped down on the armchair in the corner of Matt's office, looking tan and lithe in her bathing suit top and shorts.

"Why aren't you wearing more clothing?"

"It's summer." She leaned over to grab the papers out of the printer. "What are you doing?"

"Eh, proposals for some clients. Jim's, uh—well, Uncle Jim has been having some health problems, so he's retiring, effective now."

"I thought it was pneumonia, not anything really serious." Elizabeth fussed with the papers, lining them all up with straight edges. "Is he going to be all right?"

"Yeah. He just needs to have a stress-free life." Matt sighed as he turned his chair to face her fully. "Has to happen, but I'm feeling a little bummed."

She gave him her sweetest sympathetic face, then looked at the proposal. "I can imagine. I mean, you guys are best friends, but you know you'll see him just as much and…." Her voice trailed off. "Um, is this the final?"

Matt's gaze narrowed. "Yes. Why?"

"There's some typos," she said, looking almost guilty. "Can I give it a look over?"

He sighed, then motioned for her to go ahead. "Please."

WORK WENT faster with Elizabeth. She corrected his typos and grammar and rewrote entire paragraphs for efficiency. Setting up with her laptop at the desk next to him, Elizabeth tried to explain why she'd made the changes, but Matt just waved her off.

"I know what I'm paying for your education—I trust you."

He concentrated on floor plans until Elizabeth leaned in, scooting her chair a bit closer.

"What are you doing, exactly?"

When she started making suggestions, Matt got an excellent idea.

EVAN APPRECIATED the hearty dinner of steak and roasted potatoes that night. He also enjoyed the bottle of wine that came in the "congrats, Grandpas" basket of treats Daisy and Bennett sent.

"We have the best friends," he said, cutting into his perfectly prepared steak. "What did you guys do today?"

"Worked. Ollie and me went to the gym. I showed everyone the picture of me and Shelia." Danny eyed the wine. Evan moved it farther away from him as soon as he noticed. "Nothing much."

Matt and Elizabeth seemed to be sharing identical grins, which should make Evan nervous, but the house was still standing and Grandpa Evan was in a good mood, so….

"And you two?"

"Why do you sound like you need a pipe and sweater with those patches on the elbows?" Matt asked, reaching for the ketchup. "Is that a new voice?"

"Grampy voice," Danny muttered.

Evan ignored them, spearing a potato on his fork.

"Matt and I had the best day," Elizabeth burst out. "I helped him with his proposals and worked on some floor plans! It was just really interesting and…." She gestured for Matt to continue.

"And I have a new paid intern."

They high-fived each other as Evan rewound the conversation.

"You're working with Matt?"

"Yes!"

"And he's paying you?" Evan gave Matt questioning eyebrows.

"Of course I am. She's proven herself invaluable, and frankly if I can get her to like sports more, she can replace Jim entirely."

Evan chewed slowly, then swallowed. Clearly he needed more sleep. Was he dreaming this meal? "Well, great. It's something for you to do until you go back to school."

"Mmmm," Elizabeth said. She poked her green beans. "Are we going to see Miranda and Kent and Shelia tomorrow?"

"I figured we'll swing by there, then go to Katie's—"

"She's nesting," Matt interrupted. "Austin said so."

Sitting up straighter, Evan put his fork down. "Maybe I should call."

"Wait until after dinner," Danny said, taking a sip from Evan's wineglass.

"HOW DID you know to call?" Austin asked, sounding bewildered. "I mean, that's just so weird!"

Evan stopped midpace of his back deck. "What's wrong?"

"Katie's in labor."

THEY DIDN'T rush to the hospital because something about contractions and how far apart they were. Matt washed the dishes by hand and cleaned the kitchen so deeply Danny accused *him* of nesting. The nervous energy drove him to the backyard, where he pretended to examine the fence for loose boards in the twilight. They were just starting on this grandparent journey; at some point it would be Danny and Elizabeth reproducing, and oh God, they were going to do this so many more times. Would every one send Matt's heart into overdrive?

Matt did a circuit around their small yard, moving a pot of dried-up marigolds six inches in one direction and three in the other. Did the shed need reorganizing?

"Matt! Dad said to come inside before you get eaten by coyotes!" Danny's voice rang out.

"This is Queens, not New Jersey!" Matt called back.

Matt trudged back to the house, hands dug deep in his pockets.

"THE DOCTOR thinks it'll be a few more hours," Katie said, her breath coming fast as Evan twitched on the other end of the phone. "You should go to bed."

Evan laughed nervously. "It's sweet you think I could sleep. Do you need me to come over?"

"No, no. We'll just let you know when we leave so you can... ow. Ow." Katie's voice drifted off as Austin came on the line.

"Hey, Dad? Yeah, we're hitting another round of contractions. I'll call you back." Austin's calm voice made Evan feel a touch better. He'd been through this before with Josiah. He was a doctor, though not a medical one. Still.

"Okay. Love you guys." Evan reluctantly disconnected the call.

He lay back on the couch where he had stationed himself—fully clothed, shoes placed next to him on the floor—for the rest of the night. Elizabeth was curled up on the floor in a pile of blankets, fast asleep, while Danny texted Jane from his perch on the chair. In the kitchen, Matt rumbled around, claiming he wanted a midnight snack.

"We've got a while to go," Evan sighed as Danny grunted in response. "You should go to bed."

"I'm fine. Jane's working an overnight shift at the gym, so I'm keeping her company." He waved his phone even as he swallowed back a yawn. "She says hi."

"Hi, Jane."

Matt returned with a bottle of water, a bag of white cheddar popcorn, and two oranges.

"Are you sharing or having sympathetic cravings?" Evan asked, moving his feet to give Matt some space to sit down after he deposited his goodies on the coffee table.

"Neither." He plopped down with a sigh and lasted just long enough for Evan to get comfortable, before jumping up again. "Yeah, that's not going to work. I'll be at my desk."

Evan watched Matt go. Then he looked over at Danny, who shrugged, and then got up to follow. He checked his pocket a dozen times to make sure his phone was there on his way to Matt's office.

Inside, Evan saw the Elizabeth influence in action. Matt's desk was neatly organized, the card table from the hall closet set up in the corner with her laptop, several legal pads, and pens in a cup. The corkboard from her room now occupied the couch, and two floor plans were pinned up.

"I'm surprised Elizabeth didn't paint and add some flowers," Evan teased gently, leaning against the doorjamb.

"She's only technically been on the payroll for about nine hours. Give her until Wednesday at least." Matt spun his chair around, hands folded on his stomach. "You seemed surprised she was working for me."

"A little. I guess I didn't really see it as something she wanted to do."

"Less surprising than the police academy?"

Evan shrugged. "Good point."

"She's bored, she's smart, and I pay above minimum wage." Matt tilted his head back to stare at the ceiling. "I figure she'll help me during the summer; then, when the school year starts, I'll make a decision about the future."

Evan moved into the room. He grabbed the back of the extra chair and dragged it closer. "Can you do this by yourself? Tell me the truth." He sat down close enough for their knees to touch.

Matt's expression said "I smelled something sour," and he twisted in his chair, knocking their legs together. "Yes. I mean, on a smaller scale. No new clients unless I lose one. More traveling."

"That doesn't sound fun," Evan said gently. "And I don't think you want to be gone that much."

"So I hire someone else and hope we can work together the way Jim and I did."

Oh.

Evan leaned in, taking Matt's hands in his. "Looking for a replacement for Jim is only going to end in tears and whoever you hire being here for about five minutes. He's your best friend. Work or not, that isn't going to change. You have to remember that."

Matt sighed. "I don't want to work with a stranger."

On the one hand, Evan could easily turn Matt's frown upside down. He could solve everyone's problems (or at least the ones in this room) with a simple acceptance—*yes, I'll come work with you.*

But the security business didn't interest him.

And he really did want to be retired, focusing on his family, go on regular vacations....

"Stop thinking so loud. I know you don't want to do this." Matt reached over to flick him on the ear. "And I think I read an article in *Cosmo* that couples shouldn't work together in a small home office."

"I'll join you if you really want me."

Matt rolled his eyes dramatically, throwing himself back in the chair. "God, that was so impassioned and convincing. You're hired, young man."

"This was me being nice," Evan teased.

"Your self-sacrifice is duly noted. You'll get an upgrade in heaven, I'm sure, to a deluxe box seat."

Evan kicked him lightly. "Your religion really is baseball."

"I appreciate your faked desire to join my company but... don't worry. I'll figure it out. Maybe I should look at some ex-cops, you know? Someone who can speak the same language as me. I think that might work." Matt's phone began to ring. He spun his chair around, slamming it into Evan's knees as he lunged for his phone.

"Austin?"

MATT'S EXCITEMENT and nerves twisted together in a twitchy whirlwind. Danny threatened to put him in the trunk if he didn't chill out during the drive over to the hospital, while Elizabeth petted his head from the back seat, urging him to take deep breaths.

"I should have gotten a prescription for Valium," Evan called from the back seat.

"We should have had a beer before this," Matt responded, tapping his fingers on the dashboard.

"Drunk at the hospital—that's a classy look." Danny steered the car toward the Grand Central, his fingers tight on the wheel. "If everyone could start praying we don't hit traffic, that would be great."

"Still have time." Evan sounded tense, which made Matt drum harder. "It's only a half hour to the Upper West Side."

"As long as there's no traffic on the Grand Central," Danny muttered.

"Steven and Alexandra Cohen Center for Labor and Birth at the Klingenstein Pavilion, 1176 Fifth Avenue, between 98th and 99th Streets," Elizabeth recited from her phone. "Do you want directions?"

"No, I'm fine."

"I can get turn by turn."

"I know how to get to the Upper West Side, Elizabeth."

"Wasn't questioning your sense of direction, just offering, Daniel."

"You are both going to be so good at being married," Matt deadpanned, turning in his seat to smile at Elizabeth, then Evan.

"That's a little too *Flowers in the Attic*." Elizabeth booped him on the nose. "I know you don't know what that means, but trust me, it's funny."

"I'll take your word for it." Matt checked his phone, then his watch, then the dashboard clock. "Are we there yet?"

Danny's exact quote was "Arrrrrgh."

DANNY DROPPED them off in front of Mount Sinai, then went to put the car in the garage. The cool summer evening air was a welcome relief to Matt, who felt himself melting from the inside out. He wanted to meet Katie and Austin's baby; he wanted to head back to Queens and hold Shelia. He wanted to do a little jig as they entered the lobby.

"I can't believe this is my life," he said to Evan as they approached the information desk.

Evan grabbed his hand, squeezing tightly. "I know, right?"

You procreated—you expected this, Matt thought as Evan spoke to the pleasant-faced woman at the desk, asking for the birthing center. *I lived alone and thought I was going to die alone. Never in my wildest dreams did I imagine this.*

"Let's wait for Danny over here," Evan was saying. "Elizabeth—"

"Texted Austin. He knows we are here. Fred and Beverly are already upstairs." She threw in a salute for fun. "Matt! We need to buy balloons!"

Matt dragged his floaty brain back into the conversation. "Do they have gender-neutral balloons?" He paused. "That was a sentence I never imagined coming out of my mouth."

"We can get one each pink and blue, then something that's just 'woo, a baby.'" Elizabeth turned and jogged over to the information desk.

"You okay?" Evan asked, close to Matt's ear.

Turning to face him, Matt didn't hold back the smile budding inside him. A moment that seemed a thousand years ago flashed back to him. He and Evan sitting in a seedy bar, the intense energy between them so confusing and so intoxicating he couldn't stay away. Everything in Matt's past had told him to run away from what he was feeling back then.

God, it had been complicated. Life-changing. Like everything he thought he knew got set on fire and remade. What was left, after all the upheaval? Matt with a family, with a purpose.

The only thing Matt could think of to say, here in the lobby of Mount Sinai, was "Thank you."

Evan's face settled into an expression of concern. "For what?"

"Making me a poppy."

Evan shook his head.

"Pop?"

"Eh." Evan smiled as he leaned in to kiss Matt's cheek. "A little retro."

Elizabeth returned, trailing balloons, including two shaped like giant bottles and one like a diaper pin. "I went totally neutral, but yay baby."

"You are absolutely the best intern I've ever had," Matt said sincerely.

"Oh, thank you!" She reached into the pocket of her shorts to pull out a receipt. "I'm going to need to be reimbursed from petty cash."

IN THE green-paneled maternity waiting room, they found Fred and Beverly sitting anxiously with matching rosary beads.

"She's doing great. Austin's with her," Beverly told Evan as they embraced. Her smile was tremulous. "She's fine, just fine."

The fact that Beverly had done this once before—with a terrible outcome—kept Evan close to her, arms around her shoulders.

"Thank you for letting me know that," he said gently. "This is a great hospital. Austin was very specific about that."

"He's been calmer than I have." Beverly shook her head. "I don't know how he does it."

"My guess is, he's working very hard to remember this isn't the same situation," Evan murmured. *Because we talked about it, because he was trying to keep everyone calm, and I totally understand that*, he thought.

"True. That giant brain of his…." She gave him a quick hug. "How are you holding up? I got to see Shelia earlier today—what a precious girl."

"I feel like I haven't slept in a month," he laughed. "And all day I resented my job keeping me from my granddaughter."

"How long before retirement?"

"Four months. Which seems like a lifetime at this point."

THEY'D BARELY settled into their seats when Beverly's phone buzzed. She made a little sound when she activated the screen, and Evan, closest to her, could barely catch his breath. There was a plump little face with a full head of black hair, Josiah's nose, Katie's big eyes, and cheeks that begged to be pinched.

"What?" Matt asked as he and Fred leaned over to see. Evan felt Elizabeth and Danny crowding on the other side.

"Oh my God! He's… she's… is that a boy or girl?" squeaked Elizabeth.

With shaking hands, Beverly typed a dozen hearts, then wrote: *boy or girl?*

Our beautiful boy says hello to his family came the response. Then: *Katie sends her love. Be out in a bit.*

Evan swallowed his tears, staring at the sweet face on Beverly's phone. "I don't mean to brag, but I've got some gorgeous grandchildren."

MATT AND Fred did the macho backslapping thing, both of them crying like idiots at the same time.

"Let's wait before we do this again," Matt said to Evan after he left Fred to put his arms around Beverly. "My tear ducts can't handle all this use." He pulled a still dazed-looking Evan out of the chair.

"Mavan's a boy," Evan said with a smile. "Josiah is going to be over the moon."

"I know that's not what they're naming him, but I have to admit, it's kind of grown on me."

Evan yanked Matt into his arms. "Why did you thank me before?" he asked, his lips close enough for a kiss.

Matt took the kiss—because how could he resist? Their lips slotted together, perfectly in sync. When Matt pulled back, his smile felt like it could split his face.

"For this amazing fucking family."

IT WAS an hour before they got to see Katie, Austin, and the new baby. In the meantime, Evan texted their friends and family and called both Miranda and Ellie to deliver the good news.

Miranda wanted to come to the hospital, but Evan managed to talk her down into coming tomorrow. "Kent can watch Shelia and you can come see Katie and the baby. It's so late…."

She sniffled over the line. "I know it makes sense, but I want to see him! That picture was just…. Daddy, he's so sweet!"

"And you'll be spoiling him rotten in no time," he said gently. "I'll take more pictures when we get in there."

"Okay. Give him a kiss! And Katie! And Austin! Tell her I'll call her first thing in the morning."

"Promise. Now go to sleep before Shelia wakes up."

"Love you, Daddy."

Evan had just hung up when the door opened. Austin's exhausted face greeted them.

"Looking for the Hill-Cerelli-Haight family? We have a new member," he said, walking into the room, arms outstretched.

UNLIKE WITH Miranda, they went back in small groups. Evan sent Beverly and Fred in first, despite his itching to get back there. The twins disappeared to find bathrooms and coffee, which left him and Matt alone in the waiting room. Matt pressed against his side, their fingers entwined.

"You're handling all this very well," Matt whispered.

"What? Beverly needed to get back there to put her mind at ease," Evan said with a shrug. "I understand that."

"No, I meant all of it." Matt nudged him. "I figured you'd be missing Sherri right about now."

Evan turned his head, nearly banging Matt's forehead against his. He searched his husband's face for distress, but a placid calm and tender smile greeted him instead.

"I don't know if missing is the right word," he said thoughtfully. "I'm sad she isn't here to see this. Same way I've felt at every birthday and milestone in their lives. She loved our kids so damn much...." His voice drifted off. "I see her as a young woman like she's frozen in time. I can't imagine her... here, now." Melancholy swept through him. "It's just... sad."

Part of him braced for Matt's reaction, but the gentle kiss his husband gave him wasn't a surprise. "It is sad. And I'm sorry she's missing out on all this."

Evan opened his mouth to give reassurance—of his love for Matt, of the way it didn't diminish that because he missed his wife being here—but Matt kissed him again.

"Shut up."

"You shouldn't feel—" Evan started but Matt blew a raspberry in his face.

Well, that was startling.

"I feel grateful to be here. I love our family," Matt murmured. "Our kids have kids, for Christ's sake. And I am... sad. Because a really nice lady isn't here to see how amazing her children turned out. I'm going to go ahead and call it incredible personal growth, because that's the truth."

Evan sucked back a wave of emotion. "I have to go see my grandson. Jumping you is not an option."

Matt cackled with delight.

BRACING HIMSELF, Matt followed Evan into Katie's room. He'd pretty much emptied the box of tissues in the waiting room, transferring them into the pocket of his khakis. He had a feeling he was going to use them all.

Tucked in the hospital bed under a pile of blankets, Katie looked pale and exhausted, but the smile on her face eased a little of Matt's panic. Austin sat next to her in a vinyl side chair, a white bundle in his arms.

"Oh my God, he's like twice Shelia's size" were his first words, which triggered a slow turn and incredulous look from Evan.

"What? He's a linebacker. Austin, buy your wife a diamond necklace," Matt rambled.

"I'd argue, but I can't. Because ouch," Katie said weakly, reaching out to get a hug from Evan.

Matt's gaze flicked from the baby to Katie; he felt pulled in two directions, so he leaned down, kissed Austin on the cheek, and then peered into the blanket to see his new grandson.

"If there is a *Vogue for Babies*, this child will be on the cover," he said, feeling a coo coming on as the baby made a little mewing sound, twisting in his father's arms. "He's healthy? Everything he needs, he's got?"

Austin laughed. "Hundred percent. He missed his due date by seven days, but I think we should be grateful. Nine pounds."

"Nine pounds!" Matt straightened up, catching Katie's eye. His nose and eyes immediately became clouded with tears. "You're a champ."

Katie shrugged, leaning against her father on the bed. "I won't be recommending it as a fun exercise in the future, but when the end result is that beautiful boy…."

Matt made shooing motions at Evan. "Go away so I can hug my girl."

When he got her into his arms, Matt let go. Not crying, per se, but letting his embrace truly communicate his love for her. When things were scary, when he didn't think he could do this, Katie had his back. He'd have hers until his dying day, a promise he made in his head as he tightened his hug.

"You okay?" Matt whispered into her hair. "Really?"

"Yeah. It was just really hard," she whispered back. "A little scary."

He rubbed her back gently. "You did it, Katie. You did great."

"I HAVE four months until retirement," Evan announced as he held his grandson. "Four months until my main job is spoiling the daylights out of you." The baby made a series of adorable faces, which had Evan considering moving that date up.

"Oh, Grandpa Evan is going to be a spoiler, is he?" Katie said, holding Austin's hand as she watched her father. "I will believe it when I see it."

Evan's eyebrows folded together into a frown. "What's that supposed to mean? I spoil Josiah. I do the same with Caroline and Sadie. Shelia and uh… are we getting a name at some point, or are we keeping Mavan?"

Katie giggled, then put her hand on her stomach. "Ow."

"Mavan is not the name we decided on." Austin looked adoringly at Katie. "We spent a lot of time on this." He turned back to Matt and Evan. "We didn't want to copy Miranda and Kent. We didn't want to make any of his three wonderful grandfathers feel left out. So...."

"Hurry, please. I have things with monograms to buy," Matt said impatiently.

"His name is Nathaniel." Katie beamed at them. "Nathaniel means 'gift from God,' and we feel pretty darn lucky, so...."

"Nathaniel," Evan murmured, marveling over the weight and warmth of the baby in his arms. "That's a beautiful name."

"Is his middle name Mavan?"

"Matt, I beg you. Please do not encourage that with Josiah. Please," Katie said, using her stern voice.

"What, then?"

Austin executed a perfect deadpan. "I think we are going with LeBron."

SIX WEEKS later Matt found himself back in the Queens party space, in the same room, surrounded by approximately one hundred pink and blue balloons. A white box had replaced the table of gifts, with a little slot for cards. A sheet cake the size of a Volkswagen that celebrated the christening of Shelia Cerelli Moran and Nathaniel Cerelli Hill sat on a table, covered in six inches of white frosting.

"We have to cut into a cross? Isn't that bad?" he asked Elizabeth, who was alternating pink and blue napkins on the dessert table. "It seems sacrilegious."

She made a concerned face. "I don't think so." She stopped her napkin arranging to give him a sideways look. "We'll cut around it."

A throat clearing from behind made them both jump. Matt turned to find Ollie, Danny's ever-present best friend, standing there. In a suit, with his unruly shock of black hair combed and neat—he even shaved! And he wasn't looking at Matt.

"Oh hey, Elizabeth," he said, casually awkward. "Can I help you with anything? With uh, the napkins or carrying something heavy? You look really incredible in that dress, by the way."

Elizabeth blinked up at him, mouth poised in an open little O. Ollie's eyes were actual hearts. In his head, Matt heard a swell of cheesy violins, so he turned on his heel, heading for the table where Jim and Griffin sat.

"I would like life to slow down just the tiniest bit," he said as he collapsed into his seat.

"Do I want to know?" Jim asked.

"No, but Griffin is going to swoon dramatically."

HELENA AND Shane joined their table as Matt was explaining the actual love connection he just witnessed between Elizabeth and Ollie, a kid he hadn't seen out of gym clothes or flannel shirts in fifteen years.

"My God, you two look exhausted," Griffin said, pushing the plate of cookies they'd been sharing toward them. "When did you get back?"

Shane looked at his wrist, squinting as if his watch was there but he just couldn't see it. "What time is it?"

Griffin and Matt exchanged raised eyebrows.

"It's 2:40," Jim said gently. "You should have just gone home from the airport."

"We couldn't miss the christening." Helena rubbed her temples. "I can't keep doing this. They keep calling me, asking me when I'll be back to work, and I just... I don't know how to answer that." Tears threatened in her voice as Shane reached over to rub her back.

Matt flagged down Danny, who was across the room. He mouthed "drinks for Helena and your dad," which sent the young man running.

"What can we do?" Matt asked, drawing his chair closer. "Whatever you need."

"I... I need time to get Vic better and he and my mom up here. I have to find them a place to live they can afford. I need my job to understand. I need to be able to work on a plane at this point," Helena spit out, grabbing a napkin to wipe her eyes. "I don't mean to ruin this great day, I'm just worn the hell out."

Matt opened his mouth to say something, but someone kicked him under the table. He looked around for Evan but instead found Jim watching him intently. He got kicked again.

"What?"

An incredible smile broke out over Jim's face, a smile Matt hadn't seen in much too long.

"Helena, what do you think about a change in careers?"

It took Matt a second, but he pounded on the table when Jim's meaning clicked into place.

"That's fucking genius."

"I know."

Griffin waved his hands between them. "Could you clue the rest of us in on your weird twin thing?"

EVAN ARRIVED at the table with a double whiskey, as directed by Danny, just in time to find his husband and closest friends high-fiving each other like they'd just won the Super Bowl.

"What's going on?" he asked as he placed the glass in front of Helena—who was both laughing and tearstained at once.

"Jim just solved everyone's problems! I'm going to go work for Matt!" Helena got up, then threw her arms around Evan's neck. "It's perfect!"

"One more attractive woman on staff and Matt's got *Charlie's Angels* bingo," Griffin pointed out.

"What's Daisy up to?" Matt asked, looking around the room. "Does she need a job?"

"THAT'S A nice thing you did," Griffin said as they drove home from the shower. Caroline slept in the back seat, and Jim watched the world go by through the passenger side window.

It felt like a metaphor at this point.

"Made sense. Helena needed a flexible job. Matt needed someone who could just jump in and handle the job. She'll be great with clients." Jim fiddled with the air-conditioning to give himself something to do. "Works out."

The quiet stretched out a second too long, and Jim waited for Griffin to say what he really wanted to.

"I know how hard this is for you, to stop working."

"I don't have a choice," Jim said quietly. "I get that. Soon as I figure out how to spend my time, I'll be fine. I've changed my life before and it all worked out. I can do it again."

He watched Griffin's hands clutch at the steering wheel.

"And until then, Caro and I are going to have the best damn summer. Georgia needs a vacation, you are behind schedule...."

"Don't remind me," Griffin sighed.

"So it's me and her doing the relaxation thing together."

Griffin gave him a quick look. "You sure?"

"You're going to be jealous of how much fun we have."

11
FATHERHOOD 101

JIM USED his recovery period—also known as house arrest when he was feeling annoyed—to consider his options.

Without ceremony, he was retired. For the first time since the age of sixteen, James Shea had no job. It felt bizarre.

It felt unnatural.

He wallowed in that for a few days, in between long naps, pulling out his brave face whenever Griffin or Caroline came into the room. "I'm fine" became his go-to phrase, one that his husband let him get away with for seven full days.

"You're not fine," Griffin said, cracking open the bedroom window after dropping Jim's breakfast tray onto his lap. "You're humoring me, and that needs to stop."

Jim scowled at his Melba toast, fruit salad, and oatmeal. They could at least make bacon-flavored bland food to ease the pain.

"What would you like me to do? I'm stuck in bed, but when I get up?" He sighed. "I might as well just stay here."

Griffin sat down at the foot of the bed. "I get it. This is going to be a huge lifestyle shift for you. And I'm here to help," he said tenderly, reaching out to squeeze Jim's foot. "We'll figure this out."

Jim shoved a spoon of oatmeal into his mouth to avoid the rest of the conversation.

HIS FIRST foray out of the house since his trip to the hospital was Caroline's soccer game. The sun felt incredible on his face, and he couldn't miss the delight as he watched his little girl running across the field, hair flying and her face set in concentration.

He cheered and clapped, cleverly avoiding conversation with other parents—that was Griffin's job. When the Blossoms were victorious, he bought everyone ice cream, making himself a hero in one fell swoop.

"You should come to all my games," Caroline declared from the back seat as they drove home.

Jim turned to watch her in the back seat, dirty and tired and beaming back at him, that perfect combination of Drake genes and the exact color of his own eyes and hair. "That's a great idea, Caro."

AFTER HE solved Helena and Matt's job issues at the christening, Jim felt a weight pulled off his shoulders in a way he didn't expect. No one was disappointed in him; no one was let down. He woke up the next morning to his husband and his little girl and time spread out in front of him. Precious, precious time.

Griffin and Shane's play went into "workshopping," which meant long hours and sleeping in the city, which meant Jim was free.

"Free to do what?" Caroline asked as Jim put away their purchases from the farmers' market.

"Uh...." Was he talking out loud? Bad move. "Free for us to do whatever we want." He stopped between the counter and the fridge, hands full of fresh corn. "You don't have school, I don't have to work anymore." The pang had become just a blip. "We can do whatever we want."

Caroline's eyes sparkled. She clasped her hands together as her face went into contemplation mode—a look that Jim felt was 110 percent Drake genetics. He'd seen that from Griffin for years, mostly right before he got Jim to do something he didn't want to.

"Can we go to a petting zoo? I want to pet a goat," she said finally, a sweet smile blooming. "And feed a goat. And a cow. And a sheep."

The sheer volume of germs in a petting zoo made Jim recoil inside, but as with his husband, he was unable to withstand the big-eyed adorableness or sincerity of the request.

"Let's go to the petting zoo."

THEY FED goats and cows and a sheep. They admired a peacock and threw corn at some chickens. Caroline didn't protest as Jim made her wash her hands a dozen or so times; she obediently followed his directions, then begged for "one more quarter!" and they did it all again.

Jim actually didn't mind the experience. Caroline glowed with happiness, and it was almost relaxing, having nothing to do but make his little girl squeal and point and clap. The sun felt warm on his shoulders, and Caroline's hand in his was the definition of perfect.

"We should get a goat for the house," she said as they ate apple slices at a picnic table when he finally dragged her out. "That would be fun."

"Goats like to live at farms with other animals," Jim said. "They like company."

Caroline contemplated this as she ate another apple. "How about a cow?"

"Same thing."

"Hmm." She tapped her finger to her chin. "What is an animal we could get for our house?"

A hairless cat with a short life expectancy, Jim thought.

Out loud, he said, "Why don't we talk to Daddy when he gets home and figure it out."

"YOU WANT to what?" Griffin stood naked in their bedroom, shorts in one hand, gesturing with the other. "Do you have a fever?"

"Caro and I were talking about it, and I don't know, a pet could be good for her," Jim said, setting the alarm for seven, then settling under the covers.

"Are you a pod person now? Have I driven you insane?"

Jim gave him his best sultry look. "Insane with lust. Why don't you forget about the shorts?"

"I figured you'd go out of your mind, but I thought it would take longer."

JIM AND Caroline were eating lunch at the patio table when Daisy and Sadie arrived. Daisy's greeting was "Griffin said you've lost your mind."

"We're getting a dog!" Caroline squealed, which made Sadie squeal, and then they both began clapping.

"You have lost your mind." Daisy sat down, removing her wide-brimmed hat. "Oh no, wait. You're going to get a dog, Griffin's going to go insane, then insist you go back to work. Jesus, that's devious."

Jim placidly ate his chicken salad.

"Her name is Lois Lane," Caroline continued at high volume. "She's a beagle and she's two and she licked my face when we met."

Sadie gasped, clasping her hands against her chest.

"A two-year-old beagle? That's cruel," Daisy said, shaking her head as she stole some of Jim's grapes off his plate.

He swallowed his last bite, then wiped his mouth with a napkin. "There is no devious plan. My daughter wants a pet."

"Pod. Person."

LOIS LANE gave Jim a regular schedule, something he didn't explain to anyone. She needed to be walked, taken to obedience class, taken to the vet. In between, he took Caroline to soccer and dance. They ran household errands and went to the pool with Sadie when Daisy was in the city working. They explored every child's theater, museum, and play area within forty miles. They went to the city. They visited baby Shelia and baby Nathaniel. They spent time with Caroline's endless cousins.

Georgia took so much vacation she ended up with a boyfriend.

"Maybe we should homeschool Caro," Jim said casually one night over an adults-only dinner.

Griffin dropped his fork right into a plate of chicken cordon bleu. "Who are you?"

Jim felt Lois Lane breathing heavily against his leg. He knew if he looked down he'd be faced with pleading brown eyes. "You told me to find something to do. So that's what I did." He snuck Lois a tiny bit of chicken, which she gratefully ate out of his hand. Then licked his entire hand to make sure she'd got it all.

His husband's expression went from confused to adoring in a split second.

"Being the best dad in the world is the perfect job for you."

JIM DIDN'T win the homeschooling fight. Caroline started school in a new dress and shoes, picked out by her fathers, and ran into the elementary school with a backward wave. He waited until she disappeared with the other students, then drove home slowly.

Lois Lane looked the way he felt—bereft.

So they went for a gentle jog around the neighborhood, Jim focused on each footfall against the pavement, the beagle trotting at his side. When he got back to the house, he found a slew of cars that weren't there before.

"Uncle Jim! We're here to visit you!" Elizabeth called when he came in through his front door.

"It's a work field trip." Helena and Matt were at the kitchen table, drinking coffee and picking off a platter of fruit and vegetables the size of Rhode Island. "Griffin said we could come bother you."

"On Caroline's first day back to school?" Jim filled Lois Lane's water bowl.

Matt put his hand to his chest in "shock" and "surprise."

"That's today?" Helena asked, eyes wide. Jim realized they were all wearing matching T-shirts that said *Haight Security Worldwide*, and swallowed a barking laugh.

"You're the most fu... freaking ridiculous people I know."

Elizabeth bounced over to him, giving him a tight hug. "We're going to make sure you're not sad. Also Matt has a question about the Vericas Casino bid."

Jim's eyes narrowed. "Is this a trick? Is Griffin hiding behind the door?"

"No!" Griffin said from behind the door. He peeked out. "You can answer the question, but only if you have almond milk in your coffee."

"He drives a hard bargain, but that seems fair," Matt said. "Now sit down so we can pick your brain."

EVERY MONTH, Jim went to the doctor's.

No matter what was happening with the play, Griffin took the day off to go with him.

It took a full six months of good reports before the dark shadows in his husband's eyes fully disappeared.

Jim had the occasional thought about negotiating a return to work—part-time, consulting. No travel. But Matt and Helena made a great team, and Elizabeth's summer internship had continued into the school year. Talk of the police academy drifted off, and then Matt was asking how much they should start her off with when she joined the company officially after graduation.

"Is she going to live at home rent-free for a while?"

"Yes. Because if she says she's moving in with Ollie, I'll have to start crumbling Valium in Evan's coffee."

Jim put his feet up on the ottoman. In the kitchen, Sadie and Caroline were helping Georgia make lasagna with zucchini and soy cheese, which sounded terrible.

"He's been through this with three other children. Danny's engaged, for God's sake. Why is Elizabeth any different?"

"She's the youngest."

"By ten minutes."

"Whose side are you on?"

"Elizabeth's."

Matt made hooting noises. "I cannot wait until Caroline starts dating and I get to remind you of this conversation. It's going to be the best day of my life."

JIM COACHED soccer.

He and Caroline planted a garden out back and built a fire pit.

Georgia taught him to cook more than meat on a grill and bacon and eggs.

Lois Lane was the most well-behaved beagle in New York State.

He played tennis at the club twice a week while the girls were in school, supervising their after-school activities while Daisy and Bennett were busy with the play.

Once a week, come hell or high water, he and Matt ate lunch at a diner halfway between their houses.

And every time Griffin asked, "Are you happy?" Jim kissed him and said yes.

12
TONY

Jim 16:30
Tonys announced tomorrow. My house is overrun.

Matt 16:33
Who's Tony?

Jim 16:34
If you weren't my last oasis of nontheater talk, I'd curse at you.

Matt 16:37
Be nice. I have options. There's a riveting convo in another window about training potties.

Jim 16:40
What the hell are you adding to that conversation? Assuming you're not allowed to be crude.

Matt 16:44
I've typed "nice one!" about eleven times. No one has noticed.

Jim 16:45
I don't know what will be worse—if they get the nomination or if they don't.

Matt 16:47
That doesn't sound like something a supportive husband would say.

Jim 16:50
Press. Tuxes. Press.

Matt 16:51
Embrace the spotlight.

Jim 16:52
So far I've gotten away with "husband Jim, retired from the police force" and being called supportive. If he gets the nomination who knows? They'll want to SEE ME.

Matt 16:54
I would give a very large sum of money to see you on Ellen.

Jim 16:55
I hate you.

MAY 1

Matt 08:45
CONGRATULATIONS!

Jim 08:50
Thank you. And thank you from the crowd of people drinking champagne haphazardly in my living room.

Matt 08:51
When your husband wins a Tony, have him buy you a new carpet.

Jim 08:53
Bennett is buying me a new carpet. My husband is buying me tickets to Hawaii.

Matt 08:55
I sense a deal has been struck.

Jim 08:57
Pick up the New York Times on Sunday.

Matt 08:58
You know I'm going to make you autograph it.

Jim 08:59
Here's a preview: fuck you, Love Jim.

Matt 09:00
Have you considered male modeling? The bald dad bod is in now.

MAY 5

Matt 10:10
I can't believe I know a famous person now.

Jim 10:12
I'm going to tell Daisy you said that.

MAY 7

Jim 15:01
I AM AT A TUX FITTING. SEND HELP.

Matt 15:03
Wrong number.

Jim 15:05
Let me just say this: the measuring I just got was very thorough and might count as a threesome since Griffin was in the room.

Matt 15:07
Your life is so interesting now.

MAY 10

Jim 18:30
I am at a cocktail party. There is no beer so I am drinking champagne. The food is very tiny and weird. If you ever had feelings for me, you would call in a bomb threat.

Matt 18:35
Can't talk. Eating a pizza and watching baseball in my underwear.

Jim 18:40
Bastard.

Jim 18:42
Griffin said he wanted a picture. He might be drunk.

Matt 18:50
Matt sent a picture.
You're welcome.

Matt 18:55
Evan just threatened to take my phone away. I hope it's for reasons of the perverted kind.

Jim 18:57
Griffin said he wanted a picture of that too.

Matt 18:59
Cut him off.

Jim 19:01
Are you kidding me? That's the only way this evening is going to be redeemed.

Matt 19:04
Evan said he wanted a picture of that.

Evan 19:07
No he didn't.

MAY 15

Jim 09:10
I left two tickets at the box office for you and Evan.

Matt 09:11
Please leave a message at the beep.

Jim 09:15
You promised.

Jim 09:19
This is Griffin. YOU PROMISED. Get your ass down to the theater and get some goddamn culture. Then you can buy us all dinner because you're literally the last human beings in our lives to come and see our TONY-NOMINATED PLAY which makes you terrible friends.

Matt 09:21
BEEP.

May 16

Matt 21:10
Where are you?

Jim 21:11
Hiding backstage. Where are you?

Matt 21:14
Buying a drink, or at least standing in a line that might lead to a drink. Not sure. Might be the bathroom line.

Jim 21:15
What do you think?

Matt 21:17
There should be more bartenders.

Jim 21:19
I'll send Griffin out to sit with you for the second act.

Matt 21:22
Don't tell him this, but it's good. I like the cop character, but he seems a bit familiar if you know what I mean.

Jim 21:23
Of course. I figured even you would notice.

Matt 21:24
Even I would notice that's me?

Jim 21:25
What?

Matt 21:27
What?

Jim 21:28
Harold is based on me. As my husband is the writer of the play, who else would it be?

Matt 21:29
Yes, but Shane is the cowriter and we all know about his massive man crush on me.

Jim 21:31
Good point. I'm sending Shane out to sit with you during the second half so he can explain the metaphors. Evan can hang backstage with me. We have a full bar.

Matt 21:32
Son of a bitch.

May 19

Matt 11:11
Nervous?

Jim 11:12
Cone of fucking silence—I am freaking out. I haven't been this nervous since Caro was born.

Matt 11:14
Has Griffin noticed?

Jim 11:15
No. He's weirdly calm.

Matt 11:16
Freaky Friday Tony Edition.

Jim 11:18
He slept late this morning! I've been awake for three days.

Matt 11:20
You need to take a Xanax or something and chill out. You know this is the calm before the storm. And either you're going to be consoling a group of sad drunk artists or you're going to be getting your celebratory sex on. Either way, you need your rest.

Jim 11:22
I really want him to win. He's worked so hard for so long, got screwed over. Gave stuff up for me, for Daisy, for Caro. He deserves this.

Matt 11:25
Have you told him that?

Jim 11:27
What if he loses? Then he'll feel terrible. Like he let me down.

Matt 11:28
He's Griffin. He'll think that anyway.

Jim 11:30
True.

Matt 11:32
So tell him what you think.

Jim 11:33
brb. He's calling me from upstairs.

Jim 17:40
Sorry about that.

Matt 17:41
I don't think you can use brb for six hours.

Jim 17:43
He couldn't find his lucky cufflinks and it pretty much devolved from there.

Matt 17:44
Body switch complete?

Jim 17:45
He's a wreck. I took a nap. Everything is back to normal.

MAY 20

Evan 20:01
Good luck! We'll be watching. The girls are keeping Caro and Sadie distracted for as long as they can, but I'm assuming you'll be able to hear their screams all the way in the city.

Katie 20:02
OMG GOOD LUCK! WE ARE SO EXCITED FOR YOU!

Elizabeth 20:02
Everything is crossed and I lit a candle at three churches!

Matt 20:04
Good luck, man. Fully convinced we'll be celebrating at the beach house this weekend.

Matt 20:05
Also Harold is totally based on me.

Katie 21:02
WE JUST SAW YOU GUYS ON THE RED CARPET
LIVESTREAM OMG! YOU LOOK SO HANDSOME!

Matt 21:04
Damn. You kids clean up nice. Also I'm deaf now because the girls
have been screaming for an hour.

Matt 23:00
HOLY SHIT.

Katie 23:00
AHHHHHHHH! OMG!

Evan 23:01
Matt's crying.

Matt 23:04
Am not.

Matt 23:05
And I told you Harold was based on me.

MAY 21

Jim 11:00
*Party Bus group text to Griffin Drake, Daisy Baylor, Bennett
Aames, Matt Haight, Evan Cerelli, Shane Lowry, Helena Abbott, Miranda
Moran, Kent Moran, Katie Cerelli Hill, Austin Hill, Danny Cerelli, and
Elizabeth Cerelli*:
The party bus leaves from our house at 9:00 a.m. sharp. NO
EXCEPTIONS. If you forget anything, Bennett will buy you a replacement.

Bennett 11:01
Hey.

Jim 11:02
Please notice the latest champagne stain on my rug.

Bennett 11:04
Whatever you need.

Jim 11:05
Food's been ordered, as have libations. Georgia has kindly agreed to take an obscene amount of money to come along and wrangle the children so the adults can have a little relaxing time.

Austin 11:06
God bless you.

Shane 11:07
Do we need to bring anything?

Jim 11:08
Just your clothes.

Shane 11:09
Can I bring my Tony?

Daisy 11:10
And mine?

Griffin 11:11
And mine?

Bennett 11:12
And mine?

Matt 11:13
Who's Tony?

Jim 11:15
I hate you all.

13
A Big Bow on It

THE MEETING was an annual tradition: Matt and Evan's dining room table, Chinese food on the sideboard, lots of wine, notebooks and pens provided from whatever Bennett remembered to bring home from the office. And calendars. No one was allowed in the house without their calendars.

Evan grumbled a lot, but secretly this was his favorite part of the holiday.

The roots reached back to that started-terrible-ended-great Christmas with Matt's appendix: a holiday celebration with their beloved group of friends. The meeting started with "what do the kids want for Christmas?" and "what can I bring to the potluck?" and segued into "how do we accommodate in-laws and shared holidays and still get together?" plus the other stuff on top. They were pushing twenty-five people at this point, and with actively fertile couples in the baby-making business, there was no telling when that number would hit capacity.

Bennett and Daisy's beach house became their de facto location, with a full weekend of fun, food, and festivities for Fake Christmas. Babies were born, people were married, and Bennett built an extra wing.

"Okay, that weekend is good with everyone?" Daisy asked, giving everyone in the room a once-over. Extra chairs, the card table, and television trays filled every spare inch of floor space as all the adults sat poised with phones and paper lists. "We'll be there Friday morning and we're staying through the New Year, so—get there before Saturday breakfast and leave when you want. Leave and come back. We don't care."

Toddlers shrieked in the next room as a fight broke out over... something.

"Yours or mine?" Katie asked her sister.

Miranda leaned closer to the doorway, listening intently. "Both mine. Brigit and Clancy, you stop that right now!"

Josiah slunk into the room with his giant pair of ever-present headphones. He perused the Chinese buffet, poking around the egg rolls before taking two. Evan remembered the bouncy little boy who had come into their lives eight years before, now about to hit his teen years. He liked music and building robots and still spent occasional weekends with his grandfathers, eating pizza and getting Matt to play games with him.

"How is it in there?" Austin asked as Josiah moved one earpiece to hear him.

"The twins only want to play with the same toys, but everyone else is casual," he said, surprising Evan with how deep his voice had gotten, even in the past month. "Toni put on a show about penguins that Mattie likes, so that's good."

"Thanks for keeping an eye on them." Katie handed her son a napkin, which he took with a good-natured eye roll.

"When are the girls getting back from soccer practice?"

Griffin checked his phone. "Twenty minutes or so."

Josiah grunted as he lowered his earpiece, then headed back to the living room.

"How many times has Josiah asked when the girls are coming home?" Jim asked as Shane held up his hand with five fingers outstretched. Then he mouthed, "Five."

"Huh," said Helena.

"What's huh?" asked Bennett.

With a prelude of galloping feet announcing their entrance, Shelia and Nathaniel darted in and dived under the table, aiming for Matt's lap.

"Pop Pop, can you come play with us?" Shelia asked, bouncing next to Matt's chair once she and her cousin crawled the entire length of the dining room table. "You're more fun than Josiah."

"Shelia!" Kent admonished her. "That isn't a nice thing to say about your cousin."

Austin opened his fortune cookie. "It's actually a compliment. He's more mature than Matt, is what we're saying."

"Kent, you're my favorite son-in-law now," Matt said, putting his arms around his grandchildren. "Ollie's in second place."

Nathaniel leaned against Matt's arm. "Pleeeease. Pleeeeeease," he whispered.

"Listen, Frick and Frack, Pop Pop will come play as soon as we're done. We're planning Fake Holiday Weekend right now," Katie said, pouring another round of wine into every glass she could reach. "Go keep an eye on the twins and Mattie, please."

"If I'm not out in ten minutes, pull the fire alarm," Matt stage-whispered, giving them each a kiss on the cheek.

The cousins shared identical expressions of delight even as Kent started to explain that was just a figure of speech and please don't look for any alarms to pull....

"You're evil," Evan said, throwing a cork at Matt's head.

"I'm Super Pop Pop, and you're just jealous."

"WE CAN only stay two days," Danny told Matt as they attempted to clean off the table after all the procreating couples had headed home. Danny held the garbage can and followed Matt around the perimeter. "Jane and I both have to work."

"I get it—building the old careers."

"We manage a gym."

Matt stopped, wagging a fistful of dirty napkins in his stepson's face. "What do you do?"

"We are personal fitness consultants," Danny said dutifully.

"Clearly you need to practice that in the mirror more."

"I'm not practicing—"

"Or you can join the family business." Matt dropped fortune cookie wrappers in the garbage can.

"You can use that bad Italian accent forever, but you own a security company. You're not in the mob."

"Fun killer."

TO SAY Matt was looking forward to Fake Christmas Holiday was an understatement.

His to-do list read like a Hallmark movie—buy toys, get his Santa suit cleaned, buy another big red sack to hold all the toys while he wore his suit. More than their yearly trips to the condo in Florida, more than backyard barbecues, Matt loved FCH in all its chaotic, noisy glory.

He took the entire two weeks before it off, concentrating on his shopping, finding the perfect gift for each member of his family. They had a monetary limit, which Matt stuck to, something that drove Evan crazy.

Perfect gifts, in budget range. Maddening.

"CAN I see your list?"

"No."

"Can I barter with you?"

"What are you offering?"

"Sex."

"No."

ON THE Friday before Fake Christmas Holiday, Matt loaded the car with gifts, luggage, and trays of cookies Elizabeth and Jane had baked in their kitchen. The caravan of Cerellis and their families would begin in less than an hour, and it was all Matt could do not to break into song in the driveway.

"Did you remember the bag of stuff for the kids' stockings?" Evan asked as he came out the front door, both hands full of shopping bags.

"Big kids or little kids?"

"Both."

"Yes." Matt took the bags and filled the last square foot of space in the back seat. "Please tell me that was the last of it. Because our next option is lashing stuff to the roof." He shut the door, then waited for the entire SUV to explode like a piñata.

"Next year everyone gets an envelope of cash," Evan said, like clockwork. Matt patted his shoulder and nodded like he was considering it.

He wasn't.

Pop Pop Matt was the best damn Santa in the world, and no one was taking that away from him.

LESS THAN twenty-four hours later, all those brightly wrapped gifts were now opened and spread all over the living room of the beach house. The frenzy burned intensely, then fizzled out as everyone collapsed in exhaustion among the happy carnage.

"I can't see the floor," Matt said, leaning against the kitchen counter and looking at the living room.

Evan brought him a mug of coffee, his own clutched in his other hand. He mirrored Matt's position, pressed close as he gazed out at their family. Family, extended family, friends who were now family. Two generations of humans whose main connection seemed to be making sarcastic comments and being fiercely loyal.

How could you go wrong with that?

"Bennett might have to build another wing."

"Don't encourage him," Evan whispered.

"This is a fertile bunch, Evan. Don't be fooled by the momentary lull."

Evan sipped his coffee, trying to look casual. He suspected an announcement coming soon from Elizabeth and Ollie but didn't want to steal anyone's thunder.

"Twenty-four humans in this house. Twenty. Four."

"And a dog."

"And a dog!" Matt sounded on the verge of a rant, but one sideways look at his husband and Evan could see the absolute delight on his face. He loved having everyone here, loved spending a fortune on gifts, loved wearing his Santa costume to pass out gifts. Every time he did, Evan remembered that first Christmas, Matt buying the kids tons of presents, but then they spent it apart, broken by Evan's insecurities.

He regretted that moment so much, the panic and breaking up.

And yet.

Evan watched Griffin and Jim sharing a third of the bigger sofa, Lois Lane the beagle stretched across their laps. If they hadn't broken up, Evan wouldn't have used that rock bottom bounce to reclaim his life. If they hadn't broken up... Matt and Jim wouldn't have slept together.

How fucking weird for Evan to be thinking, *Well, glad that happened.*

"Maybe we should get a dog," Matt was saying, bringing Evan's attention back. "The grandkids would love it."

"Maybe we should get a dog so I can walk it? No." Evan elbowed him gently. "I've mellowed in my old age, but not that much."

"Mellow? Uh, no." Matt gave him a dazzling smirk. "You're still the same uptight pain in the ass you always were."

Evan knew flirting when he saw it, at least from Matt, because they'd been doing this a long damn time.

Before he could say anything, Katie ambled by.

"Why are you two being so standoffish? We have cookies... somewhere in there. You might want to check under the twins."

"That's a pass." Matt saluted her with his cup.

Among the wrapping paper, boxes, and gifts, Josiah emerged, unfolding and stretching. "Who wants to go for a walk?"

"Me!" Caroline bolted from the chair she was sharing with Sadie—who almost ended up on the floor. "Sadie, do you want to come?"

The tone and slow enunciation from Caroline got an overly blinky response from Sadie.

"No, thanks. You two go along," Sadie said with a regal nod.

Josiah nodded as Caroline rooted around her fathers to find her sweatshirt; then the two preteens left, leaving silence in their wake. When Evan heard the sliding glass doors close, he said, "All clear."

"Oh. My. God." Sadie started to laugh, leaning down to high-five Daisy, who was leaning against Griffin's legs. "Not subtle."

"What? What wasn't subtle?" Austin asked, going from sleepy to awake in a second.

Katie, returned from the kitchen with a tray of cups of coffee, made soothing noises. "Don't worry, honey."

Evan sighed, but the laughter bubbled in on the tail end of it. "Aren't they too young—"

"Josiah and Caroline?" gasped Matt. His cup shook in his hand. "They are far too young—"

"Dads!" Katie reprimanded with a look. "It's just a little mutual crush. Don't make a big thing about it. And don't embarrass them!"

"Sorry, Katie. We'll behave," Evan promised even as Matt shook his head beside him.

"Shouldn't someone be out there walking with them?"

EVENTUALLY MATT and Evan got their time on the couch. The younger folk were busy putting babies to bed or supervising almost teenagers in the game room. Four familiar couples settled around the fireplace with a bottle of wine.

"This is nice," Daisy said with a yawn, curled under Bennett's arm. "I always forget the full volume of everyone in the same room."

"Blame Evan. It's mostly his fault."

"I can't help my virile fertility."

Matt hooted, and he and Helena fake high-fived.

"Why are you high-fiving him?" Evan asked.

"I don't know. I'm sleep-deprived. My boss took the past two weeks off." Shane snored quietly beside his wife. "Also, you said virile fertility. Are you drunk?"

"Give me time." Evan kicked back, stretching against Matt, who seemed about three seconds from conking out.

"We spend so much time planning and buying stuff and wrapping stuff...," Griffin started to say.

"Who is this we?"

Ignoring Jim, he continued. "And then it's over in like ten minutes."

"You say that every year, Griffin."

"Because it's true every year, Daisy Mae."

"I like when Jim reminds everyone he's a house husband," Matt said, raising his glass.

Everyone followed suit as Jim flipped them off.

ONE BY one, they drifted off to bed. Evan felt too sleepy, too warm to move, as Matt drifted in and out beside him. Each of their friends came over to drop a kiss or a half hug before ambling out of the room.

"Breakfast at ten," Bennett reminded them. "Because we're all sleeping late. I bribed the big kids to watch the little ones."

"Good man." Evan gave him and Daisy a salute as they disappeared up the stairs. Their generosity brought everyone together. Their partnership with Shane and Griffin earned them all successful careers.

Shane climbed into Matt's lap for some wrestling until Helena hit him with a rolled-up magazine.

"Your sex games are so weird," Matt sighed, messing up Shane's hair before he got up.

"This is the scene of the crime." Helena finished her glass of wine as Evan put his hands over his ears.

"Your poor child," he sighed. "What are you going to do when she figures it out?"

"How is she going to figure it out? She's going to know she was named after Antoinette Perry, we won the Tony around that time...."

"It's a little too on the nose."

"Evan, our other choices for names were *lawn chair* and *beach house*. I think Toni was the nicest thing we could do."

Matt smacked the side of the chair. "I'm tapping out of this discussion. Go to bed, Shane."

Griffin hauled Jim off the couch; they wrapped around each other like handsy octopi. Evan watched them share a kiss, then murmur to each other as they gathered empty glasses.

"Leave them. We'll take care of it," Evan said.

"Nah, old man needs water to take his pills," Griffin said lightly. He took the glass from Jim's hand, making the same scowl face.

"Can I make a Viagra joke?"

"No." Griffin gave Matt a kiss on the cheek, then Evan. "Night, guys." He paused, considering. "Okay, just one."

Matt threw his hands in the air. "Goddammit, I forgot what I was going to say."

Griffin left them in the living room, heading for the kitchen with the glasses. His laughter rang out, leaving Matt muttering under his breath.

"You believe I had a great line, don't you?"

Jim held his hand to his ear, squinting in the firelight. "Eh, speak up, sonny. Can't hear you."

"Jerk."

"Dickhead."

Jim and Matt did a half hug, Jim bending down and Matt pretending to rough up Jim's hair at the end.

"Oh. Sorry."

"Keep it up, asshole." Jim hit Matt with a throw pillow. "I'm still in better shape."

"He's right," Evan pointed out and got an indignant look from Matt. "What?"

"I'll let you two work this out. Try not to stare as I walk away."

"James Shea, how much did you have to drink?" Griffin yelled from the kitchen.

The night ended in Daisy coming down to tell them all to shut the hell up before they woke a child.

UNDER THE covers, Evan poked Matt as he continued to break into peals of laughter. "Daisy's going to come in here and yell at you."

Matt choked, tears streaming down his face. "She's so fucking tiny, but when she yells…."

"It's terrifying." Evan tried not to join Matt's ridiculousness, but it wasn't easy. "Stop!"

"I can't!"

Evan lay there, letting the bed shake as Matt let it all out. This was his life, married to a big kid who never missed an opportunity for a smile. "You're nuts. I don't think you can handle your liquor anymore."

"You think Jim's hot," Matt hiccupped, wiping his eyes on the sheet. "If I had a Breathalyzer, you'd be in trouble, buddy."

Plumping up his pillows, Evan rolled over to face his husband. "Is this role-play?"

"If I said yes, can we consider it my Christmas present?"

"So I'm cancelling our trip to Maine?"

Matt made a face. "Can we role-play in Maine?"

"Matt, you know we've never done that, ever. And to be honest, I don't know how to do that," Evan said. "But I can promise you lots of shower sex."

The smile he got was wide and bright.

"This is why I love you. And why I wrote you a poem for Christmas. It's called 'Ode to Evan's ass'...."

AT NINE fifty, Evan rolled out of bed. He grabbed his sweater and socks and left Matt snoring away under the pile of blankets. Outside in the hallway, he encountered a stampede of grandchildren as Josiah herded Nathaniel, Shelia, Brigit, Clancy, and Mattie toward the stairs.

"You need help?" Evan asked, observing his grandson's patient herding.

"No, I got this, Grandpa Evan." Josiah grabbed Mattie right before she toddled into a wall. Matt's namesake didn't quite have her sea legs yet—champion crawler, so-so walker. Katie's youngest wasn't going to run until she was good and ready. "I hear there are pancakes and bacon."

"Pancakes!" Brigit shouted.

Through an intricate series of bargaining—"Shelia, hold Clancy's hand. Nathaniel, you got Brigit. I'm carrying Mattie. Go slow, hold the railing!"—Josiah got them down the stairs.

Evan smiled as he oversaw their trek all the way down. He cherished each individual sparkle of their personalities, the way they got along. The cousins were best friends, traveling in a pack despite their different ages, fighting and making up sometimes in the same breath. They lived in the same neighborhood, went to the same schools and day cares.

And now they were running into the kitchen, yelling "Pancakes!" with Josiah at the lead, waving Mattie's little hand.

"Oh my God, so much noise," Sadie said, coming out of her room with a dramatic sigh. "Hey, Uncle Evan."

"Morning, Sadie. Sorry if the gang woke you."

She shrugged, swanning past in her furry pink robe, blonde hair tucked under a beanie. "Don't tell anyone I said this, but I love those weirdos."

"They're the best weirdos."

They shared a smile; then she headed down the staircase. A second later Josiah's head came into view, peering around the corner. When he saw Evan still on the landing, he jumped back.

"She's not up yet," Evan mock whispered. "Maybe you should come up, bring her some orange juice."

Josiah's eyes widened and he shook his head before disappearing again.

A door opened—not Caroline but Matt, lumbering down the hallway in a hoodie that proclaimed him "the boss" and truly ugly pajama pants featuring chili peppers wearing elf hats.

"I might have been dreaming, but an army of children was screaming about pancakes. No. Wait. That was definitely real." He stretched and yawned before wrapping his arms around Evan's shoulders. "Merry Day After Fake Christmas."

Evan relaxed into Matt's arms. The sounds of breakfast prep rose up, a clanging of pots and pans and the happy shrieks of children, the laughter of their friends. They'd eat, then head out to the beach for a bundled-up walk, working off some of the calories consumed. Movies, hot chocolate, the annual Scrabble tournament—which gave way to strip poker after the kids went to sleep, but it all depended on how much wine Evan drank.

Wholesome family insanity.

"What?" Matt whispered, resting his head against Evan's shoulder.

"I was just thinking how much I love this," he murmured. "Every crazy bit of it."

"That's because our resistance has worn down over the years."

"Shut up, you love it too."

Matt snickered. "I love it. I love you. I really love pancakes."

Evan didn't want to let go of Matt just yet. There was coffee and delicious food and family to be a part of, but this in-between felt... nice. More than nice. Like contentment encapsulated into a single moment.

"Did you ever imagine," he said softly, turning his head to look at Matt.

"This?" Matt's smile lit up from the inside. "Hell no."

"Me either."

They were quiet for another moment, just watching each other. Evan broke the gaze with a kiss.

"How lucky are we?" he asked.

"The luckiest sons of bitches on the planet." Matt sealed the words with another kiss, slanting their lips together in a perfect fit.

AND THEY lived happily ever after.

The End

TERE MICHAELS unofficially began her writing career at the age of four when she learned that people got paid to write stories. It seemed the most perfect and logical job in the world, and after that, her path was never in question.

(The romance writer part was written in the stars—she was born on Valentine's Day.)

She writes happily ever afters in the big city—with heaps of snark, angst, and humor. Her focus is on characters and all the ridiculous ways they trip through life and love. She has written fifteen books including her popular Faith, Love, & Devotion series and the superhero saga The Vigilante.

Her home base is a small town in New Jersey, very near NYC, a city she dearly loves. She shares her life with her husband, her teenaged son—who will just not stop growing—and two exceedingly spoiled cats. Her spare time is spent watching way too much sports programming, going to the movies and for long walks/runs in the park, and buying more books than she can read.

Nothing makes her happier than knowing she made a reader laugh or smile or cry. It's the purpose of sharing her work with people. She loves hearing from fans and fellow writers and is always available for speaking engagements, visits, and workshops.

Find her at:
Website: www.teremichaels.com
Twitter: @teremichaels
Facebook: www.facebook.com/tere.michaels.9

TERE MICHAELS

Faith &
Fidelity

Faith, Love, & Devotion: Book One

Reeling from the recent death of his wife, police officer Evan Cerelli looks at his four children and can only see how he fails them. His loving wife was the caretaker and nurturer, and now the single father feels himself being crushed by the pain of loss and the heavy responsibility of raising his kids.

At the urging of his partner, Evan celebrates a coworker's retirement and meets disgraced former cop turned security consultant Matt Haight. A friendship born out of loneliness and the solace of the bottle turns out to be exactly what they both need.

The past year has been a slow death for Matt Haight. Ostracized from his beloved police force, facing middle age and perpetual loneliness, Matt sees only a black hole where his future should be. When he discovers another lost soul in Evan, some of the pieces he thought he lost start to fall back in place. Their friendship turns into something deeper, but love is the last thing either man expected, and both of them struggle to reconcile their new and overwhelming feelings for one another.

www.dreamspinnerpress.com

TERE MICHAELS

Love & Loyalty

FAITH, LOVE, & DEVOTION: BOOK TWO

Faith, Love, & Devotion: Book Two

Seattle Homicide Detective Jim Shea never takes work home with him—until now. A judge banged his gavel, declared a defendant not guilty, and laid waste to a family. The emotional fallout of the trial leaves Jim vulnerable and duty-bound to the victim's dying father.

It's that man's story that screenwriter Griffin Drake and his best friend, actress Daisy Baylor, see as their ticket out of action blockbusters and into more serious fare. But to get the juicy details, Griffin needs to win over the stoic and protective Detective Shea. Their attraction is immediate, and Daisy encourages Griffin to use it to their advantage: secure the man, secure the story. Neither man has had much luck when it comes to love, and when their one night together evolves into a long weekend of rapidly intensifying feelings, both Griffin's fierce loyalty to Daisy and his very career is put to the test.

Because the more Griffin is drawn into a new life with Jim, the more his Hollywood life falls apart. Secrets and broken trust threaten Griffin's relationships, and he'll have to choose between telling the truth or writing a Hollywood ending.

www.dreamspinnerpress.com

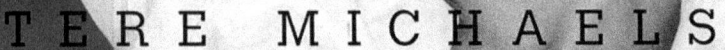

TERE MICHAELS

Duty
Devotion

FAITH, LOVE, & DEVOTION: BOOK THREE

Faith, Love, & Devotion: Book Three

A year after deciding to share their lives, Matt and Evan are working on their happily ever after—which isn't as easy as it looks. As life settles down into a routine, Matt finds happiness in his role as the ideal househusband of Queens, New York, but he worries about Evan's continued workaholic—and emotionally avoidant—ways. Trying to juggle his evolving relationship with Evan and his children, Matt turns to his friend, former Seattle Homicide Detective Jim Shea.

The continued friendship between Matt and Jim is a thorn in Evan's side. Jealous and uncomfortable with imagining their brief affair, Evan struggles to come to terms with what being in a committed relationship with a man means, and the implications about his love for his deceased wife, the impact on his children, and how other people will view him. His turmoil threatens his relationship with Matt, who worries that Evan will once again chose a life without him. But now, the stakes are much higher.

www.dreamspinnerpress.com

TERE MICHAELS

Cherish & Blessed

FAITH, LOVE, & DEVOTION: BOOKS FOUR & FIVE

Faith, Love, & Devotion: Books Four and Five

Cherish

After several years of happy coupledom, Matt and Evan can relax in the knowledge that their little family has survived the worst of it. The two older girls are away at college, the twins have yet to fully hit teen angst, Matt is doing well with his part time security consulting, and Evan is about to be promoted to captain—it seems like things are calm and bright.

Until they aren't.

As the holidays approach, Evan and Matt get a shock no parent is ever prepared for: feisty Miranda, Evan's eldest, has a new boyfriend, Kent, and they are talking marriage after just three months together. In fact, Miranda wants to bring him to Thanksgiving dinner—along with his parents, Blake and Cornelia.

Blessed

Lives are in transition as everyone gathers at the stunning Hamptons beach home of Daisy and Bennett to celebrate the christening of their new baby. Griffin and Jim—secretly growing tired of their rootless lifestyle—are in a rocky spot in their relationship. And as the godfather, Griffin finds himself yearning for something he's sure Jim won't be interested in.

Fatherhood.

Matt and Evan are looking to reconnect during the long weekend, as their respective careers pull them in separate directions. With less time spent together, Evan grows concerned about what will happen when the last two kids leave the nest.

www.dreamspinnerpress.com

TERE MICHAELS

Truth & Tenderness

FAITH, LOVE, & DEVOTION: BOOK SIX

Faith, Love, & Devotion: Book Six

Newly promoted police captain Evan Cerelli takes command of his own precinct as Matt Haight's security business begins to expand at a rapid rate. Both of their careers require more and more of their time—away from home and each other. When his most famous clients, Daisy and Bennett Ames, suffer a traumatic breakup, Matt is drawn into a dangerous and dramatic situation. With attentions diverted, Evan and Matt's tight-knit home life begins to unravel.

As Griffin Drake's movie nears final edit, his thoughts turn toward building a home with his new fiancé, Jim Shea—and maybe even starting a family. Before he can think of a new family, Jim is caught up in his past. The possibility of putting Tripp Ingersoll in jail once and for all beckons, and Jim wants the closure that has long eluded him. As a new lead spurs him on, Jim begins to lose sight of the future by chasing an old ghost.

Both couples struggle to remember that "happily ever after" requires hard work, trust, and tender, open hearts.

www.dreamspinnerpress.com

The Heir Apparent

Tere Michaels

The heir apparent to a vast international company, Henry Walker has focused his entire life on pleasing his cold and distant father, a futile effort that's left him no time for life, love, or making his own decisions. He has just one friend—one dirty little secret—Archie Banks. Raised on the Walker estate alongside Henry, Archie is now Henry's driver, bodyguard... and occasional lover. Archie is loyal, but he's about to graduate from college and has plans for his life that don't include living every moment at the beck and call of Henry's father. Not even for Henry.

With no warning, a shocking kidnapping leads to tragedy and chaos, thrusting Henry and Archie into a dramatic struggle that threatens them individually and as a couple. Can they find a way to heal the hurt of the past, save the company that is Henry's birthright, and find a future together?

www.dreamspinnerpress.com

FOR MORE
OF THE
BEST
GAY
ROMANCE

www.ingramcontent.com/pod-product-compliance
Lightning Source LLC
Chambersburg PA
CBHW051638260626
47170CB00004B/1222